for Chr

My friend and

The Case of the Angry Auctioneer

daughter of one of

An Auction House Mystery

my biggest emotional
supporters, Kay

Sherry Blakeley

"Jonesy" Jones.
(I wouldn't be here

First in a New Series

without her!)
With love,
Sharon ["Sherry"]

New Light Productions, LLC

Cover design by Tina Lenz-Mandt

Dedication

For David Lundahl, artist extraordinaire and the most unusual person I have ever known, with love, gratitude and admiration

Prologue

When Jasper Biggs crossed that first threshold to the basement, she held her breath. She expected the stench of death, like the rotting sweet stink of a drawerful of mice, but when she breathed again, it was only the old tired smell of dust and mold that the whole house held. Plus an overlay of urine. The police detective Glenn Relerford said, "Put your hand on my belt and follow me nice and slow." She did as she was told and inched her way down the steep stairs, illuminated by the detective's flashlight. At the bottom she looked around warily, thinking maybe she wouldn't be able to recognize her stepfather in the gloomy light. But she saw him lying there on the ground and was surprised that even before she focused on his features, she would have known his slightly chubby shape, the length of his legs, his overall shortness, anywhere. His height, breadth, width. His very Jimminess.

She moved in closer, her skin crawling with emotions: worms of fear, centipedes of grief. The musty clutter in here had been moved out toward the walls, piles of National Geographics, the bowling ball that had rolled downstairs when she and Jimmy had first viewed the basement, a broken pseudo Chippendale chair with only two legs, and lots of unrecognizable debris. Jimmy lay in a circle cleared of junk, like a fallen gladiator at the bottom of the amphitheater. Dizziness compelled Jasper to sit on the cold floor. She eased herself to her knees and crawled over to Jimmy. She inhaled a hint of sweat and the strong aroma of some cologne she didn't recognize. He was always helping himself to cologne found in auction clients' houses. Jimmy had several bad habits. Jasper and her twin sister had long suspected that the perfumes he gave them birthday after birthday probably came out of housefuls of stuff destined for the auction. "Is it okay if I touch him?"

Glenn nodded. "Take your time."

Having asked, Jasper suddenly felt awkward. Jimmy had never been much of a hugger. She touched his face. Cold. Shouldn't a hothead like Jimmy have stayed warmer even in a cellar? She drew her hand back, then reached forward and stroked his thinning hair. She patted him on the shoulder. "What was he doing here alone?"

"I was hoping you could tell me."

Up close, Jasper could smell the flowery dryer sheets Jimmy was so fond of adding to his laundry. The rough-and-tumble auctioneer had always been a stickler for personal cleanliness. He wore his favorite watch, a Tag Heuer he'd gotten for a song at the auction. That night he had left a proxy bid, then did the bid-calling himself so he could control how the sale went. "What were you doing here, Jimmy?" she asked the dead man. A chill vined up her back. Maybe Jimmy hadn't been alone when he died. She turned to the detective "Did you check his pockets?

"Yes, ma'am," Glenn said.

"Was anything there?" Jasper asked in a small voice.

"This was on the floor near him." He handed her a Biggs Auction House key fob, one of the freebies they kept on the counter at work. He crouched down next to her. He pulled a wad of something from his own pocket and passed it over. He shone his flashlight on it. Jasper's hands shook. It was a roll of bills that relaxed open to reveal Ben Franklin's tight-lipped smile. Jasper spread them apart. Four hundred dollars plus a George Washington.

"Looks like you've been dealt a little gift hand there," he said.

"My sister and I get to keep this?"

"Later. But why $401?"

Jasper sighed, relieved that Jimmy hadn't died at the hands of a robber. She handed back the money. "It was just one of those Jimmy things. For luck, I guess. Or maybe just out of habit. When we were girls, he used to take us out for ice cream sometimes. He made us splurge on triple-decker cones even if we weren't hungry. I always got butter brickle. I think he liked to impress the people at Moo'n Goo when he whipped out a hundred doll bill."

The detective remained quiet.

"Sometimes though he'd just pull out the extra $20 he always kept in his wallet. Oh my gosh, where's his wallet?"

"Easy now, easy. It's right here."

"Oh, thank goodness," Jasper said. She opened the worn leather billfold and ran her fingers over the plastic covered driver's license, foggy in the flashlight beam. Jasper slipped her fingers under the license. Nothing.

Jasper said. "It was his emergency plan. He always told us we should tuck $20 away for emergencies. $401 but no 20? That's kind of odd I guess."

"True that," he said. "It is odd." He opened his palm to her. "I found this too."

The flashlight revealed a small silver figurine with some kind of sparkly stone in the center. Jasper brought her face in close. "It's from a necklace, I guess. What is that – a crab or a lobster?"

"So it's not familiar to you? "

Jasper shook her head. "Where did you find it?"

"Next to him on the floor."

"Oh-h-h. Were you cherry picking, Jimmy?" she whispered.

"Cherry picking?"

"Sorry. That's auction speak for picking out the most valuable items ahead of time. Before the regular auction crew comes over for the pickup."

"To protect the good stuff, so to speak."

"Uh-huh. So to speak." She got slowly to her feet. Glenn held out his ringless left hand to help her up. "That's okay, detective. I can manage on my own."

"Jasper."

"Now that we know Jimmy fell in the line of duty, more or less, I guess we should get back upstairs to the others," Jasper said. She stumbled forward. The detective caught her in his muscled arms. Jasper began to cry, and he drew her in closely.

"It's okay, baby, it's okay," Glenn said. "I'm really sorry. But it'll be okay."

It felt good to rest for a moment in his protective hold, but the rest of her life was waiting for her and she had to get on with it. "Let's go," she said.

"It's your world," he said. He kissed her palm gently then guided her to the stairs.

Chapter 1

Two weeks earlier, Candace Jasper Biggs Rowe had stood next to her husband The Right Reverend Timothy Rowe in front of the cheerful group in the basement of the Truman Free Church. The hall, as it was called, was nearly full of parishioners come to wish her well on her last day of full time duties as the pastor's wife. There was a polite silence for the most part. They were a polite group, made up almost exactly half and half of Social Security-ites and young farm couples. The children and grandchildren did what children and grandchildren do anywhere, making Jasper feel sad and relieved at the same time that she didn't have any of her own. The kids ran around the hall, laughing and dashing between tables, until the admonishments of the adults and slices of the chocolate-frosted marble cake brought them back to the white oil cloth covered tables. The air smelled of sweet and spicy Sloppy Joes and vinegary potato salad with traces of incense around the edges. Several church women moved among them, offering cups of burned coffee to the adults and more lemonade to the children.

The pastor's wife's stomach growled. She'd never liked church hall food. And she hadn't been able to find any pink medicine to tuck in her suitcase. Her nerves were bad enough without the bad food. She was about to embark on a solo adventure. The Right Reverend had wronged her too many times. She fingered the synthetic diamond wedding ring she still wore, the cheap one Tim had put on her finger long ago with a promise to make it better when he could.

In spite of her best intentions to stand on her own two feet, she leaned a little against her husband's muscled body. She supposed she'd miss that. His body. Being able to lean on someone. Even a man like Tim. Tim loomed a head higher than her five and a half feet, and he kept his former football player musculature toned and ready for action. He wasn't a handsome man but his big blue eyes could go from pleading to understanding in a blink. His eyes were what first drew her to him, up in Madison at the University of Wisconsin. His eyes and his build were what attracted all the girls. But he seemed to focus only on her. She was Communications. He was Religious Studies. Two years apart. When he got his calling to attend divinity school, he invited her along – as Mrs. Timothy Rowe of course.

That had been nearly two decades and three churches ago. The Rowes couldn't seem to settle in. Every time she thought her husband would leave the women of the new church alone, he'd come confessing his guilt and remorse first to her, then to the wronged other woman and cuckolded husband. On rare occasions he extended his flirtations and assignations to unlucky men who might have been even more heart-broken than the "gals," as Tim termed them. Jasper would step into one of her roles in her time as Tim's wife: consoler of the deserted lover. She had not signed on for that back when she was a naïve young "gal" herself. Tim's resignation would follow. And off they'd go to another small town, another denomination. This last one was non-denominational. And when long-suffering Mrs. Rowe found out about the latest wooing of the youth services director, she realized she could go on no longer. What could possibly follow "non-denomination?" No denomination. She felt just too demoralized to go on.

There'd been only one pregnancy, followed by one miscarriage. Tim did not want to try again. "I don't know what would happen to me if something happened to you," he had told her. Somehow that rang in her ears as another of Tim's selfish remarks. So no children. She was free to go.

"Candy?"

She tuned in to the voice of her still-husband Pastor Tim. He was holding the microphone toward her, but when she reached for it, he drew it back toward him.   He was all for show.

Thanks, anyway, she mumbled. "You're kindly welcome," he said right on mike. He used that pseudo folksy tone that he thought would carry the day wherever he landed in the Midwest. Why, if the folks of Truman knew what all he subscribed to on the Internet, one, they'd be suspicious of his hidden radicalism both right-wing and left, two, they'd be horrified by his fondness for soft porn, and three, they'd be mad at him using the church's computer for all of the above. She longed for a laptop of her own where she would not be bombarded by advertisements for hot guys and gals every time she wanted to e-mail her sister or read the Aquarius horoscope for the day.

"Well, folks, as you know, we're here today for a fond send-off for one of my favorite people. My wife."

There were titters in the crowd. Nerves, friendliness, confusion.

"Candy will be going to tend to her aging father over in Forest Grove."

"Stepfather and he's not all that old," she mumbled.

"And doing a fair amount of soul searching along the way. It's kind of a modern vision quest, wouldn't you say so, honey? Thirty days in the desert and all that."

"Jesus."

"What's that, honey?" Again, he made as if to hand her the mike, then snatched it back. He waggled his finger at her as if keeping her from being heard was just a playful routine between a happy husband and wife.

A hand went up in the crowd.

"Yes, ma'am?"

Snoopy old Mrs. Bachmeier asked, "How long will you be away, dear?"

"That depends," she said quietly.

"What? What's that, dear?"

Pastor Tim said, "An undesignated period. Any rate, let us now bow our heads in prayer."

If she had to hear him say "any rate" instead of "at any rate" one more time, she would…she would probably just take another ibuprofen and drown her annoyance in something sweet and chocolaty. Maybe salty too. Chocolate covered pretzels sounded pretty good at the moment. She sighed and refocused.

He led them all through an appeal to the Almighty to look out for loved ones especially his wife and keep them all safe in their travels and travails. Mrs. Rowe couldn't even shut her eyes. She had walked through life with her eyes closed for far too long. She was so over all his B.S. If he and the Almighty were such good friends, then she didn't even care to be on speaking terms any more with God or Whomever in the Sky.

Just get this over with and get me out of here, was her prayer.

A short while later the women and men gathered around her and said they'd be praying for her father and for her speedy return.

She did not correct them. "Thank you, thank you, thank you," she repeated. What was the point in trying to tell any of them the truth of her life, as a stepdaughter not a daughter, as Rev. Rowe's wife? Her motto as a door mat would be, *Go away and let me be myself. By myself.* That would probably not all fit on an average welcome mat. She would probably have to settle for something shorter and more to the point like *Wipe your feet on me. That's what I'm here for.* Oh, too many words again. *Let it go, let it go, let it go,* she told herself.

If the faithful church-goers only knew she planned on filing for divorce, they would feel shocked and...hurt. She just couldn't stand to hurt their feelings. And although they were modern people, some of whom themselves had endured family crises of one kind or another, they would feel so betrayed if they knew what a rat their pastor was and the more conservative would blame her if the truth about his wayward ways came out. When rattled, the residents of Truman could revert to that old rotten prejudice: Isn't it always the woman who leads the man down the wrong path?

How did she ever come to be living out only part of her personality in a place like that? What had happened to her young dreams of occupation and activity and intellectual stimulation?

So surrounded was she by well-wishers and consumed by her own sad secrets, that she lost track of her husband. Where had Tim gone? The clock on the wall with its numbers big enough for even her myopic eyes to make them out, said 1:25. She would have to get on the road if she expected to reach Forest Grove in time to meet the auction van with some furniture inside for her new apartment.

"Now you pack up some of this good food for yourself, dear. I'll just pull together a few things for you in the kitchen," one of the ladies said.

If she let them help, she would be there all afternoon. Jasper felt fresh out of patience. Her skin itched. "No, no, you've been too kind. I'll go wrap up a few things myself. Be right back."

"Don't forget the potato salad!"

"Don't worry," she called back over her shoulder. Who could forget that potato salad? She could finally admit to herself that she detested pseudo-German potato salad laden with apple cider vinegar and sugar. *That's a real declaration of independence*, she chided herself. Then she told herself to stop being so self-critical. Even that sounded so negative. She had to escape this land of self-abasement and guilt before her head started spinning around in complete circles.

Pushing open the swinging door to the kitchen, she wondered about the life she was leaving for the one that lay ahead. Would living in the same town as her cranky stepfather be an improvement over pretending to be happily married to a two-timing, small town minister? Of course her twin sister Cookie would be nearby.

As the door swung fully open, she caught sight of a tangle of humans over near the sink. It was Pastor Tim intertwined with the Director of Youth Services. Tim pushed Elaine away from him. The gray-haired woman began to stammer, "Mrs. Rowe, oh, Mrs. Rowe." Then she was crying.

"Oh, for Pete's sake," was all Jasper could muster. To Tim she said, "Hadn't you better do something? Give her a paper towel or something?"

She marched back out to the main hall and, ignoring the people who again began to mass around her, picked up the microphone and flipped the switch on. "I want to thank you all for your kindness." She glanced toward the kitchen. Tim was headed her way. "You should know that Rev. Tim is on his own kind of quest. Isn't that right, *honey?* "

Murmurs of "whatever does she mean?' started through the crowd.

Tim reached her and grabbed for the microphone. But for once, she was too fast for him. She walked to the length of the microphone cord and said, "I just want you to know…"

The worn, working faces of the crowd looked up at her puzzled. She couldn't do it. Even though her own heart had broken long ago, she couldn't break theirs. "I want you to know that my stepfather is not all that aged."

Tim mouthed *thank you* to her and again reached for the microphone. Jasper put it away from him. She continued, "Oh, and if I ever see you again, no more 'Mrs. Rowe.' Please call me Jasper Biggs." Finished at last, Candace Jasper Biggs Rowe, now plain Jasper Biggs, handed the microphone back to her soon to be ex-husband, and turned to go.

"Who's Jasper Biggs?" someone in the crowd asked.

One of the children ran up to her with a platter of cranberry cookies. "Mom said you should take these." She smiled and thanked the girl.

Jasper nearly tripped over her long skirt as she marched up the steps. Just as she reached the door at the top, the newly christened Jasper Biggs heard Mrs. Bachmeier saying brightly into the microphone, "Well, it's been quite a day!" The microphone screeched.

Footsteps raced up behind her. "Candy! " Tim stood there looking up at her with beseeching eyes. "Can you give me just one more minute?"

She nodded and he climbed the stairs toward her.

"I just wanted you to know that I'm really grateful for what you did, or rather, what you didn't do back there. Any rate, I wanted to say thanks."

"It was more for them than you," Jasper told him.

"Be that as it may. Thanks." He gave her one of those bluey looks that could melt the heart of any straight woman or yearning man within sight. "How 'bout a little kiss for the road?" He snaked his arms around her. "Hmm. Candy?"

"Stop!" Jasper gave him a little shove. He stumbled down a step or two. A few cookies flew after him. He recovered his balance.

"You'll need to get somebody else to clean up your mess!" she shouted at him. "Oh, and Tim?"

Some of the church people had gathered below, watching the drama wrap up.

Tim's voice was falsely calm. "I'm fine, I'm fine. What were you saying, Candy, dear?"

"Don't ever call me that again! 'Candy' or 'dear!'" Jasper Biggs and her mostly full platter of cookies reached the top of the stairs and marched on out.

Chapter 2

Driving away in her secondhand Ford that she'd gotten from a choir member for a song - $550 from her personal savings account - Jasper couldn't help but glance in her rear view mirror again and again as she neared the edge of Truman the village and entered the countryside of Truman Township. Would Tim come after her? Or, more like him, send an emissary like the Youth Services Director to make sure she was calm enough to drive away safely with Tim's latest sexual secret intact. But nobody followed. No church bus. No holier-than-thou gray Buick. No earnest Subaru wagon.

The Midwestern countryside in the early spring appeared moist and bruised to Jasper. The plants and ground either dead from last year's season of growth or birthing into small greenery and the mud of raw fields, not yet put to order by farmers and their machinery. Old oak trees twisted and reached out from their century-old cores. The sky, a tender blue protected by a screen of clouds. You knew it was daytime but you couldn't pinpoint the sun. A good day for driving. No need for sunglasses. A good thing too. Although Jasper always kept the public rooms of the manse – it was just a plain old ranch next to the church but Tim always liked to call their homes "manses" - in company-ready condition, she let her indifference toward housekeeping show in the messiness of her car's interior. Thank heavens for tinted window glass. Her new old car had its perks.

Up ahead some large dark object suddenly showed on the side of the road. Garbage bag? It moved. Jasper braked. "Thank you, angels, for driving my car," she said, her faith being an on-again, off-again thing that cropped up during moments of high stress or drama. She'd been driving on automatic pilot, half her mind still back in the Truman Free

Church hall kitchen, watching Pastor Tim waxing amorous amidst the leftovers.

The garbage bag alongside Highway X, closer now, showed itself to be what it was in reality, a wild turkey. Even with her finely tuned contact lens prescription, Jasper remained near-sighted. She could never achieve her twin's near perfect vision. She waited for the turkey.

The big tom gave her and her car a sidewise glance, then led his flock from the wooded side across the two-lane road to the wide open field all gold stubble from last fall's corn harvest. It was too early to plant this year's crop. Jasper counted each of the iron-colored birds, some only slightly smaller than the feathered parade major, others inches shorter and smaller boned, as they followed their leader. She sure did enjoy watching these strange creatures. Jasper was a born-and-bred Midwesterner. And although she had visited several important American cities, and while in college, even enjoyed a semester living in London, she remained at heart, a Midwest girl with a liking for the changes in the seasons and an appreciation for empty country roads and prehistoric-looking birds that kept to their mission in spite of human presence.

Two, four, seven, eight... The turkeys kept coming like cars on a freight train which she also enjoyed watching pass whenever she got stopped at a railroad crossing and didn't happen to be in a hurry. Jasper was the sort of dreamy, patient person who liked contemplating the lives of turkeys and train engineers alike. They probably both – the turkeys and the engineers – saw a lot of the country. Arkansas probably and Indiana at least.

There on the quiet Highway X with her Ford pointed west, Jasper sat still, daydreaming for several minutes after the turkeys were safely crossed. She pictured the colorful tags on the sides of the boxcars. They'd read something like "Hobo Stew" and "Metro Retro." Tim had told her they were gang signs and irreligious symbols. And he objected to the property damage. But Jasper wondered what all his fuss was about. She couldn't see the graffiti as blemishes on the tame old boxcars. What was the harm in admiring someone else's handiwork, their art and the only canvas they had maybe, their wild scrawl and design of pride? There was no law against looking and marveling, was there?

Jasper rummaged at the foot of the passenger's seat in the cooler she'd packed last night back at the manse in Truman. She felt the bottle of water, but opted for the less healthy but perkier tasting diet soda. She popped the lid and sipped. Wasn't there some kind of hypocrisy in Tim's inability to enjoy a display foreign to his own life? She couldn't work it out logically. She had never felt particularly logical in spite of her years spent in serving out her term as the wife of a minister with lots of dirty secrets. Being able to be practical and appear respectable was not the same as being logical. Tim's attitude was, *If it ain't mine, it ain't right.* Not a point of view Jasper had ever shared.

The turkeys off to her right were having a field day, oblivious now to her presence. Even with her myopia, she spotted the leader – the big tom who had led the exodus. Were all those not-so-big turkeys his hens? Would one male turkey get to have a dozen hens to himself? Maybe some of the smaller birds were other toms. Did the big tom have rights to them as well? Or didn't turkeys fly that way? Maybe younger males hung around their role models before mating season arrived full on and set them into rivalry one against the other.

Jasper shook her head, focused forward, and started driving again. Probably I'm just run down, she said to herself.

She popped an auctioneering instructional CD she'd ordered from Worldwide College of Auctioneering in Mason City, Iowa, into the car's player, and chanted along as she drove. "One-dollah-bid. Now two-dollah-bid. Now three-dollah bid and four." The instructor's voice at the beginning had told her to relax her diction, to let herself go Southern even if she wasn't from the South, to let her Midwestern twang melt into honey, so that the distinctions between words and numbers slurred. The practiced auctioneer on the CD even said to take bids off the telephone poles. Jasper liked the sound of that, "Taking Bids off Telephone Poles." But she didn't quite get it. The telephone poles were bidders? Or was she supposed to sell the poles? She slurped her pop, and carried on as best she could.

The telephone poles went by and her bid-calling went on. "Five-dollah-bid, now six-dollah-bid, now seven-dollah bid, now eight," she sang as the miles and the poles went by.

Three hours later she was closing in on Forest Grove when she saw a car pulled over on the gravel shoulder just ahead. A person stood behind it. The car was a rusty orange color. The person – it was a woman, she could see now – wore all black, slacks and long-sleeved shirt. She turned to the side, waving, and Jasper could see the bulge of a baby-to-be. Jasper checked her rear view, signaled and pulled over alongside the woman. She cut her engine so the woman could hear her easily. "Need some help?"

"I'm due soon."

"I see!"

"I mean at work, at the restaurant where I work," the woman said. She was laughing and so was Jasper.

"Hop in. Or rather, get in slowly, then rest," Jasper said. "Where's your restaurant?"

"Over in Forest Grove. Right downtown."

"I'm going to Forest Grove! If you give me directions, I'll get you there right away." Jasper moved the cooler out of the way.

The woman exhaled a big sigh as she released the seat belt, and adjusted it for her extra bulge up front. "I'm so relieved. You're very nice to do this."

Jasper smiled over at her reassuringly. "It's no trouble. But what about your car?"

She sniffed. "My boyfriend will take care of it. I'll call him from work, and he'll come over to get it started. Again. It's really his old junker. Let him take care of it."

"Okay, then," Jasper said. Today she felt reluctant to hear someone else's troubles.

With the passenger door secured, Jasper turned the key in the ignition and the auctioneer's rhythmic chanting sounded. "Five-now-ten-now-fifteen-twenty…" Jasper pushed off the sound.

"I love auctions!" the woman said. "You must like 'em a lot to listen to them in the car."

Jasper glanced over at her new traveling companion. The woman was younger than Jasper, she could tell that. Her red hair and freckled face gave her a pleasant farm girl charm, like an old painting of a little Dutch girl or maybe an Irish lass from days past.

"I'm studying to become an auctioneer."

"Huh. I didn't know you had to study to be an auctioneer!"

"It's one way to do it. Is this your first baby?" Jasper asked pleasantly.

"I dated one once."

"What?"

"An auctioneer. Ted Phillips? Maybe you know him. He's at – "

"Biggs Auction House," Jasper said. "That's my stepfather's place. That's where I'm going to work."

"Oh-oh. I don't know about your stepfather. But watch out for Ready Teddy."

Jasper cringed. "One of those, huh?"

"You'll be okay. I'm just saying. Oh, it's my third," the woman said.

"Pardon?"

The woman patted her expanded tummy. "My third baby! I have two girls already. Maybe number 3 will be the lucky charm. I love my girls, but I s'pose a boy would be nice for a change. I'm Molly by the way."

"Candy – I mean 'Jasper.'"

"Hi, Candy, I mean Jasper." Molly giggled. "Are you a spy? Witness protection? That sort of thing."

Jasper looked again at young Molly's face. So young, with three children, a broken down car, a boyfriend and working as a waitress, and amazingly cheerful. "Well, I've just left my husband and I'm on my way to my new life."

For a few key seconds, Molly said nothing, and Jasper feared that she had shocked her into silence. Jasper felt woefully out of touch with social mores when it came to truth-telling.

But then Molly said, "It happens. We have about 20 minutes here. Why don't you tell me about it?"

So Jasper did. By the time they reached the outskirts of Forest Grove, Pop. 7,830, then drove through the college town with its industrial overtones, she had unburdened herself – revealing the years of covering up her husband's misbegotten romances, just leaving out the fact that some of them had been with men. A philandering minister was bad enough. A philandering minister with multi-sexual tendencies might shock her temporary car guest. Jasper found that her feeling of being wronged didn't require her to exact revenge on screwy Pastor Tim. He'd have enough to deal with just because of her absence and the forthcoming news of their legal separation. Then the big D that would follow.

She left Molly outside the door of The Forester, a posh looking place next to the Forest Grove Inn. The young waitress invited her to come there for dinner sometime. "You bring a friend – anybody but that bad husband of yours – and just ask for me. I'll treat you."

Jasper thanked her. The offer was so warm-hearted that it brought tears to her eyes. It gave her hope for her new life in Forest Grove. "And you'll have to stop by Biggs Auction House. You can see a lady auctioneer in training." They waved good-bye.

Jasper pulled away, heading confidently in the direction she thought would take her to her apartment.

Owing to her poor sense of direction, Jasper made a wrong turn off Riverside Avenue where The Forester and the Forest Grove Inn backed up to the Honey River, then another wrong turn meant to correct herself, and ended up driving across one of Forest Grove's three main bridges from the more prosperous East side of town to the West.

What would make it so, she knew from Cookie's and Jimmy's citings of local history. Although their differences and vocal arguments were the stuff of family legend, Cookie and Jimmy had found common ground in their love of local lore. When Eastern industrialists and Western pioneers with inventive spirits created their millworks, their foundries and machining works (paper making machines and corn curls came later), they needed housing for the scores of late 19th, early 20th Century blacks and poor whites they induced to come north and work in their factories.

The one-story, two bedroom homes all made from the same plan sprang up across the west side of the prospering town. They weren't slums. Rather, working class homes with tidy yards front and back. Individual families had altered the fronts of their cottages. Some trimmed the front windows with maroon shutters, or painted the wood blue or yellow instead of the original white. Gingerbreading decorated the overhang above one front door.

As she drove up 4th Street, then back down 6th, Jasper could easily picture a young couple, he in suspenders, she in housedress with a babe in arms, proudly surveying their new home. "Well, sweetheart, it ain't much but it's all ours," the man would say. "Why, dear, I think it's sweet," his bride would reassure. And they'd go in and set to making their own Brasstown Cottage all their own.

Jasper's cell phone brought her back to real time. From its entombment in her purse which she'd shoved under the driver's seat, it sang out, "Alleluia!" Time for a new ringtone.

She pulled over and scrambled but missed the call by a heartbeat. It was Cookie. She quickly found Cookie under Favorites and called her back.

Cookie didn't say hello. She said, "What do you think?"

Jasper smiled. It was simply reassuring to hear her sister's voice. "About what?" she asked. Out her window, some kids were bouncing and missing and bouncing and missing baskets with the ball they flung toward a garage hoop. It should be lower for such little children, Jasper thought, but the kids were better than she would have been.

Cookie's voice at her ear woke her from her reverie. "Your new neighborhood! Your house! Your apartment!" There was a suspicious pause.

Jasper could read her sister's silences as clearly as any spoken comment.

Cookie said, "You're not there yet, are you?"

"Uh-uh." Outside, the tallest child missed a basket. The Alpha male missed. That was sort of gratifying, Jasper thought, and felt instantly guilty.

"Where are you?"

"Maybe you can help," Jasper said.

"OK. First let's figure out where you are."

"Sis, if I knew where I was – "

"Right. Can you read the street signs?"

One of the kids lost control of the basketball and it rolled into the street in front of Jasper's car. She jumped out and stopped it from rolling further with quick foot work. She picked it up and flung it back toward them. It landed on the grass, and the smallest child scampered to pick it up. But the kids didn't return to their game. They just stood and stared at Jasper.

"Hey, you guys?" she called, all friendly and mild. In Truman she'd grown accustomed to children talking to her. Even there the schoolchildren had been drilled in Stranger Danger, but most of them knew her as the pastor's wife, a safe bet. But here where people, especially on the west side of the river divide, or so it was said, had more worries and mistrust and no one knew her as Mrs. Rev. Rowe anyway, it was different and more dangerous.

Alpha Boy yelled back, as belligerent as it was inquisitive, "Whaddya want, lady?"

"Could you tell me where we are exactly? I got a little turned around."

The boy spat on the ground near him. His own yard. Jasper felt sorry for a child angry enough to defile his home ground. But maybe that was just a boy thing. She liked to think that if she had had a son, she would have raised him not to spit in public. Maybe he was going through a spitting stage… The front door of the squat gray house opened. A stringy looking woman in shorts and unbecoming tank top stepped outside, carrying on an argument with the phone at her ear. She broke off her phone dispute to yell at the children. "Get in here! What're you doing? No talking to strangers! Playtime is over! Get yourselves in here."

The older boy spat again – this time in Jasper's direction, then marched with the other two past the cross woman into the house. The woman turned momentarily toward Jasper. "What're you staring at, huh?" Then into the phone, "I don't care what he told you, it's the time we had that counts."

She disappeared back inside the house. "Close the damn door!" she yelled. And the door slammed shut.

Jasper retreated to her car. She heard Cookie calling her name. Jasper grabbed the phone.

"Sorry."

"Are you okay? You were there and then you weren't there."

"Fine. I'm fine." She told Cookie about the brief scene with the children and mother.

"You've got to be careful, Sis." Her voice held real concern. "You've always been a little too open to other people's energies, and you're vulnerable right now."

"Yes, ma'am!"

"No, really, Sis. I'm telling you," Cookie said. Some people might think that being a professional psychic medium, which was Cookie's calling, meant that one was flakey. Dizzy. Ungrounded. And that someone who has been a pastor's wife and a responsible hard-working, loyal one at that and was now entering the practical realm of auctioneering, would have her feet on the ground. And the feet would be encased in heavy, no-nonsense shoes. But Jasper had long been the twin with the wandering mind. While Cookie prided herself on her own down-to-earthness. "Put me on speaker phone," she told Jasper.

Jasper did as she was told. She was obedient to a fault – a quality in addition to loyalty and caring too much about what other people think – that had helped imprison her in a flawed marriage for 15 too-long years.

So with Cookie on speaker phone, riding shotgun as it were, and Jasper moving up close on street signs for her myopic eyes which would reveal the actual lettering when it was almost too late to matter. G-O-D-3-Z would become Grant St. at the very last second.

Jasper zigzagged through the west side, where people were outdoors in their yards enjoying one of the first breaks from the long winter just winding down. She passed a Stop-Ngo, a bright red Chicago style hot dog stand, Taco Jack's, and a drycleaners with what looked like a large green jungle barely held in by the plate glass window on the front.

"Sis! Sis, are you there?" Cookie's voice interrupted her sightseeing. "You need to turn left at the next intersection! Are you in the left lane? Get in the left lane!"

Jasper signaled, looked over her shoulder – for the rear view mirror had suffered too many off course reverses and was being held in a permanent unusable position by epoxy and duct tape – then jumped when the driver behind her honked. "Thank you!" She smiled into the mirror and waved. She made it fully into the lane just in time for the turn. She told Cookie, "The bridge! I'm back on the bridge!"

Cookie laughed fondly. "Just so it's the same bridge." Later she could tease her sister about her lack of directional sense. Right now they shared a mission. "Okay. Now focus. This next part gets tricky."

Ten minutes later, Jasper glided steadily at 27 mph down Milwaukee Road. Cookie announced, "Prepare to turn right."

"I'm all about right turns."

Chapter 3

Jasper turned onto Hickory Lane. A big white box van with *Bid & Buy at Biggs!* waited in the driveway of the second white house from the corner. Its tires actually straddled the narrow drive. Jasper hoped her new landlord didn't mind a few ruts in the yard and boulevard of grass separating the property from the next door neighbor's. She told Cookie that she had arrived, and they made plans to talk again later.

She pulled in by the curb in front of the house. Things had been so tense and busy for her the past six weeks that Cookie had done the house hunting for her and found her an upper apartment in this nice old two-story in what she described as a peaceful neighborhood. This was Jasper's first view of her new home. Taller than the single family houses that flanked it, the white sided Victorian with yews flanking the front steps and plain yard looked simple, without frills. Blank. The better, Jasper hoped, to make it her own. 320 Hickory Lane. $3 + 2 + 0 = 5$. A good number for someone in transition, Cookie had told her, numerology being one of her side interests.

"Are you asleep in there?" a man's voice asked outside her window. He knocked sharply on the glass. Jimmy Biggs, a 65-year-old man of average height, stomped back toward the truck.

He signaled Jasper out of her car with a choppy thumb jerk like a coach calling a player back to the bench.

Jasper got out and hurried to comply.

"Sorry I'm late." She tried to kiss him on the cheek, but her stepfather moved out of reach.

"It's about time too. Where the hell have you been?" Jimmy was a barking dog of a man. Not especially tall. Maybe that's why he'd developed into the tough guy he was. He radiated largeness – a largesse of energy that he shared with the world on a *my way or the highway* basis. He'd been grumpy and badgering for decades, and in spite of that, had built up a solid business reputation in the community and a good middle class income from the auction house he'd founded. His eyes were a watery blue behind glasses. He won every stare-down contest that Jasper had witnessed since he first came into her life as her mother's husband. The twins, Jasper neé Candy and Cookie were six at the time.

"I got a little turned around," Jasper told her stepfather.

"What else is new?" The two helpers smirked, then hid their smiles.

Jimmy had aged certainly. Decades did that to a person. His face had fleshed out of that hungry dog look he used to have and his skin looked a little yellower than the last time Jasper remembered. His ever observant eyes looked slightly less piercing now behind their glasses, but Jasper bet he still didn't miss much. He'd been sober for many years now, so his belly was still flat under the polo shirt he invariably wore. Maybe his hairline had receded a couple more inches than the last time she had seen him. *Never call Jimmy Biggs bald.* He was long-waisted with short legs, and Jasper knew he was vain about them. As soon as the weather warmed, he'd switch from long khakis to shorts as much to show off his muscular calves as for comfort. His sort of footwear varied from L.L. Bean sneakers to L. L. Bean boat shoes. Only an evening benefit auction would force him into the one expensive pair of dress blacks that he owned and a mismatched but professional looking brown suit jacket and tie. Jimmy Biggs had an in charge personality, to say the least. No doubt about it, Jimmy Biggs ruled as pack leader.

"Where's your key?" he asked Jasper.

She handed over her key ring which contained some seven keys too many and Jimmy passed it along to one of the helpers.

The dark-haired man introduced himself to Jasper as Esteban. Carrying along the souvenirs from past places at least made it easy to find her key ring. Finding the correct current key was a different matter. "It's that one," Jasper said.

"You wanna unlock the door?" Esteban asked.

"Go do it!" Jimmy ordered.

"Sure, boss. But it is her place."

Jasper smiled at him and took back her keys. She put her hand out to the other man, fair-haired. "I'm Jasper."

"Tony. I thought your name was Candy?"

"Jasper was my mother's maiden name. I'm kind of tired of being called Candy."

"Not a candy ass anymore, huh?" Esteban joked.

"Watch your fucking mouth," Jimmy said. He turned to Jasper, "I gotta go. I'm looking at some real estate. These two are fine. A little rough around the edges. But they're all right."

Esteban and Tony made faces behind his back, then sobered up fast when Jimmy shot them a look. Jasper decided it might be fun to have younger brothers types like these guys around.

Jimmy strode to his black SUV which he'd parked behind the auction van.

"Thanks, Jimmy!" Jasper called after him.

He waved. He said, without turning around, "I'm glad you're here." He swung into the SUV and yelled out the open window at Jasper. "Come over here." He handed her a $20 bill.

"You can give it to the guys when they're through. Don't tell them it's from me."

Jasper thanked him and started away. "

"Be on time tomorrow!" he yelled after her. "Nine sharp. Make that 8:30." He started out of the driveway, then backed up. "Wear something practical for God's sake!" he yelled. Then he tore away.

Jasper watched him go.

"Let's get moving," Esteban said. "We can catch part of the game if this doesn't take too long."

"Sorry. Sure." Jasper hurried up the steps to the house and fumbled for the key to her new front door

Jasper crossed the dark wood threshold. Inside, the entry way was pretty bare bones. The walls were chalk white, the carpet, a deep green, and the banister leading up to her apartment as well as the closed door, she understood, to the ground floor apartment, were painted dark brown. She heard a TV going behind the dark door. Some loud mouthed preacher. Oh, lord.

Esteban and Tony were on her heels. So she climbed resolutely up the stairs. Three-quarters of the way up, a jut-out covered in plaster nearly grazed her head. "Low one," Estaban said.

They reached a small landing where the stairway made a sharp turn to the left for the last few steps. There was a second door here, with multi-paned glass.

"You gonna be here by yourself?" Estaban asked.

"But I hear it's a nice safe neighborhood," Tony said.

Jasper shivered a little. Put her key in the lock, and turned open the door to her new apartment. She stepped inside. It smelled a little dusty but not bad.

She felt like whispering. But the men's voices were loud and echoing in the empty apartment. She let them wander as she made her own way around to check out her new home.

The bathroom with an old claw-foot tub and pedestal sink was just to the left and across the hall was the bedroom. Her room. It had a one door closet, but a deep one she was happy to discover. Two windows on adjacent walls that were letting in a good amount of afternoon light. And nothing else. She would need curtains, a bookshelf. A bed!

Jimmy had sent over a few things from his last auction to tide her over until she could afford more on her own. She'd never in all her adult life been faced with decorating decisions on her own. She trembled a little. Not quite overwhelmed. Not quite excited. Something at a confusing point in between.

Esteban and Tony were already removing the door from its hinges, and taking down the banisters on either side of the last short flight of steps by the time Jasper finished her tour of the apartment. There was a small living room and, through an arched doorway, another room whose windows looked down to the street and next door to the neighbor's. The houses here stood a little closer than they had in Truman, but there would still be plenty of privacy. She wanted time and space to lick her wounds. To what use could she put this extra room? A library? She loved reading. A sewing room? A place to set up as an art studio? She'd always wanted to learn how to sew and paint.

And the kitchen. An oddly arranged room with a two-part white sink from the 30s, one set of cupboards, an apartment sized gas range and a white refrigerator alongside. There was a nice area for a kitchen table and chairs. Why, she might even someday maybe if possible invite people or at least one person over for dinner. It could happen.

Another door off the kitchen held steep steps that Jasper knew from her sister's description led down to the basement laundry room. The couple living in the ground floor apartment owned the washer and dryer but maybe she could work out something, Cookie had said. Jasper didn't want to negotiate with anybody. She would just as soon go to a laundromat for the time being so as to avoid any potential conflicts. There was one next to the auction house.

The guys were efficient carrying up the furniture, banging about a bit on the narrow steps and cursing as they went. She could tell they were frustrated for a few seconds here and there and tried not to take it personally. They asked her did she want the sleeper sofa in the living room or the bedroom? Living room. Along with the TV and chest of drawers. She thought the TV might soothe her to sleep while she adjusted to living alone.

She helped them carry up the dinette table and chairs plus two boxfuls of kitchenware and dishes. Then they put the door back on its hinges and screwed the banisters back in place alongside the stairs. Jasper walked outside with them.

She thanked them profusely and shook their hands. "Here's twenty," she said.

They stared at the single bill.

"Oh, I've got something in the car for you," she said. She ran over and brought back the plate of cookies from the church send-off.

They exchanged glances with each other. Jasper read their minds. *We gave up our afternoon off for this?* "Wait, there's more." She fetched her purse and handed them each a $5 of her own. Tim would have given them a God Bless, no cash. "Is that okay?"

"Yeah, yeah, this is great. This is great," Esteban said.

"You don't have to," Tony said and tried to hand her back the five.

"No, no, it's not much. But you guys were really helpful and very nice about it."

"Taco Jack's, here we come!" Esteban said. They told her they'd see her tomorrow at the auction house. Then they pulled down the door on the back of the truck, climbed in, and rolled out of the driveway.

There were ruts. There were definite ruts. But they weren't too bad, Jasper told herself. She watched the guys drive away, waving as they went. Then she headed back to the house. It was time to start helping herself feel at home.

Chapter 4

As she started back up the steps to her place, the door to the ground floor apartment opened. A cloud of menthol cigarette smoke blew into the shared entryway.

"I see you," said the voice of a middle-aged woman. "Don't think you can sneak on by without saying hi!" The voice held a teasing, sing-song quality.

Jasper came back down to meet her new neighbor. She introduced herself.

The woman said her name was Mrs. Margie O'Neil. She stepped into the entryway and closed the door behind her. Fifty-five, 65, 70 years old? Jasper couldn't tell. Mrs. O'Neil had a plump, old-fashioned figure encased in a powder blue going to church dressy dress covered in a floral bib apron. She might have been younger than Jasper's mother would have been if she had lived beyond her daughters' childhood, but the clothes she wore reminded Jasper of small town life 25 years ago. Mrs. O'Neil fanned the air with her plump hand. "That's my husband Mr. Dick O'Neil in there. He's a chimney." From her apron pocket, she extracted a spray can. She began misting the hallway with floral air freshener.

Jasper felt like a mosquito under air raid attack. "Oh, please, please, you don't have to do that! Not on my account." She covered her hands and mouth with her hands.

"I wouldn't want our nice new neighbor complaining about smoke the way the last one did." Mrs. O'Neil aimed a roguish spray Jasper's direction and squawked in delight.

"Could you stop now, Mrs. O'Neal? Please?" Jasper pleaded.

The spraying petered out. Mrs. O'Neil shook the can. "All gone. I'll pick up some more next time I'm out. That is, unless you want to buy the next round?"

Jasper said she would try to remember.

"Bye now." The door closed, then reopened before Jasper could move. Mrs. O'Neil stuck her head out. She eyeballed Jasper's long, chaste skirt. "We attend service every Sunday. You're always welcome. Mr. O'Neil and I would just love that."

Jasper thanked her. The second the door closed, she dashed upstairs. She opened the bathroom window and both of the ones in the living room. Then she grabbed a sweater and padded downstairs and out the front door. It seemed like the perfect time to take a look around the neighborhood.

The air outside was cooling with the approach of evening, and Jasper, quick to chill, wished she had a heavier wrap. But the air smelled so fresh after the menthol cigarette meets lilac stink back inside, that she didn't mind. She'd just walk faster, that's all. She hoped that if she met up with anyone, her own clothes didn't reek with the foul blend. Pastor Tim always told her to windmill her arms, shake out her hands, do jumping jacks. None of that actually helped her icy hands warm up. But that didn't stop his *suggestions*. She turned herself into a human pinwheel for him. She tried. She really had tried.

She found tears coming to her eyes. She forced herself to focus on her new surroundings. There were indeed lots of trees here in Forest Grove. They still stood bare branched from the winter but they promised blossoms soon and lots of shade for the summer.

Two joggers went by and nodded at her. A couple walking a Great Dane and a bulldog maneuvered by. She moved into the grass, but they were nice and pulled the dogs far from her. "Nice evening for a walk!" they said cheerfully.

Jasper smiled back. "Yes! Isn't it?" It was comforting, these little public exchanges. By the time she had passed the swing set on the length of lawn between sidewalk and the cemetery fence which was set well back from the road, and reached the gate to the cemetery, her loneliness had eased.

She decided to walk a little ways into the cemetery. Forest Lawn it was called, according to the sign at the entrance that displayed a list of rules. Winter hours were 7 a.m. to 6 p.m., she noted. Nothing about springtime. She wondered how diligent the local police were in enforcing this. With a twinge of slight guilt, she followed the red brick pathway inside. She liked the uneven feel beneath her feet of the old paving bricks. She admired the old granite markers and statues. "For Our Soldiers Dead" read the inscription on one that showed four men in Civil War uniforms. None of their backsides showed and they carried canteens and flagpoles to cover the fronts of their pants. *Oh God*, Jasper thought, *have I started to get odd about sex already?* Fifteen years of life next to Pastor Tim with little to no sex between them had finally caught up to her now that she was free of him.

Jasper studied the headstones. *Bliss, Key, Peet and Love*, she read. Suzannah Reynolds had lived for only 14 days.

Cemeteries did not sadden Jasper. She felt at home there, curious about the lives lived in other times, liked knowing that in Victorian days families would picnic in the park like settings.

Forest Lawn had huge oaks growing and Jasper, squinting, could practically see a family in warm weather cottons sitting happily on a blanket. Jasper's heart panged with Family Envy.

Before she knew it, she had walked far down the first long brick road. A wave of tiredness washed over her. It had been a long day. She looked for a second gate she might not have noticed earlier but did not find one. Maybe she could climb the fence and shorten her route home. She peeked around but could see no living person. She giggled. She felt so naughty. Then she felt chagrinned at how this little thing was such a big deal to her. Her world, until this very day, had shrunk to such a small repressed size. She approached the fence. A chain link one. High enough to keep intruders from hopping over easily but not too tall to climb. In or out.

There wasn't anything nearby to stand on since the closest grave markers were at least three feet away. After a moment's deliberation, Jasper approached the barrier, reached up and grabbed the top rail, then stuck the toe of one shoe inside the metal mesh as far up as her leg would reach. She hiked her skirt up above her knees, then boosted herself up and flung the other leg over the top. She centered herself atop the fence. She'd have to catch her breath and figure out how to extract her foot from the inside hole of the fence before she could drop to the other side. Easier fence climbing probably took practice.

Then she saw a man walking across the grassy yards of the park between the cemetery and the sidewalk near Milwaukee Road. Her toe was really stuck. He drew closer. Jasper smoothed her skirt down as best she could. She pretended to admire the view from her fence top perch.

"Hi," the man said with a friendly smile. "You just hangin'?" He was a handsome dark-skinned man, slim, in jeans and a blue shirt with the sleeves rolled up. Maybe 40 years old, Jasper assessed.

Darn it, oh darn it. "Might as well," Jasper said.

"You need a hand?"

There was nothing she would have liked better, but she felt much too embarrassed to accept help from this stranger. This strange man. This handsome stranger.

"No. I'm good. I think. Ouch." Jasper shifted uncomfortably on the fence. She tried to get her shoe free. She just about had it out when her hem caught on one of the strands of metal.

"Uh-huh."

"I'm good. Really." Jasper wriggled her left foot free of the cemetery side of the fence, balanced again, and had nearly gotten her outside leg cleared when she completely lost her balance and tumbled down to the grass outside the fence. She felt the back side of her skirt rip. The man hurried over and helped her to her feet.

"Ah, you might want to tie your sweater around your waist," he said. "Sorry I don't have a jacket to offer you."

"Th-thank you. I think."

"You do this a lot?"

Jasper stared at his solemn face which cracked into a wide friendly grin. She smiled back. "My first time. I'm new to the neighborhood." She hoped the nice man would go away soon before her deep intrinsic shame – shame on general principles – rose to the surface along with the blush she was already showing.

"Oh. Are you the new lady in the two-family?"

She nodded.

"Word travels. Or at least Mrs. O'Neal's words do. I'm Glenn Relerford. Two houses down."

"I'm Jasper. Jasper Biggs." They walked together back toward their block of Hickory Lane. "But weren't you taking a walk?" she asked.

He smiled easily before he answered. "I was just finishing when I saw your dilemma and I just couldn't leave you stuck up on that fence all night."

She thanked him. They chatted amiably, and Glenn told her about the neighborhood. She was relieved to hear she wasn't the only singleton. Although he didn't say whether or not he had a family, he mentioned several other neighbors on their own. He wasn't wearing a wedding band.

There was a Mrs. Beyer, a banker's widow, and Ginny Gardener, the widow of a doctor. These were older ladies, Jasper knew, who had defined themselves for many years as the wives of important professional men. She felt glad to know she was breaking free of her role as Mrs. Rowe, the minister's wife. She would never be the minister's widow. She gulped and rubbed her skinny wedding ring. "I'm sorry. Did you ask me something?" They paused on the sidewalk in front of 320 Hickory.

Glenn nodded toward the downstairs picture window. "Good ol' Mrs. O'Neil. She's having the time of her life right now," he said. "'That new girl is talking to the black policeman,'" he said in falsetto.

"You're what?"

"I'm black," he said with a straight face.

Jasper laughed nervously. "No, the other part."

"I'm a police detective. You look startled. Should I be worried about you?"

"Okay. I was in the cemetery a little late. But that's why I was climbing the fence."

He stood silently.

Guiltily, Jasper continued. "That's why I was climbing the fence. To get out faster."

Glenn remained silent.

"Well, okay, here's the thing. I was just plain tired. You know? And, to tell the truth, I was just taking a short cut home." She shifted from one foot to the other. She checked out the curtains on the ground floor picture window. Sure enough. They fluttered.

"Uh-huh. You were saying," Glenn said.

"Am I in trouble?"

"Well, let's see. After hours occupation of cemetery. Possibly disturbing the peace of a bunch of dead folks. Fence climbing."

Jasper actually found herself sweating.

Glenn burst out laughing. "Hey, I think that Forest Grove can overlook these minor infractions, Mrs. Ex-Minister's Wife."

"What?" That wave of tiredness she'd felt earlier washed back over her. She took a step away from Glenn.

"I'm sorry. I shouldn't have said that," he offered.

"I guess I better get used to my new title." Jasper waved a hand at him over her shoulder as she trudged toward her front door.

"Wait!" he called after her.

"Nice to meet you," Jasper said without turning around. She unlocked the door and went inside.

The combined odors of cigarette and lilac lingered like indoor smog. Tiredly, Jasper climbed up and beyond the cloud and let herself in to her apartment.

Her footsteps echoed across the bare wood floors. In the living room, she sagged on to the sleeper sofa. She sat and sat until the light faded all around her. She heard a mumble of voices from below. Something strange and yet oddly familiar. She got wearily to her feet and tiptoed to her apartment door. She cracked it open and could hear more mumbling, indiscernible voices from downstairs. *It sounds like...*

Jasper retreated, closing the door behind her and locking it. She retrieved a stemmed glass from the kitchen, brought it into the front room, and turned it upside down against the bare floor. She got down on her stomach and laid her ear atop the base of the glass. The loud gibberish she thought she had heard was amplified now. It was what she had thought. Glossolalia. Speaking in tongues! "Oh, God, can't I get away from this stuff?" Jasper asked the nobody in the room. Her cell phone Alleluiaed. It was Cookie. "Hi, Sis, I'm so glad to hear from you." Jasper flopped back on the sofa and settled in for a comforting long chat.

Chapter 5

Jasper kicked all her covers off the sleeper sofa during the first night in her new apartment. So when her cell phone chirped her awake at 6:30 a.m., she took her goosebumped arms and icy feet to the bathroom for a hot shower. No shower, only tub. She'd forgotten. She sniffed back a second of self-pity, her life felt so reduced, ran a couple inches of water into the claw foot, and took a quick sitz bath, only long enough to warm her purple toes to deep pink and give her time to soap down her vital parts. When she stepped out, she saw no towels. She wiped herself semi-dry with her nightgown and draped it on the towel rack. Her mouth tasted foul so she ran her tongue over the wet bar of soap, scooped up a handful of water from the tap, and gargled until suds leaked out her mouth. She had no idea where she had packed her toothbrush and toothpaste.

Jasper rushed to her suitcases and boxes to find something suitable for her first day of work at Biggs Auction House. She dug through a box labeled "Church Donations" and found a pair of neutral slacks either black or navy; she couldn't tell from the dim overhead bulb in the bare bedroom. Further down in the box full of items parishioners had sent to the manse, she discovered a plaid shirt that reminded her of a Country Western tune she liked, "For Crying Out Loud, I've Got You to Thank." She sang a little bit to keep herself company. In her own things, she found a cache of clean panties. She grabbed up a balled pair of dark hose and one-inch pumps that were almost the right size and, sprinting naked back to the living room, found her bra from yesterday where she had dropped it alongside the sleeper sofa.

A quick glance at her cell phone showed that she had unbelievably used up a half hour already. The eastern light poured in the living room windows. Even the proximity of the house next door couldn't block the sun. A second floor curtain across the way twitched. Jasper clutched her clothes over her breasts and her flats across her crotch. A gray-haired woman smiled and waved. Jasper smiled automatically and waved back. She dropped to her knees atop her fallen clothes, and scooted along on top of them to the arched doorway between living room and the empty possibility room. There she lay on her back atop the painted wood floor and shimmied into her clothes.

A buzzer sounded from the hallway inside her front door. Fire alarm? Jasper sprang upright in a hurry and went to check. She heard voices talking downstairs, so she turned the deadbolt and opened her door. A ribbon of cigarette smoke curled inside. Fanning the air, she stepped out on the landing in her stocking feet and closed the door behind her.

"There you are!" Her downstairs neighbor Mrs. O'Neil stood near the open front door in the ground floor entryway. She wore a red and blue plaid bathrobe. She aimed a spray of gardenia-scented air freshener up through the clouds of cigarette smoke toward Jasper. "You have company!" She slammed the front door and marched off into her own apartment.

Jasper padded downstairs. That same buzzer sounded from over Jasper's shoulder.

"Next time you'll know the sound of your own door! Mr. O'Neil and me get the bell," Mrs. O'Neil shouted.

The first five knocks of shave-and-a-haircut came from outside.

Jasper flung open the door. On the porch outside stood a familiar looking woman of 70 years or so.

"I'm sorry – "Jasper began.

"I'm sorry to bother you," the woman said. "And that other person." She giggled. She held a stuffed animal of some kind up to the screen. "Welcome to Hickory Lane."

"Oh! You're from next door." Jasper fumbled with the lock on the screen door.

When the woman was inside the foyer, she handed over the toy which turned out to be a fluffy orange and white cat. Jasper immediately dissolved into tears. She sank onto the second step from the bottom and clutched the toy cat to her heart.

"Mrs. Rowe, you're overwrought." She edged onto the step next to Jasper. "I'm Ginny Gardener from next door."

"Jasper," Jasper said.

"No, Ginny. There, there." Ginny Gardener draped her arm gently around Jasper's shoulders and pulled her into a motherly side hug.

Jasper rested her tired head against the other woman. "You don't understand," she blubbered. "My old name is Rowe. My new name is Jasper. Jasper Biggs."

Ginny Gardener reached for the toy cat. "I think I've made a mistake."

Jasper held on tight. "Don't take the kitty!"

"You don't have to keep it to make me feel better. I know you've been through a lot lately. I don't want to add to your burdens."

Jasper hugged the toy cat. "How do you know? My name – my old name?"

"That's what neighbors are for. At least they are in an old-fashioned neighborhood like ours."

"I love the kitty, Mrs. Gardener." Jasper felt about ten years old hugging the stuffed cat and, for the moment, she did not care how she was coming across to her new acquaintance.

"Ginny."

"Call me Jasper."

"Of course, dear." The older woman cleared her throat. "I wanted to warn you about that policeman who lives on the other side of me," she said. "He's married, you know."

"Oh?" Jasper snuffled back the last of her tears.

"I've never met the lady. They don't live together. But I believe it's the real legal deal and all that."

Jasper swallowed her disappointment. *Told you the world was a wicked place. Better get used to new heartaches,* that wicked old familiar voice inside said. "I suppose he has a bunch of kids too," she said.

"That I couldn't say. Although sometimes there are young people visiting next door. I believe he has other family in the area."

Jasper squared her shoulders. "Thanks for sharing that with me."

"We're a close-knit little neighborhood here," Ginny said.

"Yes, I see that," Jasper said. She helped the older lady to her feet and linked her arm with hers. She escorted her next door, explaining en route how she had to hurry to leave for her first day on the job. The front lawn felt crunchy under her feet, but warmed by the morning sun, soaked the soles of her hose.

Ginny pointed at the footprints that trailed them across the adjacent driveways. "Oh, dear. I've caused you problems."

"It doesn't matter," Jasper said. She hugged the friendly neighbor good-bye and promised to come over for a longer visit when she could find time.

Ginny opened the side door to her house. A fluffy animal resembling the toy that Jasper still clutched came toddling out.

"Oh, Buddy!" Jasper, who had never been allowed a pet as the wife of the persnickety and often on the move Rev. Rowe, stood still not knowing how one approached a cat new to one's acquaintance.

"That's Alice."

"Alice."

Alice chirped a very small meow for such a big feline.

Jasper was won over immediately. She reached down to stroke the pet but it ambled just out of reach.

"I'm so glad you like cats."

"I didn't know I did but it turns out I do."

"Not like the other people in your house."

"The O'Neils."

"I don't know about him. I've never met him. But she brings out the broom every chance she gets."

"She goes after Mr. O'Neil?" Jasper glanced back over her shoulder and saw Mrs. O'Neil glowering out the window of the lower apartment directly at her and Ginny Gardener.

"No, I meant Alice." Ginny cleared her throat. "Ah, when you saw me at the window earlier."

"Oh, well, not really. Not for long."

"It was by mistake. People look out their windows in this neighborhood but I never expected to see you....I mean...in the ....I mean the way you were. I just wanted to see what color of curtains you had hung."

"Well, we'll both know soon!" Jasper did her best to sound light hearted. She made a mental note to buy the heaviest curtains she could afford. After all her years as a minister's wife, she was tired of having the details of her life scrutinized by others. Nice or otherwise. "Gotta run!" she called as she hurried back to her house.

"Dear!" Ginny called. "You might want to rethink those shoes you were planning on wearing. I expect at the auction house, you will be on your feet all day long."

♦

Biggs Auction House was just where Cookie had told her it would be, on the corner of West and Lincoln. It took only 20 minutes and one quick call to her sister before Jasper pulled into the big blacktopped parking lot. A former Piggly Wiggly grocery store, the gold brick building still boasted large display windows. Jasper parked in front of them since the lot was empty of other vehicles and she didn't know where to go. Old-fashioned furniture that looked heavier than all get-out took up the display area inside. A cherry red sign hanging down from the one-story roof announced the building's new identity. The auction house stretched nearly the entire length of the lot. Two big dumpsters stood side by side at the far back.

8:20 on her Ford's clock whose digital display was working this morning for a change. Jasper glanced in the visor mirror. Yikes. She had forgotten to do anything with her hair. She took one of the rubber bands she always kept on the gear shift, ran her hands back over her scalp, and pulled her long dark waves into a ponytail. The morning sun did nothing to hide her paleness. She slapped her cheeks and chewed her lips to bring out a little color.

A black SUV charged over the curb and roared to a stop alongside her car. The SUV's passenger window powered down. Jasper cracked her door open. She heard the radio blaring out early rock music. "Got a pen?" Jimmy Biggs yelled.

Jasper switched off the car and started rummaging through her purse. Tissues. A Forest Grove map. Peppermints. A religious tract titled, "God has a Plan for You."

"Leave it. We're late." Jimmy's voice boomed out and echoed against the sides of the auction house. The plate glass windows rattled.

"I just need a moment."

"We don't have a minute. Lock your goddamn door. Get in."

Suddenly feeling sweaty in the palms like the 21-year-old she had been nineteen years ago when she had to break the news of her impending marriage and the end to her college career to her angry stepfather, Jasper felt her 40 years of life and all her starting over courage evaporate. She got shakily out of her car, leaving behind her purse, pressed the lock button, and stepped up and into Jimmy's vehicle. It smelled strongly of some musky male cologne.

"What the hell took you so long?" he asked.

"How are you this morning?" Jasper asked.

Jimmy roared out onto Lincoln Avenue.

The force of the car slammed her back against the seat. She scrambled for her seatbelt. Jasper realized that she had left her keys locked inside her car. She told Jimmy.

"Don't whine," he said.

"But I need my car. It's all I've got."

Jimmy put in a quick call on his cell phone. "My brilliant stepdaughter locked her keys in her car. Open it for her, will you? Don't worry about it. It's a piece of crap." He tossed his cell on the dash.

"Thanks. I think."

"You see a yellow pad in here?"

"A pad? You mean, like a pillow?"

"Oh, for Christ's sake."

"There's no need to swear."

Jimmy swerved the SUV over to the curb. The car behind sounded its horn and pulled past. Jimmy yanked off his seatbelt, threw open the door and marched to the back where he retrieved a legal pad from among the packing boxes and paperwork, and brought it back inside. He threw it onto Jasper's lap. There was an address scrawled across the top page.

"Thank you." She was nice to a fault.

"Don't be sarcastic, missy. Remember who's boss here."

Jasper started to protest, but Jimmy cut her off. "We're on our way to a look-see," he said.

"Is that like a looky-looky?" Jasper asked, trying for a light-hearted note.

"Why don't you just be quiet and learn something?"

"Yessir."

Jimmy cut her a look. Even in three-quarter profile, Jimmy's glares had always cut her down to size. He had aged since she had last seen him. But even with liver spots and thicker glasses over his rheumy blue eyes, Jimmy was still the Man in Charge. He ruled his auction kingdom the way any despot does. Absolutely, with few kind words meted out to anyone in close association – family, employees, auction-goers.

He explained to Jasper that a look-see was an informal survey of stuff that a potential client wanted to sell on auction.

"An appraisal?"

"What?"

Jasper reached for the radio knob to turn down the volume. Jimmy pushed her hand away. Jasper raised her voice. "A look-see? It's an appraisal."

"No. We're just gonna look at their stuff and see if there's anything we want for the auction."

"Oh, a pre-auction estimate." Jasper had heard that term on her CD from the auctioneering college.

"No."

"An evaluation?"

"Look-see. What's our address?"

Jasper studied the handwriting on the pad. "I can't make it out."

Jimmy jerked it out of her hands. "311 Emerson Court. Or 811." He called the auction house on his phone and soon they pulled up in front of a bungalow at 819 Emerson. "Come on," he said. He was already out the door.

"But what do I do? Do I bring the notepad?" Jasper asked. She wiped her palms down her dark slacks.

"Yeah, bring the pad. Do what I tell you to do. Don't say anything."

Jasper scuffed along the cracked sidewalk toward the squat frame house. She felt about five years old. Was this what having a job felt like? Or was it just working for her stepfather? When she had worked alongside her soon-to-be-ex, she felt old beyond her years. Would she ever feel simply like herself?

The seven steps leading up to the front door were pink concrete, to Jasper's delight. She loved visiting other people's homes. Jimmy took no notice. He raised his hand to knock on the wrought iron and glass door but the interior oak door swung open. A woman with ferocious black hair stuck her head out. "Can I help you?"

Chapter 6

"We're here to help you," Jimmy said, turning on the charm. "You look familiar. Have you been to the auction?"

Jasper plastered a friendly smile on her face.

"Oh, you know me all right," the inky-haired woman said. "You both from Biggs Auction?"

Jimmy pulled out a business card from his bright red "Bid and Buy at Biggs" windbreaker.

"I know *you* are," the woman said. She woman disappeared into the interior and Jimmy followed her inside. The doors closed in Jasper's face. Feeling foolish, she knocked tentatively. She spent a moment sizing up her options and decided that no action was the best response. The doors opened and Jimmy yanked her inside.

"Stay right behind me," he hissed.

"There you are! We thought we'd lost you!" The woman smoothed her blunt cut hair into place. She radiated the strong scent of flowers; Jasper couldn't tell what kind. She stood several inches taller than Jimmy. She held her hand out to Jasper. It was a meaty hand. "Mary Clippert. This is my father's house."

Jasper shook hands. Mary Clippert delivered a real bone crusher. "Jasper Biggs. This is my stepfather."

"We go way back," Mary Clippert said.

"Really?" Jasper asked politely. Jimmy stepped on her foot. "Ow!"

The air reeked of garbage and dirty old clothes. A faint undercurrent of mildew lurked. Boxes and plastic bags, several microwaves of different vintages, random cabinets and chairs. Stacks and stacks of magazines and newspapers. It looked like a house of moldy old cards had collapsed. Jasper looked all around. The three of them seemed to be standing in the only level space available. "You have my sympathy. So has your father been gone awhile?" Jasper asked.

"Gone where?" Mary Clippert stood stiffly with her arms at her side as if she didn't want to come in contact with any of the dirty clutter that filled the room.

"I mean – ow!"

Jimmy had planted another shut up hint on the top of her foot. Jasper regretted not taking her neighbor's advice and wearing sturdier shoes. Jimmy was in brawny L.L. Beans and they were heavy. He said, "This is the living estate of Ray Clippert."

"I've just moved Father to assisted living."

"Well, I'm sure he needed the help. There sure is a lot of junk. Stuff. I mean, estate items." Her voice trailed off.

Jimmy turned his back on Jasper. Since Mary Clippert was so tall, close to six feet, Jasper could still see her face looming over the back of Jimmy's head. She had the kind of vivid coloring, or makeup at least, that would have made for a lively look. Lips painted cherry red. Big brown eyes lined with black and sculpted eyebrows tweezed to high arches, the left one a little higher than the right. Her mouth was slightly downturned at both corners, indicating a life of habitual disappointment, Jasper thought.

"– living room," Mary Clippert was saying when Jasper woke from her momentary reverie.

"Let's start in the basement and we'll work our way back," Jimmy said.

"Are you sure?" Mary Clippert asked. "Do we all have to go down there? I mean, she doesn't need to traipse all the way down there, does she?" She gave Jasper's length the evil eye.

"I can handle it." Jasper squared her shoulders. "It's part of my job."

"She's right. It's her job," Jimmy said.

"It may be your job but it's my father's life. He's lived here 50 years." Her lower lip quivered. The quiver looked like something she had practiced in her bathroom mirror. "He's accumulated a lot of things."

"Why? Why do you think he had to gather up so much?" Jasper stopped to rub her shin where Jimmy had just landed a backwards kick. She had forgotten until now how she went through much of her adolescence in long sleeves and slacks to cover up the many small bruises.

"This is 50 years of accumulation," Mary said. Her voice was steady.

"Was he like this when you were young?"

"Frankly, I can't remember."

"Well if people didn't accumulate, we'd be out of business," Jimmy said. He and Mary laughed.

Jasper just nodded. *Don't explore the psychology of the client.* Noted.

Mary marshaled them down a narrow trail winding its way from the front room into the next room with a centrally hung chandelier. Jimmy fingered it on the way past. Jasper sneezed. Jimmy said, "Craftsman. Swirl glass. Cherry wood. Original?"

"It's always been here," Mary said.

"It might bring a bit on auction."

"I want it to stay with the house. It goes with the woodwork."

"What are you going to do with the house?" Jimmy asked.

"Sell it, I hope."

"No chance your dad will want to move back?" Jasper asked. She stepped away from Jimmy to avoid another foot stomp.

"No. He's grown a bit confused and has started to wander off on his own."

"We have a good track record with house sales," Jimmy said.

Mary Clippert sniffed. "Sure you do. I don't want it to go for peanuts."

Jimmy brought out his ever-present handkerchief and polished one of the glass shades. "We sell all kinds of houses and we always get fair market value."

Jasper was bursting with curiosity about the world of auctions. "What does that mean – fair market value?" She took a quick step back away from Jimmy. "Sorry. I'm just learning," she told Mary.

"I think that's a very good question," Mary said. Her red mouth quirked sideways the other direction. She probably did quirk practice on alternate sides. "What is fair market value?"

Jasper could feel Jimmy's anger washing back toward her. Wow, just like the olden days. She knew her stepfather would not show his irritation in front of a potential client. With Jimmy, money had always been his master.

He said, "It means the price you achieve on any given day when you have two or more interested parties bidding against each other."

"Hmm. I bet you can teach me a thing or two." Mary got the parade started up again. They entered the kitchen, recognizable by the sink which held a gold plastic bucket and the dishes caked with dried on food piled on counters plus an old chrome-legged table.

Jasper was surprised it didn't stink as much as she would have expected. People could adjust pretty quickly, and diminished smell in the face of major odor must be a built-in survival mechanism. How else could people live like this? She had smelled many a dairy farmer sitting in a pew on Sunday mornings. The dairy farmers had grown accustomed to the smell of manure. They had become one with their cows. She supposed a hoarder like Ray Clippert, for whatever reasons he had to pile up all this junk over the years, had become one with his possessions. Most days, he probably didn't notice how he was living. Jasper wondered if Ray Clippert had been lonely.

"So your Dad's ready to part with, with all of it?" Jasper asked.

"He's in assisted living now. Well, here's the way to the basement." Mary flicked the light switch on the wall just inside the door which was propped open with a cast iron kettle filled with a jumble of old knives. "Dammit. This house eats light bulbs."

Jasper wondered what else the house had eaten in its lifetime.

"Go out to the car and grab the flashlight from the back," Jimmy ordered Jasper. He whispered, "And shut the fuck up."

Jasper wasn't so sure she could run the gauntlet of junk again on her own. "There's a candle over there. At least I think it's a candle. See?"

"We're not lighting any damn candle in here. Get the flashlight."

Jasper scuffled her way back to the front door and out to Jimmy's SUV. She tried the back door. Locked. She returned to the house. The outer door was open, but the interior oak door would not open. Jasper raised the round copper knocker and banged it down three times. She was feeling the chill of the March morning by the time Jimmy peered out. Something was on his cheek, cherry red lip imprints. Jasper scratched her own cheek. Jimmy pulled out his handkerchief and scrubbed at his face. "Where's the flashlight?"

"I need your key."

"Of all the – "Jimmy reached into his pocket and pressed the remote to unlock the SUV doors. "Hurry up." He disappeared back inside.

Chapter 7

Jasper had just retrieved the rubberized flashlight and slammed the car door shut when she saw an older man making his way carefully around the side of the house. He headed for the front steps. He wore a green and gold Green Bay Packers jacket that was much too big for his skinny frame. He hoisted himself up the pink steps one at a time, using the iron railing in a grab-pull motion. Jasper hurried over.

She tucked her arms around his right one and said, "Let me help you."

"Get your dad-gum pesky hands off me!" He shook her off and wobbled in place, clutching the rail to steady himself.

"Relax!"

"Relax yourself, you young bitch. Who the hell are you?"

"I'm with the auction company." Up close the man smelled like the house's interior.

"Are you Mr. Clippert?"

"What's it to you?"

"No reason. Where did you come from?"

"This is my house!"

"Yes, it is your house. But I understood you had, uh, moved away kind of recently."

"You been talking to my daughter?" He shook an angry finger in Jasper's direction.

She took an instinctive step away. So far, her new job was proving a bit of a challenge.

"Uh-huh."

"This goddamn nursing home crap. Man, oh, man, life goes on too long."

"I know what you mean."

"How the hell do you know anything about it?" He continued hoisting himself up the steps. He paused at the top. "Auction, huh? Is that what she has planned for me?"

"Well, it's just one option."

Jasper followed him inside, the old man grumbling as he trailed down the narrow pathway.

"Where the hell are you?" Jimmy yelled. He came charging into the dining room and stopped face to face with the older man. "Jimmy Biggs." He held his hand out.

The old man spit toward some overflowing bushel baskets on the side.

"Ray Clippert, I presume." Jimmy said. He reached past him and Jasper handed him the flashlight. "I'm just talking to your daughter about how to get you the most money for your houseful." His voice was extra loud.

"I ain't deaf. You the auctioneer?"

"That's right. I run Biggs Auction House. Here." He handed over a bright red key fob with Biggs Auction House emblazoned on it.

"Crap. Heard of it. Nothing good."

"Everybody's entitled to their opinion."

Jasper hated scenes. Especially those that might escalate into violence. It looked as if the 80-something-year-old was getting ready to punch the 65-year-old.

Suddenly Mary Clippert entered the scene.

"You!" Ray Clippert tried to move past Jimmy in the narrow pathway. Jimmy steadied him like they were Robin Hood and one of his not so merry men trying to settle the rights to cross a swinging bridge.

"I told you to wait in the car," Mary said to her father.

"So you could sell my belongings out from under me," Ray said.

"I'm sure we can work out everything," Jimmy said. "Jasper, come here."

Jasper crawled across a pile of magazines and continued on the side trail to Jimmy. He joined her on the side path and left Mary and Ray to settle their differences. "We'll just go take a look in that basement!" Jimmy called back as he and Jasper hurried for the cellar.

An angry slap sounded from the dining room, followed by the sounds of falling objects. Something heavy thudded to the ground above them.

"Aren't you worried?" Jasper asked as she followed Jimmy down the uneven wooden steps.

"She can take care of herself."

"But what about him?"

The basement looked like the aftermath of an earthquake in a dollar store. Or an explosion in the cereal aisle of a grocery store. At first Jasper could discern only colors: cherry red, orange orange, lemon yellow. Old dried out chocolate brown, poison mushroom gray, bile green. "I think I'm going to be sick."

"Don't be such a priss. I've seen worse. The trick is to focus. Look for anything other than the crap that's on the top."

"I'll try."

"Atta girl." Jimmy's moods had always been unpredictable. Grumpy, angry, belittling, then suddenly a small word of praise.

Jasper lifted away a foot-deep stack of old National Geographics. Even with their exotic locales and beautiful photos, they never brought much on auction. Her stepfather had been complaining about them for years. Underneath staring up at her sideways was a bathing beauty who had lost her bra. Jasper couldn't make out the date in the semi-dark but she could see that the picture on the cover of a PhotoPlay magazine was from the pre-implant era. Underneath was another. As she dug down through the stack, Jasper felt like an archaeologist unearthing layers of someone else's life. The further down she went, the more revealing the covers became.

"I think there's something here you should see" she called over to Jimmy.

"What?"

"Magazines."

"NGOs? I've told you a million times."

"Nope. Not unless NGO stands for No Gowns On or Nude Girls Only."

"Hm. If they're in good condition, get me a count. Mark the spot. Then get moving. We've gotta find some big ticket items in here if we're gonna make anything happen."

Jasper counted up to 103 until she got to the damp bottom layer. She wondered if Mary Clippert knew about her father's collection. She hoisted the short stack of National Geographics back on top. *Five feet out from the stairs, left side, angle of approximately 45 degrees.*

She worked her way around the basement. Several feet away from the paper goods she came across a piece of furniture. Its dark wood poked out of a pile of petrified sponges, ragged towels and an assortment of coffee makers missing their glass pots.

Jasper didn't know a Victorian breakfront from a 20th Century sweet gum piece but she did recognize quality. She pushed some of the junk to the side. This piece reminded her of one of the pulpits in an old church where she and Rev. Tim had ministered. This was real wood, not a cheaply veneered copy. More magazines and books waited behind the glass-fronted doors. "Jimmy, you've got to see this."

Jimmy grumbled his way over to her. "Give me some room."

He and Jasper did an imbalanced do-si-do and she retreated to the steps where she took a seat. She was almost 30 years younger than her stepfather but she was going to have to start some serious exercising if she was going to keep up with the dogged auctioneer.

More knocks and bangs sounded from upstairs. Jasper glanced toward the doorway at the top of the stairs.

"Don't even think about it."

"I didn't do anything."

"You were thinking about it. Take it from me – don't mess with other people's stuff."

Jasper glanced around the basement full of other people's stuff that they were pawing through.

"Come over here," Jimmy said.

"How?" Jasper asked, a little weary of the mess. But she stood up ready to obey.

Another large noise came from upstairs. Suddenly something struck the top step and rolled rapidly downward. Without thinking, Jasper dived into the nearest pile. The bowling ball just missed her. It slam-bounced its way down the trail between the clutter piles and struck Jimmy low. He went down like the last pin that had been left standing.

"Dammit."

"Jimmy, are you okay?" A mouse ran over Jasper's hand and disappeared. She stifled a scream with her clean hand. She tottered to her feet.

"Did it get the Stickley?"

"Did what get the what? I'm coming over to help you."

"The Stickley, dammit. The bookcase. The Stickley Mission Oak Bookcase. What the hell!" Jimmy had scrambled to his feet and stood brushing away soot from the front of the item in question. "Looks alright."

"You're bleeding."

"Can't find a label in this light. Might have to sell it as Stickley *style*."

"There's blood on your khakis," Jasper said.

"So what else did you come across down here?"

"I was busy dodging bowling balls and mice."

"The bowling ball is shit. We'd have to give it away."

"How about the mouse? It was kind of cute – except for its being disgusting."

"Cute don't count for shit in this business. *Cute* won't bring much at auction. *Disgusting* - maybe. Let's go talk to the owner."

"Aye-aye, Boss!" Jasper gave him a snappy salute.

"Does everything have to be a game with you? When we get up there, I'll do all the talking. If the old guy is still inside, distract him."

"How?"

"How the hell did you get to be this old without any common sense? You talk too much. You always have. Go talk too much to the old guy."

Upstairs they found Mary Clippert alone in the kitchen. Her cheeks were flushed red but neither side was brighter than the other. Ray Clippert must've been the one who'd gotten slapped. Jasper tightened her mouth.

"Everything okay up here?" Jimmy asked. "There was a lot of commotion."

Mary rolled her eyes. "It's always something with him. Oh, what happened?"

"The bowling ball got him," Jasper said. Jimmy shot her a look. She shrugged. Rev. Tim was always telling her how passive aggressive she was. It was the best way she'd figured out to handle bullies.

"You poor man!" Mary knelt down in front of Jimmy and began to roll up the leg of his pants.

"Whoa, Whoa," Jimmy said as if he was trying to stop a horse back in his native Nebraska.

"Don't say no."

He stumbled backwards and landed on a stuffed black garbage bag. "Man, my back," he moaned.

"Jimmy?"

"Let me help," Mary said. "I'm used to this kind of thing."

Before Jasper could move, Mary grabbed up Jimmy and pulled him into a bear hug, her big breasts pressed along his spine, her arms wrapped around his shoulders and chest. She arched backwards and took Jimmy with her. It was like tandem skydiving meets chiropractic for couples. A loud pop sounded. Jimmy groaned. The two-headed chiro beast stood up.

Jasper released her breath with a sigh.

Jimmy rubbed the back of his head. "Wow, what did you do to me, woman? My back feels kind of good now."

Mary chortled deep in her throat. She released him but stayed behind, still pressing her top half against him. "I bet you have a lot of aches you don't let on about, Mr. Auctioneer." Mary gave Jasper a wide, sidewise wink.

"I'll just go out there now," Jasper said. *Ew.* The basement mouse was not the only disgusting thing she had witnessed on her first morning of work.

Chapter 8

"Well, ten-ta-ta-ten-ten, who'll go ten? I have seven-and-a-half, now ten!" Jimmy called bids. He stood on top of one of the three long tables bunched together. Two of the tables were mostly clear of stuff behind him. He was like a giant Gulliver stomping his way through a Lilliputian village of junk. He left emptiness and unwanted bric-a-brac in his wake. "Ten-now 15,ta-teen-teen, 15, now 20!" he said into his microphone head-set.

A crowd of auction-goers pushed in as close as they could get. Everybody had to worship at Jimmy's feet. Most were men. Sweat hung heavy in the air. The man in front of Jasper farted. She waved the air in front of her face.

"You bidding?" Ted asked. "Ready Teddy" Phillips was a barrel-chested man with black hair, crafty green eyes and a hale-and-hearty manner that pleased the men in the crowd. He used a winning smile on the women whom he called "girls" no matter what their ages.

Jasper yelled, "No!" People around her laughed.

People were jostling each other. Esteban who had helped her move into her apartment held the old-fashioned meat grinder up in the air. Sweat trickled down Jasper's side. She fought to stay focused.

Esteban's wife Kelly gave her a triumphant grin from where she stood across the table. She waved a bidder card. "You got ten!" she shouted. Covering for absentee bidders was her main job at the auction and she took it seriously. Her red hair was already sleek with sweat. While she had been a little bitchy toward Jasper ever since she joined the auction house, Jasper herself had come to admire Kelly's strong work ethic.

"Now 20,20,20. Twenty back to you, Kelly. Want back in?"

Kelly drew the card across her throat in a slashing motion.

"Don't cut me. I'll take 20!" Jimmy said.

Kelly made a vinegar face. She nodded.

"Sold! Twenty dollars! Number 87. Bid left."

Even though Kelly worked for Biggs Auction, when she stood-in for absentee bidders, she applied her innate ferocity to try to get them the best deal possible.

Ted grabbed the meat grinder from Esteban's hand and shoved it at Jasper. "87," he said in her ear. "Tag it in the back!" She clutched the meat grinder to her bosom. He gave her a small shove. She lost her footing, and stumbled in to the farting man who let out another big whoopee in her face.

"Ooh-ee! Carl's trying to scare us off again," a short man in overalls said.

A little space opened up around Carl the farter and Jasper escaped. She excused her way through the milling bidders. She got a strong whiff of cigarette smoke, maybe the same kind favored by her downstairs neighbors. She had no idea that auctions could be so odiferous.

Folks not interested in items on the first tables were either seated in the folding chairs or looking over things they would bid on later. She thought she spotted Mary Clippert and her father Ray in the audience but she was in too much of a hurry to double check. When it came down to it, all the auction goers were turning into one Big Blurry Bidder.

"How much?" Grace yelled her question from up on the auction block where she sat at a keyboard clerking the sale. A seasoned auction worker, Grace kept her straw-like hair cut the same way Jasper remembered her wearing it 25 years ago –

bangs and a chin length pageboy. Grace was a heavy smoker and she had permanent pucker marks around her mouth. She was tough on the outside, but Jasper knew from experience that Grace was a soft-hearted women who would do anything for the people she loved.

Jimmy kept going. "Who'll start me off on the old phone for fifty?"

Blond-haired Tony raised an oak wall phone for the crowd to see.

"I need the amount for the last item!" Grace yelled.

Jasper turned and yelled, "She needs to know how much!"

"How much, Jimmy?" another, familiar woman's voice asked from the other side of the block.

"The girls are ganging up on you, Jimmy!" one of the auction-goers heckled.

"Twenty, Grace, twenty. The rest of you – butt out! Where was I?"

"I'll give you ten bucks!" the heckler told Jimmy.

"Like hell you will!" Jimmy said. "I've got 20 bid right behind you. Now 30-ta-30, 30, 30, I have 30!" His tongue rolled over the numbers. "And now 40!" Jimmy was off and running again.

Jasper ducked behind the auction block. A handsome wheat-haired man checking out the art work gave her a quick smile and stepped out of her way. Jasper came face to face with her twin sister Cookie.

Jasper clenched her lips so she wouldn't squeal out loud. She set the meat grinder down on the steps leading up to the block. The twins danced into each other's arms. Jasper hadn't been hugged with such familiar sweetness for a good long time. They broke out of the hug and giggled at each other.

Cookie, actually an inch shorter than Jasper, looked taller. She was 10 pounds heavier than Jasper who had always envied her sister's curves. Cookie wore a blue ruffled jacket, jeans, and knee-high boots. Her chin-length hair had gotten shorter and blonder than Jasper remembered. "You look great!" Jasper said.

"You look – like my favorite sister!" Cookie said.

"The one and only!"

"Shhh," Grace said.

Jasper grabbed Cookie by one hand and the meat grinder by the other, and pushed through the silver door behind the auction block. This former food storage area now housed auction house gear and items won by proxy. Jasper placed the meat grinder next to a yardstick collection and a cast iron doorstop already won by #87.

The sisters perched on the table.

"So tell me everything," Cookie said.

"Where is that girl?" Jimmy's voice said on microphone.

Jasper leaned her weary head against Cookie's shoulder.

"Everything you can in ten seconds or less," Cookie said. "I've seen you looking better, Sis."

Ted burst through the door. "Well, well. Hey, Babe."

"Ted," Cookie said.

"This ain't no time for a coffee clutch, girls."

"Coming." Jasper eased back onto her sore feet.

Cookie stepped in front of her. "Why don't you get back to assisting the auctioneer or whatever it is you do, Ted, dear?"

"What're you talking about, Miss Cookie? You may be a cute little mind reader but you ain't tuned into your stepdad's head. We've pretty much drawn up the partnership papers."

"Oh, honey, you've got something on the back of your jeans," Jasper said.

Cookie looked over her shoulder while Jasper brushed away the dirt.

"Can I help?" Ted asked.

The twins glowered at him with quite similar glowers.

Ted gave a mock bow. "See you back on the floor. Pronto." The door swung in his backwash.

"Same old Ready Teddy," Cookie said.

"He hits on married women too?"

"He hits on everybody. I don't take it personally," Cookie said. "So, do you have any time tomorrow?"

"Working. I think."

Cookie's hazel eyes widened. They had both inherited polka-dot eyes from their mother. Hazel. Cookie's were mostly green, Jasper's brown. Cookie said, "You can't get fired, you know. You're the boss' daughter."

"You heard Ted. If he and Jimmy are going to be full-fledged partners, where does that leave me? It's bad enough having Jimmy as a boss. If Ted gets more power here, the two of them will turn into total Nazis."

"Get your butt out here! Now!" Jimmy roared on mike.

"We'll be the resistance movement then." Cookie and Jasper exchanged one more hug.

Cookie said, "I'm staying to bid on furniture for my new office. See if you can come along on the delivery tomorrow."

"They deliver to you?" Jasper asked. "I'm impressed."

"We have more power than you realize," Cookie said, giving Jasper an affectionate poke in the side.

The sisters re-entered the auction room with matching grins.

Working with renewed energy, Jasper returned to the auction floor. She called out a loud "Yep!" as bid spotter whenever Cookie raised her number. Cookie won her bid for a velvet settee and matching wingback chair. She waved good-bye to Jasper from the checkout area where she had stopped to pay the college student who came in to cashier during auctions. Then, Cookie was gone, and Jasper called out another enthusiastic "Yep!

Chapter 9

Cookie's new office was on the second floor of one of the old buildings in Forest Grove's downtown. The stairs were steep and Jasper struggled a bit to drag the armchair up, while Esteban and Tony managed the settee without apparent effort. The frosted glass door announced Psychic Medium Rare – Confidential Clearings, Coaching & Classes. An In-Session sign hung from the doorknob.

Esteban and Tony had just settled in for a quick slouch on the settee with Jasper perched on the wingback chair when the door opened. Out came a familiar looking brunette dressed in a black and white geometric print suit, sensible buckled loafers, and a necklace of Bakelite cherries. Diamond studs shot sparks from her earlobes.

"Mrs. Clippert!" Jasper leapt to her feet. Would she ever get over her excessive politeness?

Esteban rose. Tony remained unmoved. "Hey, tall lady," Tony said.

Esteban cut his eyes Tony's way. The younger man got to his feet.

"It's Ms. Clippert. But *you* can call me Mary," she said to Jasper.

"Tony, haul ass," Esteban said.

Cookie emerged from her office. Today she wore a smock of swirling paisley over gray linen slacks. Her blonde hair haloed her face. "Hi, everyone. What's the fuss?"

Esteban said, "Excuse me, ladies." He said good morning to Cookie and eased past her. He and Tony went to work with a screwdriver prying off the door hinges.

"Hey, Sis." Jasper felt like a slouch next to the other women. She adjusted the elastic waistband of her denim-look pants over her red Bid and Buy at Biggs shirt. Jasper had long been in the habit of tucking in her tops, thanks to Rev. Rowe. Tim never liked to see her shirttails hanging out.

"Be right back," Cookie said. She placed a gentle hand on Mary Clippert's waist and guided her toward the stairs. The two exchanged a few quiet words. Cookie beckoned Jasper over.

Jasper patted a few dark tendrils that had come loose from her pony tail back into place. "At your service," she said. She felt like a well-schooled Japanese lady set adrift in a foreign land without knowing the local customs. Cookie was her sister and an equal. Mary Clippert was an auction house bidder and potential client. She also seemed to be consulting Cookie. Jasper kept her eyes from rolling and her shoulders from shrugging.

"Did you notice anything unusual when you and Jimmy were at Mary's father's house yesterday?" Cookie whispered.

"There sure was a lot to look at," Jasper said, trying for a diplomatic note.

Mary Clippert and Cookie huddled in close.

"Did you *feel* anything strange?" Cookie asked.

"Vibration wise," Mary said.

Jasper glanced down the long stairway behind Mary. She pictured the bowling ball crashing down the basement steps.

"You're remembering something, aren't you?" Mary's frosted nails fondled her cherry necklace.

"Well. I mean – "

Cookie stepped closer and draped an arm around Jasper's tight shoulders. "With your permission, I'll share your concerns with my sister."

Mary glanced over at Esteban and Tony who were turning the settee this way and that trying to get it through the doorless doorway.

Cookie and Jasper held index fingers to their lips. Jasper admired Cookie's manicure. Cookie had the hands of a saint with long tapered fingers, their mother Laura had always said. When her other little girl looked on enviously, Laura had reassured Jasper. "Yours are small but mighty. You have big dreams and the power to make them come true." *Maybe I could get a manicure sometime*, Jasper thought.

Mary turned her wrist over to look at her watch. She wore the gold links facing out. "I'm due there now."

"At your father's house?" Jasper whispered.

"*Your* father is meeting me." She started down the stairs. "He wants to do a little cherry-picking." She fingered her necklace. "Whatever that means." Her laugh echoed in the stairwell. The street door creaked open, then slammed shut behind her.

"Ewww," Jasper and Cookie said with one voice.

"How's your tea?" Cookie asked. "I can't believe you like it with milk. I'll have to keep some in stock now that you're so close."

"I can live without it," Jasper said.

"You don't have to live without anything anymore, Sis. I'm so glad you finally got out alive."

"Alive?"

"I mean while you have plenty of your life left to live."

Jasper and Cookie sat side by side on the velvet settee. It and the matching burgundy wingchair gave the office a semi-Victorian look. Combined with a roll-top desk, lace curtains at the windows, a ginger jar lamp and a Japanese shoji screen, the office looked just right for a professional psychic medium, Jasper thought. As far as she could tell. Her sister was the only professional psychic medium she knew. How had they ended up leading such different lives? Jasper wondered.

The month after Jasper started college at age 17, Cookie got married. She and her husband had their first child eight months later, a son, and two years later, a daughter. Cody and Kayla were now in their twenties, and Cookie and her husband Will Swanson were still happily married. The successful architect had stuck by Cookie all through her various careers – hairdresser, interior designer, and assistant high school guidance counselor. Sometimes Jasper wondered how her life would've turned out if she hadn't run into Timothy Rowe back in college so long ago.

"So you like it?" Cookie was asking.

Jasper sipped her tea. "I love orange spice."

"It's pomegranate. I mean, how do you like your new apartment?"

"Pomegranate, huh?"

"Uh-huh. You're stalling."

"Well, it's a little smoky."

"Ah-ha! I bet the landlord got those downstairs people on their best behavior for the day I went through. If you want, we could feng shui your place to help protect you."

"I'm sure I'm safe. They smoke a lot but I don't think they're Bonnie and Clyde."

"Just the same." Cookie's mouth took on that firm, determined set that Jasper knew meant business. "I cleared it for you before you moved in, you know."

"No, I didn't know."

"I went through with sage and incense and made sure there weren't any spirits hanging around."

"Well, I appreciate that." Jasper had never been sure what she did and did not believe about the supernatural and life after death, even though Rev. Tim had always avowed the existence of the traditional heaven and hell. There probably was something that went on after people passed out of this life but Jasper had never wanted anyone from the other side to come back and explain it to her.

"By the way." Cookie set her mug of tea down and scooted in closer to Jasper. "That Mary Clippert – she wants us to unhaunt her father's house."

"Us?"

"Well, me. But you can help."

"Thanks for including me, Sis. But I'm learning the auction trade. No offense but you're the psychic in the family."

"Psychic medium. You've always had the same gifts. You've just decided not to hone your skills. Do you think there's anything going on at the Clippert house?" Cookie asked.

"I didn't notice anything but a whole lot of junk and some tensions between Mary and her father."

"Maybe the house has a disturbing history."

"I'll tell you what's disturbing – Mary Clippert flirting with Jimmy. I've always wondered, do you think he has, I don't know, any special sexual proclivities?"

"I don't know how special they are, but I bet he has lots of them," Cookie said.

The sisters dissolved into a giggling fit there in the Victorian style office of Psychic Medium Rare.

Chapter 10

The week sped along for Jasper. Friday was a day full of auction house busyness. She helped Jimmy sort through boxloads of stuff from several pickups. "Which lot is this?" Jimmy would holler to double-check here and there. "Number 127!" would come the answer from Kelly working in the office. "Run these things up to Grace," Jimmy ordered Jasper. "No, not one thing at a time! Jesus! Use the cart, use the cart." And Jasper would scurry to comply, filling one of the big metal carts with boxes of items and maneuvering it up to Grace who arranged the front tables each week. She had to group as many of one consigner's items together as possible while maintaining an attractive theme at each table. Glassware by glassware, whenever possible. Dolls all on one table. Items that might go high such as Waterford crystal seeded in among things of lesser value, such as random hand-painted plates.

There was nothing to preview at this point in the week, but customers who'd won their bids at Wednesday night's sale stopped in to pay for their purchases and haul them away. Jasper already knew some of them by name. There was Myrus Kornhauser, whose liking for lawnmowers of all ages and workability belied the suits and ties he wore. April Bendham came in to pick up the boxfuls and flats of linens she left bids on. While Chuck and Terri Suiter stopped in to pay for felinabilia they'd won. *They go for anything cat, Grace the clerk* had whispered to Jasper before the last sale. *Keep an eye on them when those showcase items come up.* And sure enough – whenever a cat item, whether cookie jar or calendar came up for bidding, she watched for Chuck and Terri to flash their bidder card. "Yep!" Jasper would holler, louder each time as her confidence as a bid catcher grew.

Friday closing time meant Jasper's first paycheck from Biggs Auction House. Jimmy stood near the front door, handing out payroll one envelope at a time. "You think you deserve this?" he asked Tony.

"Yeah, boss."

"Get outa here," Jimmy said and thrust the check at him. He aimed a near-miss kick at Tony's backside.

Next came Kelly and Esteban.

"Well, if it isn't Man and Wife Martinez. You want one check or two?"

"Come on, Jimmy. We gotta pick up the kids," Kelly said. She jumped for the checks and Jimmy raised them high overhead.

"Come and get 'em," Jimmy said.

"Oh, yeah?" Kelly said, stepping in close and resting her palms against Jimmy's chest.

"Yeah, baby," Jimmy said.

Jasper hadn't seen that coming. Her face flaming, she turned to Grace. She stood waiting as if all this was the norm.

"Ouch! Goddammit – she bit me!" Jimmy yelled.

"Thanks, Jimmy. Have a good night," Esteban called, waving the checks in his hand. He and Kelly hurried out the door.

Grace accepted her check from Jimmy. He put his hand on her ass. "If you weren't such a roughneck, you wouldn't get in so much trouble." Grace removed his hand "Now give your daughter – "

"Stepdaughter."

"Give your stepdaughter her paycheck and let's all go home," Grace said.

Jimmy shrugged. "Everybody gangs up on me," he said.

Sweat trickled down Jasper's sides. She was tired, she was hungry, and she wanted to escape the workhouse atmosphere of her father's auction house. How would the little king make her sing for her supper?

Jimmy held out an envelope. Jasper reached for it, and he snatched it away. "You think you can learn this business?"

Jasper had her doubts. But she crossed her arms and stood her ground. "I'm gonna try." *What choice did she have?*

"Atta girl!" Ted walked through the front door. "Just getting rid of one of our favorite dumpster divers," he said to Jimmy. He plucked the envelope out of Jimmy's hand and held it out to Jasper. She grabbed it and walked toward the door with Grace.

"Hey, little lady!" Ted called after her. "You owe me one."

"For my paycheck?" Jasper asked.

"Just pretend you didn't hear him," Grace said.

"Bright and early tomorrow, girls," Jimmy said.

Saturday was not a day off for any of the auction employees. Jasper didn't mind so much. Her apartment was still largely unfurnished and, since Jasper returned most evenings tired out from a long day side-stepping Jimmy's rages all whilst learning the ropes of appraisals and look-ats and auction set-up, largely unlived in. She'd usually microwave a semi-healthy frozen dinner, then open out her sleeper sofa and nod off to whatever she found on TV. So, Saturday, she helped out at an afternoon coin auction attended mostly by intense looking men who crowded around the locked showcases and bid on first editions, limited editions, proof sets and a variety of metal money that Jasper had never known existed. It was a quieter sort of auction than the weekly sale on Wednesday night. Jasper thought she might like that. But she found that she missed the noise and the crowd of people from different walks of life. *Surprise, surprise, Jasper Biggs,* she told herself. *And you thought you knew all about you.*

On Sunday morning, Jasper woke out of habit at dawn. Then realized there was no Pastor Tim to cater to, no congregation to think of, nor Sunday School to see to, or, or, or…anything. Her downstairs neighbor, Mrs. Smoky O'Neil as she'd come to think of her, had invited her to attend the couple's Pentecostal church, the sincere one over on the West side, not the more popular one just a couple miles out on Milwaukee Road. Jasper declined. She'd had enough of churches to last her another 15 years. And when and if she ever returned to one, she wanted it to be after she'd fully settled in to her new life and come to know herself on new terms, not out of obligation. She drifted back to sleep until a buoyant Yoo-Hoo from halfway up the stairs wakened her. She pulled a pillow over her head and stayed quiet. So far, the O'Neils had not ventured over that invisible border into her territory. It was only their cigarette smoke that trailed all the way up to her second floor digs.

"She must not be home!" Margie O'Neil said loudly. Minutes later, the front door slammed. Jasper reached over the bed and grabbed her cell phone's recharger cord. She fished it up next to her to check the time. 9:39! Wait. Relax. Nothing to do for hours. She set the alarm for 11, then let herself drift away again until the sailor's hornpipe woke her. She'd spend the afternoon helping Jimmy and Grace at a benefit auction down at the River Center. Butterflies Unlimited or something like that.

She was in the bathtub when she heard the Alleluia of her cell phone – she had to get that ringtone changed soon to something more appropriate like I Am Woman Hear Me Roar or maybe even something more modern once she'd caught on to modern...Cookie could help in the music-for-phones dept. The phone went off a couple more times while she was searching through her modest choice of clothes for something appropriate.

When she finally decided on a bib dress with an embroidered butterfly she'd forgotten she owned and fastened the buttons on the side, the phone Alleluiaed again. Good thing too. She'd forgotten that she had left it on the kitchen table.

Caller ID showed Jimmy's cell. She picked up. "Hello there," she said.

"Where the hell have you been?" he yelled in her ear. "I called you five times."

"Hmm. I only see three messages."

"I got tired of hearing your stupid recording."

"Sorry. I've been getting ready to go."

"Well I hope you made it. I'll pick you up in five minutes."

Jasper put him on speaker and carried the phone back to the bathroom where she ran a brush through her wavy hair and daubed some colored moisturizer on her cheeks and forehead.

"Why so early?" she asked him.

"You know I hate being late. Not like you."

A horn honked outside. Jasper peered out the bathroom window which faced the street below. Jimmy's SUV sat in the driveway. Jasper left the phone on the toilet seat and ran barefoot to the bedroom to grab a pair of pumps. With them in hand, she started down the stairs. She made it to that mysterious halfway point, then slid on the carpet. She travelled on her backside the rest of the way down. She sat for a minute, mentally checking that nothing was broken. Bruised maybe but not broken. She pushed her feet into the pearl-colored pumps, checked her pocket for her keys, and let herself out. She climbed into Jimmy's SUV and he roared back out of the driveway. "Took you long enough," he said.

The benefit auction went without a hitch although after three hours in her nice pumps – for Jimmy's compulsive earliness meant they arrived at the River Center a full hour before the start of the sale – Jasper's feet hurt like the devil. Jimmy loosened his tie, but he showed no compassion for his stepdaughter and required her presence for dinner at the same restaurant where he had insisted throughout the week that she join him for each and every lunch. Her stepfather didn't seem to like her, Jasper, the individual very much but he hated eating alone.

By the time, he dropped her off in her front yard, Jasper felt all used up. Luckily, the O'Neils' door was closed when she let herself in. She tiptoed carefully upstairs where she undressed, pulled a nightgown over her head, and retreated once again to her bedroom cum living room. *I'm in bed exhausted. I was in bed and exhausted last night, and I don't even have anyone to be in bed exhausted with. Is this all there is?* Jasper asked her plain white ceiling.

Chapter 11

Monday and Tuesday brought more of the same. The final sorting and set-up in time for the auction preview all day Tuesday and Wednesday before the sale. A couple look-ats that didn't amount to much. "It's not worth my time or yours for me to send the truck out," Jimmy told the older couple with a garage full of rummage sale leftovers, and the doll collector who only bought Limited Edition modern dolls. All three people looked crestfallen but Jimmy didn't waste words. "You can bring some of it to the auction house, but I don't think it'll bring anything much," he told the two households in identical language.

"Why can't you put that differently?" Jasper asked him back in the SUV, passing slower vehicles right and left on the way back to the auction house. "Do you have to hurt their feelings? You kind of insulted them, maybe, don't you think?"

"They'd be more insulted if I sent the truck out. You know we have to charge them for that. Then on auction we'd end up having to box-lot all their crap, and hand them a bill afterward instead of a check. You can't be nice to people in this business, Candy."

"Jasper."

"I don't care if you call yourself Lady Jane. You gotta get over some of this niceness, kiddo. Toughen up. I never got anywhere being nice. And neither did you."

"Wow," Jasper said. "That stings. And pretty much stinks too."

"The truth hurts – until you get used to it," Jimmy said.

"What if it's not really the truth? There's more than one way of looking at things, I think."

"You gotta cut the philosophy shit too," Jimmy told her as they pulled into his regular parking space in front of the plate glass window at Biggs Auction. "Those people will come back to us."

"Why?"

"They always come back for more," Jimmy said. "You came back, didn't you?"

Well. Nothing like a typical Jimmyism to remind Jasper of life's repeating miseries.

♦

Wednesday afternoon rolled around and the auction preview was in full swing. Members of the auction crew, Jasper included, wore the uniform of khaki pants and red polo shirts emblazoned with *Bid & Buy at Biggs!* Kelly accompanied people around the auction floor, speaking quietly to them and jotting notes on the backs of their bidder cards. They would name the top dollar they wanted to pay for an item, and during the auction a few hours hence, Kelly would do her best to win what they wanted just as if the absentee bidders were there in person. Of course someone could outbid them, as Kelly patiently explained to each and every one of them. Even the regulars got the spiel. Kelly was as careful about that as she was about the bidding itself.

The women in the office, along the wall at the back of the big room where the main event took place, kept busy registering bidders and answering questions about the bidding process for newcomers.

Jasper walked among the browsers, doing what she could to radiate friendliness even though she didn't yet feel very knowledgeable about many of the items. "Hi, Jasper!" many people called. She shook hands and patted backs. She was already on a hugging basis with several of the women.

Ted Phillips's jocular bass voice sounded out even among all the hubbub. "Well I don't know about that, Charlie, but you can give it a go, give it a go! Why the hell not!"

Jasper knew that if Jimmy or Ted saw her lingering too long with any one customer, there'd be hell to pay. So she kept moving, circulating. She knew how to do that well. She never thought that any of her training to become the perfect minister's wife would come in useful out in the bigger world. But here she was and it was working for her. No wonder job counselors urged people to list whatever it was they'd been up to regardless of seeming relevance. Life could take some funny turns.

Kelly approached her. "Jasper, have you seen your father?"

"Stepfather."

"Whatever. Jimmy? I need to know whether he's going to sell the souvenir bells piece by piece or as a collection."

Jasper looked around the room, which was rapidly filling with people as the hour for the auction neared. "Didn't he and Estie go out on a couple calls a while ago?"

"Yeah. But I thought they'd be back by now," Kelly said. "Hey, Ted! Got a sec?" She moved away with her bell bidder in tow.

Jasper left the auction floor and hurried past the snack machines and the restrooms to the back door of the auction house. She went outside into the chilly March afternoon. She knocked. No answer. She tried the doorknob. Locked tight. She shivered and hurried through the crowded parking lot toward the street and the auction house's main entrance. Nope. Jimmy's parking spot was vacant. The regulars knew to leave it free for The Boss.

Inside again, Jasper spotted several people in the crowd whom she'd met with Jimmy on look-ats and appraisals during the past week. She waved hi to the older folks who'd had the garage full of rummage sale leftovers. The woman turned her head away, pretending to study a floral sofa that sat waiting for sale along with chests of drawers, dining room sets and mattresses in varying degrees of "Like New-ness" lined up against the wall. The rummage sale husband glared at Jasper.

Okay. She could see that Jimmy's rejection had stung the old folks, as she'd thought. But they had come back to Biggs Auction. Just as he said they would. When she noticed a woman crouched down in front of a boxful of toys in front of the auction block, she knew that Jimmy knew how to read people. It was the Collector Doll lady! Jasper started up toward her, thinking to say hello and reintroduce herself. But as she drew closer, she saw the scowl on the woman's face. *Oh, oh, another one.* Jimmy knew how to bring people out for an auction but he won them over through sheer force of will, certainly not friendliness or kindness.

Jasper couldn't help but think about Pastor Tim who cheated on her time and again. Pastor Tim who criticized her clothing, her appearance, the way she laughed. And how, for 15 years, she kept coming back for more. She glanced back toward the faces of those already seated for the start of the auction. There were a good number of friendly faces in the crowd. But at least a third of the people she saw looked mad, annoyed, aggravated. Arrogant, gruff Jimmy might not be able to win friends but he sure knew how to influence people.

One man thumped his cane and called out, "Let's get this show on the road!" Jasper saw that it was Ray Clippert, sitting alone. A bidder number was taped to the seat of the empty chair next to him. Jasper squinted toward the clock on the wall behind the counter. She couldn't make it out. But she felt sure it was still early. "Mr. Clippert!" she said, walking up to him and extending her hand. "I'm glad to see you again. Jasper Biggs. My step-dad runs this auction house. Remember me?"

He looked at her blankly. He said, "Sure, sure. When the hell does this thing get underway?"

"It won't be long now. Where's your daughter?"

"Somewhere. She's around here somewhere. Little girl's room. She'll turn up. She always does. I'm parked here for the duration no matter what. Came to see your old man in action. He's a son-of-a-bitch. But a pretty good auctioneer."

"Thanks," Jasper said politely.

"Yoo-Hoo!" a familiar voice called to her. On the other side of the aisle sat her downstairs neighbor Mrs. O'Neil.

Closer up, Jasper caught a whiff of that familiar dual scent of menthol cigarettes and flowery air freshener. She stifled a cough. Lately, all she had to do was think of the Smokey O'Neils and she'd cough. "Well, what a surprise. It's nice to see you. I didn't know that you and your husband were auction-goers."

"Well not so much anymore. Dick's health, you know. But we used to go all the time. And I've known Jimmy for years." Mrs. O'Neil smoothed her gray permed hair.

"My Jimmy?"

"At one time, he was My Jimmy," Mrs. O'Neil said. She winked.

Jasper took a step backwards. "You don't say?"

"Oh, my, yes. The stories I could tell!" She covered her mouth like a Japanese geisha and giggled. "But that was before I found Jesus. And Dick found me."

"Well, okay then! You tell that husband of yours I said hi," Jasper said, inching away. She backed into some tall man's backside. Ted Phillips looked over his shoulder.

"Nice running into you too!" he said loud enough to bring guffaws from the crowd around him. He draped an arm over Jasper's shoulders and drew her in alongside him. "Folks, this little lady is studying up to step into her daddy's shoes."

"Well, that's not exactly –. " Jasper tried to wriggle free of Ted's clasp but he held on tight. His strength and muscularity reminded her, embarrassingly, of Pastor Tim's, and she felt both drawn to him and repulsed, an icky sexual entanglement of feelings.

The men and women clustered around Ted showed real interest in her, reaching for her hand, introducing themselves.

Ted teased them about their special interests in auction items. "Now, Charlie here, wherever you see Royal Doulton, there's Charlie."

"No, no," Charlie said. He moved away into the crowd.

Ted went on "And Edith and Ardith, these girls love their jewelry."

"We have a shop," the taller of the two sixty-something women said. "You'll have to stop by sometime, Jasper." They nodded to Jasper and stepped away. Ted steered Jasper off behind the steps up to the auction block.

When they were alone, he said earnestly, "I want to know if you feel ready to get up on the block for a while tonight."

"What?" Jasper shook her head. "I'm way not ready, Ted! What are you thinking?"

"Jimmy said you've been practicing."

"But not in front of people! I've been selling to telephone poles! Or selling telephone poles. I'm not sure," Jasper said. Her usually cold hands had gone sweaty.

Ted's dark brows moved together toward the bridge of his nose.

I wonder if he plucks his eyebrows. I bet he broke his nose in a fight or falling off his motorcycle, Jasper mused irrelevantly.

"Jasper! What do you say? Atta girl!" Ted slapped her on the back, and when she stumbled, drew her to him in a quick hug.

"Ted!" Kelly came around behind the auction block. "Well, well," she said. "One big happy family!" She laughed. Ted joined in. And Jasper climbed up the steps to the elevated auction block.

Up there were the portable headsets and controls for the wireless sound system, along with a computer at the clerk's station and a chair. Jasper rested her trembling hands on the surround wall and looked out over the auction house floor. From this elevated perch, she could see the entire room, from the tables covered with white paper and smaller items to be sold on either side of the block, to the ones set up straight across the front with their displays of small appliances, assorted glassware, folded quilts, and cases of silverware.

Two sections of folding chairs with an aisle down the middle now held some fifty people. The ones not engaged in conversation with their neighbors looked up at her expectantly. "Are you going to auction tonight?" a man with rosy cheeks and a mild smile called out. Jasper shrugged. *I hope not, but it's beginning to look that* way, she thought. *Where the heck, no, where the hell was Jimmy?* Jasper joined the auction team on the ground.

"Anybody seen Estie?" Ted's voice bellowed. "Man, where's everybody gone?"

Jasper was in the office, helping latecomers register for their bidder numbers when a large Boom! sounded from the back table. Jasper jumped.

"We better get moving. Ted's dropped the step," Kelly told Jasper. The clock read 4:33.

Jasper followed the more experienced woman through the crowd packed in tight around the back table. Kelly and Jasper worked their way up toward the bid catchers. "Try to keep people from looking over my shoulder," Kelly said into Jasper's ear. She didn't want prying eyes to know what her top bids were.

Ted tugged on his headset and tapped the mouthpiece. "Run up there and switch me on, Jasper!" he ordered and gestured toward the auction block.

Jasper hesitated.

"You know an on-off switch when it you see it, Girly?" Ted said loudly.

"Go! I'll be fine," Kelly told her.

Jasper elbowed her way through the crowd at the table, saying "Sorry, Sorry," all along the way. Then she hurried up the lane between the seated bidders and the furniture and made her way up the steps to the top of the auction block. She kneeled down in front of the box of electronic equipment. "Oh, Lordy," she said.

"It's somewhere on the right side," Grace said from where she sat ready to type in all the winning bids.

Jasper pressed her face in close so she could read the various labels. And there it was, On-Off. A simple toggle switch. She pushed it up. Then got to her feet.

"There she is! Back from the dead! Can you hear me okay up there, Jazz?" Ted's voice was now amplified and bigger than ever.

Grace handed her the cardboard megaphone she sometimes used to get the auctioneer's attention when she missed hearing the item description or bid. Jasper held it to her mouth. "A-OK," she said.

Some of the crowd applauded. Her first words from the auction block.

Before she left the block, Grace whispered to her, "Where are Jimmy and Esteban?"

"Don't know." Jasper hurried down the steps and ran back to the table.

"Get back here," Ted ordered her. "You're Esteban."

"Hi, Estie!" a gnarled man with a friendly, crooked smile said.

"We're a few minutes behind the clock tonight, folks. But it's business as usual from now on." People wanted to know where Jimmy was, and Ted said that he was still on a call. There was friendly joshing among the bidders. *Maybe he's taking a nap. Maybe he's having a little lee-ay-zon!* There were snickers and chortles. Letting off steam. Jimmy wouldn't like to hear those comments.

Ted cut them off. He quickly introduced the auction crew, saying that tonight the part of Esteban was being played by Jasper who was here studying up on how to walk in her Stepdaddy's shoes, then gave the order of the sale followed by terms and conditions. "We're gonna try to stick to the way we usually do things here at Biggs. This back table first. Then we'll move up front for the purty stuff." He told the crowd to use their bidder cards. "If we can't see you, you're not in," he said. "There's a 10 percent buyer's fee on all purchases. Settle up tonight with the girls in the office. All items are sold As Is, Where Is."

"What if we find a chip or a crack and you haven't mentioned that?" a newcomer asked.

"Folks, we look everything over pretty careful before the auction. If we find a problem, we're gonna call it. If we miss something, well, we've missed it. That's what previews are for."

Jasper caught the eye of the man in suspenders who'd asked the question. His face had flushed red. She smiled kindly. The man shrugged and turned his attention to the item Tony was holding over his head.

"Okay, let's get started! Tony, what've you got there?"

"First item up! Monkey wrench, boys. They don't make 'em like that, anymore! Who'll give me 25 and go? Now 25-25-25? Bid 'em in at 25! Let's go, folks!"

Kelly studied her stack of bidder cards. She held up five fingers.

Ted said, "Make it ten, and go!"

Kelly waved her card and nodded.

"I've got ten right here, with Kelly. Who'll go 15 now? 15 there! Now 20, and 25. Bid 25-25-25? Sold it. Twenty dollars. Right there. Number 102 bought it, Grace. 102 for $20." 102 was the man who'd embarrassed himself with the question about chips and cracks. Maybe, thought Jasper, he was winning back his self-respect by winning the first item of the auction.

The crowd stuck close as Ted walked his way down the table, the way Jasper had seen Jimmy do it the week before. Tony would pick up a flat full of license plates or a cast iron doorstop and hold them high, turning to show some of the people, mostly men. The bidding moved quickly. The doorstop brought $37.50 and a mason jar full of buttons went higher than Jasper could've imagined: $55 to a long-haired brunette named Hillary. "There you go, sweetheart," Ted said before he handed her the jar himself.

Ready Teddy, Jasper thought, remembering the words of his ex-squeeze, the pregnant waitress.

Jasper helped as much as she knew how, handing up items for a quick look-see by Ted before he launched his attack again. When Kelly won the bid for one of her absentees, Jasper took turns with Tony, running the item up to the storage room behind the auction block, scrawling a bidder number on one of the scraps of paper there and tucking it under the item, then racing back to the table to help catch bids with a hearty Yep! or run the next item back the way she'd come.

Ted raced through the back table items one after the other. Postcard albums. Old empty milk and medicine bottles. If he couldn't get a bid, he'd say, "Put 'em all together. OK, all for one money!"

Jasper was sweating. Her head was reeling. How could Ted keep up with all the bidders, and the objects that Tony or Kelly scooped up from the table, marbles, and calendars and rusty old tools? How could Grace up on the auction block possibly understand all this keep and type an accurate record of each winning amount and bidder amount into her keyboard?

And the question that most made Jasper sweat: *Where, oh were, was Jimmy?*

Before she knew it, Ted had reached the end of the table. "Jasper's gonna sell for a little while," he announced. Then he pressed a button on the black box he wore on his belt. Unclipped it, and handed it to Jasper with the attached headset. "Put this on. Get up on the block. Switch the switch and sell a few things. I need a quick break."

The crowd at the back table broke up, many of them going to chairs they've saved earlier with empty boxes on the seats or jackets or a copy of their bidder number taped on.

Jasper felt a hot hand on the back of her neck. Tony said in her ear, "Come on. I'll tell you what we're selling, and you just go through the motions."

"My bid-calling stinks!" Jasper said.

"You'll be fine." Tony said. He hurried her up the aisle.

She climbed the steps, feeling as if she were ascending to her own hanging. She fumbled the headset on. Grace helped her snug it down for her smaller head size. It was moist with Ted's sweat. Maybe I'll get electrocuted and this nightmare will end, Jasper thought as she switched the button the little black box she'd tucked into her pocket. Unlike Ted, she wasn't wearing a belt.

Since she didn't instantly go up in smoke, she faced the expectant crowd spread out below her. "Okay, everybody, same terms and conditions," she said.

Grace whispered, "Same auction. You don't have to do that. Just sell. You can do it."

Jasper had spoken from the pulpit before – only a couple rare times when Pastor Tim relinquished control – so she knew she could address the crowd.

"Let's get started then. Tony, what do we have first?"

"Art glass!" Tony called out. "Choice off the table!" He gestured at the globular bowls and stalactite vases in oranges, yellows, bright blues that covered one of the front tables.

"Who'll give me five to start?" Jasper asked.

Two different bidders raised their cards.

Jasper hesitated. What did she do now?

"You got five!" Tony called.

"Now seven-and-a-half?"

Both bidders raised their cards again. Jasper, not sure which one to pick, just pointed at one of them and kept going. "I have seven-and-a-half. Now ten. Okay, there's ten. Now 15. Who'll go 15? One of you ladies want back in at 15? 15? 15?"

"Sell it!" Tony yelled.

"Sold for – " Jasper turned to Grace who whispered, "Ten." "Sold for $10 to buyer number 67." The winning bidder got to her feet and walked up to the table. She picked up one of the bases and a bowl.

"Takes two!" Tony called. "Anybody else?"

"Say that," Grace whispered.

"Anybody else?" Jasper echoed.

The other woman, the one who'd been outbid moved up to the table. With whispered instructions from Grace, Jasper announced, "Bidder 112 takes two. Anybody else?"

The crowd sat still. Some of them moved impatiently in their seats.

"All to go!" Tony yelled and punched the air.

"All to go!" Jasper called over the mike. "How about five for it all. There's five! Now ten! Who'll give me ten?"

Number 67 made a cutting motion across her throat with her bidding card.

"She's cutting your bid. Seven-fifty," whispered Grace.

"Do I take it?"

People in the crowd snickered. A few groaned.

"You have seven-fifty!" Tony yelled. "Go ten!"

"Ten, anybody, ten? There's ten! Now 12…12-and-a-half! Got it! Now 15. 15, anybody? 15? Sold – twelve-and-a-half to number 67. Whew!" Jasper said on mike.

There was a smattering of applause, but Jasper knew she was supposed to keep the auction under control. Hadn't the nice auctioneer teacher from WorldWide College of Auctioneering said just that on her study CD? So she looked to Tony down below. He'd moved over to the front table on the other side of the block.

"Got some nice quilts here, Jasper!" Tony shouted.

Poor Tony. His voice was growing hoarse. Jasper decided to try harder to take up the slack so he didn't have to use himself up. She eyed the quilt that Tony was holding out to his full wingspan. "Show me!" she ordered Tony. He turned quickly with a sideways glance up at Jasper.

"Madame," Tony said with a bow. Esteban hurried in the back doors and took his place by the other ringhand. He belched loudly.

"Nice of you to join us. Keep that quilt up off the floor," Jasper ordered. "Show them now."

"The lady's got herself some new nards." Esteban spoke quietly but Jasper caught his words. She shrugged them off. "Very nice quilts," she told the crowd. "This one is wedding ring pattern. See the pink and rose colors intertwined? The background white is spotless, meaning that this quilt was cherished and protected." Tony seemed to be taking in her words and stood straighter, held the quilt higher. Visible on either side of him, the crowd lifted its diverse heads as if it had become a single-minded entity.

Kelly, seated in the front row so the auctioneer would always see her holding up bidder cards for the absentees, got to her feet. She stood up on one side of the quilt and faced the crowd. "Let's sell 'em one at a time, Jasper!" she shouted. "These ain't blankets, folks. These are some damn fine handmade quilts!" Kelly turned Jasper's direction and mouthed the words, "What am I bid?"

Jasper took a deep breath. "What am I bid for this one fine quilt?" she asked the crowd. Then she took off, her bid-calling growing stronger by the second. It was as if she were channeling the soul of Jimmy Biggs, Master Auctioneer. "One hun-hun-hundred dollar bid, now 125, and 150!" The bidding finally topped off at $225 and Jasper called, "Sold!" while Tony and Kelly called out a simultaneous, "Number 107."

"One hundred and seven," Esteban said.

"107 takes it," Jasper said.

Kelly turned and winked at her. "My oh my," Jasper thought to herself. She nodded gratefully at Kelly. "My oh my, we might become friends after all."

"Good job, Jasper," Grace whispered from the clerk's spot next to Jasper.

Tony shouted, "Next quilt up, Jasper. We got another good one here!"

Jasper paused for a quick slurp of water from the bottle, and in those few seconds saw the entrance of the next real, hard, phase of her life.

Glenn Relerford dressed in somber brown marched up the central aisle. "Talk to you," he said.

"Me?" asked Jasper on mike.

Glenn pointed at her and signaled that she come down off the auction stand. Estie stepped in his way and spread his arms wide like he was going to stop him.

"Don't let him take Jasper!" a man in the crowd shouted.

"We'll protect you!" a woman said.

"It's okay, it's okay," Jasper said, still speaking into her headset microphone as she walked down the steps at the back of the platform and joined Glenn. She fiddled with the switches on the side of the microphone box at her waist. "It's Jimmy, isn't it?" she asked and her voice boomed throughout the auction house.

"I'll take you to him," Glenn said. He placed his hand lightly on her shoulder.

Ted stomped back into the room and rushed over to Jasper and Glenn. "What the hell is going on here?"

Jasper took off her microphone and handed it to him. "Sell something," she said.

Chapter 12

Jasper left the auction house in a squad car with Glenn and a uniformed officer who said to call her Sheila.

"Sheila," Jasper said.

"You just relax back there."

Deal with death much? Panicked was how Jasper felt. All body parts that registered in her overwhelmed brain felt sweaty: hands, feet, face. Even her brain was sweating. Not only had something happened to Jimmy, but here she was on her first night of auctioneering sitting in the back of a police car. There was nothing like the smell of other people's lies and fears and a bullet-proof window between police and prisoner section to heighten her already off-the-charts emotion. She fidgeted. Her knees bumped up against the back of the front seat.

"Got your seat belt on?" Glenn asked kindly.

"Uh-huh."

"Would you like a pop or something? We could go through Mickey D's on the way over," Officer Sheila offered. "There's no real hurry here."

"No hurry?"

Glenn turned to the other officer and said something in a low voice. Sheila whispered back.

Jasper pretended they were not talking about her. *Sticks and stone may break Jimmy's bones...* She studied the lights in other people's houses as they sped by. What were these other normal people doing this evening? Fixing the kids mac and cheese? Kicking back for a lazy evening on the sofa? Jasper would have killed for a big bowl of cheesy pasta and a remote control. She would even be happy if she could auctioneer for another round. Nothing like an emergency to put the rest of life in perspective.

There was no siren going, but when another vehicle slowed them down, Sheila would reach toward the console and jab a button that made that *wah-wah* sound she knew from TV cop shows. The civilian would clear out of the way. Glenn would step on the gas. Jasper was getting a little car sick.

The officers argued sotto voice. *You told her, didn't you? Yeah. She knows. But just the same.*

"Sorry," said Officer Sheila.

"No, nothing for me, thanks. And there really is no hurry, is there? I mean, maybe we could take a drive around the park on our way. Hmm?" Jasper didn't want the nice police officer to feel badly about anything.

"Which park?" Officer Sheila asked.

"I think that's a line from an old movie," Jasper said. "I guess I'm not very funny, am I?"

Sheila murmured to Glenn.

"Just sit back," Glenn told Jasper. "We're almost there."

The back windows of the squad car were steamed up. Cars did that when the heat was high and the night was bone chill lonely. The Midwest knew how to do heart-breaking spring rains really well. But why wouldn't a police car have special window de-steamers, she wondered. Of course if you thought about it, you realized that Forest Grove police cars were just Chevies refitted with the accoutrements of law enforcement – the prisoner barrier, the radios, the siren and light equipment.

Jasper felt as if she were under arrest herself. She did yoga breathing to steady herself. She had never been in trouble. She was a good girl to a fault. A good woman. Girl. Sure, she got angry. But she didn't rage like her stepfather Jimmy. No, her crimes, if any, were of the passive aggressive type. Could you be arrested for secretly spitting in her soon-to-be-legally-ex-husband's communion grape juice? Was there a law, an obscure law it would have to be, somewhere, one of those that state legislators had forgotten to erase from the books that forbade misplacing a minister's last clean clerical collar so that he had to borrow one's own white dickey? Probably pressing a dime into a bowl of December morning oatmeal and then claiming it was an old Norwegian custom when one's then more-or-less-full-fledged husband bit into it and chipped a tooth bordered on criminal intent. But no, Scandinavians did do something like that – but maybe it was a gold coin or just an almond – and okay, she wasn't Swedish, Danish or Norwegian although a lot of people around these parts were and heaven knows she could've picked it up from them, Your Honor.

The squad car pulled to a stop.

There was one second of silence. Then from somewhere came an indecisive noise– a whine. Like a chainsaw that can't make up its mind or a ghost that's new to haunting.

"Neighbors?" Jasper asked.

The whine started up again. A saw in somebody's garage shop down the street, no doubt.

"The Camry belongs to the Austrings," Glenn said.

"Aren't they Japanese?" Jasper pulled Kelly's borrowed sweater closer around her shoulders. Even though the squad car was toasty warm, her hands felt icy. They'd turned yellow and purple. Raynaud's Disease. Nothing to worry about. Lots of women especially had it. Not her twin. But worry brought on the poor circulation and Jasper was prone to worry.

Glenn spoke slowly. "The Austrings. They're the people who want to buy this house. They're the ones who found your father."

"Stepfather. Did you know we always called him Jimmy?"

"We'd better get inside." He got out and came around to open her door.

Jasper sat. Then with a sudden longing for cold fresh air, she thought *Rise and walk* and stepped out into a puddle on the uneven sidewalk. "Sorry," she said. Jasper was well practiced in apologizing for things not her fault.

It was a quiet street. A lone car drove by. Jasper heard the crunch of its tires against the gravel wash on the opposite side of the road. Glenn escorted her up the walk. The short march felt familiar. Ah. That old familiar processional. Jasper was well practiced in processionals – up and down the aisles of many churches in many towns.

Processionus Gravitatus.

The small house looked more worn out tonight than when Jasper had first viewed it alongside Jimmy two days earlier. Now it looked its age and its history. Generations of hard working factory folk had lived their lives here. Its wooden sides looked thin as if they provided little protection from the Midwest's notorious cold and damp.

The detective's brown and gold trainers seemed to lift him above the puddles. Her own sensible sneakers hit every small pond. They climbed three steps to the porch. Up close, the house breathed out a smell of rotting wood, a poor smell like nothing for dinner but bowls of thin soup. Glenn reached for the doorknob. Jasper hesitated, drops of water from the overhang torturing the back of her neck. Then she scraped her feet rightleftrightleftrightleft on the Beware of Dog unwelcome mat and followed him in.

Jasper shivered. She sneezed three times into the sleeve of her borrowed sweater. "Sorry."

The lighting inside was indifferent. Jasper automatically reached for the light switch she remembered was on her left. Nothing. She looked up at Glenn's face, almost invisible now except for his gleaming eyes and teeth.

"The old guy, the owner, had it cut off. We checked with the power company."

"That wasn't supposed to happen – not until we get the house sold, I think." Jasper said, happy to think about a practical problem for a few minutes.

"Yeah, and it's damn inconvenient!" said a male voice from the direction of the sofa.

Jasper turned. Her eyes were adjusting now to the half-light and the curtains stood open to let in the weird orange of the street lamp outside. The man, a stranger in his late twenties, sat by a woman of the same age next to him.

"Hush," the woman said. "That's her. You know."

"Oh, yeah."

Jasper stared at them wordlessly. Then something of her usually polite self resurfaced. "You're the Austrians?" she asked.

"Austrings. Emily and Kiefer," the young woman said. "We're buying this house"

"You still want to?" Jasper asked.

"I knew it! I knew it!" Kiefer Austring said, starting to get to his feet. "There is something wrong with this place."

Jasper glanced at Glenn. *Can you believe these people?*

He shot them a professional policeman on the job look that pinned young Mr. Austring in place.

Jasper mustered her last remaining ounce of professional courtesy. "There's nothing wrong with this house.

The man who owns it is ….old and a little confused. He told Power & Light to switch off the electricity. It'll be back on tomorrow. It works fine. OK?"

"Well," the man began, still a little grumpy.

"Kiefer!" hissed his wife.

Officer Sheila stood keeping an eye on the young couple. She crouched in front of them and spoke in firm tones. Jasper supposed she would let them go when she finished taking their statements.

"Are you ready?" Glenn asked Jasper.

She nodded.

He led the way, directing his flashlight along the floor like a theater usher. Clutter lined the uneven path. Jasper had forgotten what piles of stuff this house contained. Ray Clippert was one major hoarder. The dust kept her sneezing. She wiped her nose on the sleeve. She'd have to wash Kelly's sweater before she returned it. Jasper tripped over a toppled stack of old magazines. She righted herself by holding on to Glenn's shoulder. She hoped he wouldn't take it personally.

"There's a lot to get hurt on in here, isn't there?" Suddenly tired, she felt it could take all night to traverse the distance to her stepfather's body. She stuck close to the detective until they reached the basement door in the kitchen.

He ducked and descended onto the landing. "Take your time." He thunked the overhead beam with his palm so its location became apparent. "Watch your head now." Jasper moved forward and he placed a hand atop her hair, as if she were a suspect being helped into the back of a squad car.

When she crossed that first threshold, she held her breath. She expected the stench of death, like the rotting sweet stench of a drawerful of mice, but when she breathed again, it was only the old tired smell of dust and mold that the whole house held plus an overlay of urine. Glenn said, "Put your hand on my belt and follow me nice and slow." She did as she was told and inched her way down the steep stairs, illuminated by the detective's flashlight. At the bottom she looked around warily, thinking maybe she wouldn't even be able to recognize Jimmy in the gloomy light. But she saw him lying there on the ground and was surprised that even before she focused on his features, she would have known his slightly chubby shape, the length of his legs, his overall shortness, anywhere. His height, breadth, width. His very Jimminess.

She moved in closer. The clutter in here had been moved out toward the walls, piles of National Geographics, the bowling ball that had rolled downstairs when she and Jimmy had first viewed the basement, a broken pseudo Chippendale chair with only two legs, and lots of unrecognizable debris. Jimmy lay in a circle cleared of junk, like a fallen gladiator at the bottom of the amphitheater. Dizziness compelled her to sit on the cold floor. She eased herself to her knees and crawled over to Jimmy. She inhaled a hint of sweat and the strong aroma of some cologne she didn't recognize. He was always helping himself to cologne found in auction clients' houses. Jimmy had several bad habits. Jasper and her sister had long suspected that the perfumes he gave them birthday after birthday probably came out of housefuls of stuff destined for the auction. "Is it okay if I touch him?"

Glenn nodded. "Of course. Take your time."

Having asked, Jasper suddenly felt awkward. Jimmy had never been much of a hugger. She touched his face. Cold. She drew her hand back, then reached forward and stroked his thinning hair. She patted him on the shoulder. "What was he doing here alone?"

"I was hoping you could tell me."

Up close, Jasper could smell the flowery dryer sheets Jimmy was so fond of adding to his laundry. The rough-and-tumble auctioneer had always been a stickler for personal cleanliness. He wore his favorite watch, a Tag Heuer he'd gotten for a song at the auction. He had left a proxy bid, then did the bid-calling himself so he could control how the sale went. "What were you doing here, Jimmy?" she asked the dead man. A chill crept up her spine. Maybe Jimmy hadn't been alone when he died. She turned to Glenn. "Did you check his pockets?

"Yes, ma'am."

"Was anything there?" Jasper asked in a small voice.

"This was on the floor near him," Glenn said. He handed her a Biggs Auction House key fob, one of the freebies they kept on the counter at work. He crouched down next to her. He pulled a wad of something from his own pocket and passed it over. He shone his flashlight on it. Jasper's hands shook. It was a roll of bills that relaxed open to reveal Ben Franklin's tight-lipped smile. Jasper spread them apart. Four hundred dollars plus a George Washington.

"Looks like you've been dealt a little gift hand there," Glenn said.

"Cookie and I get to keep this?"

Glenn shrugged. "Later. You are his closest relatives. But why $401?"

Jasper smiled. She felt better knowing that he hadn't died at the hands of a robber. "It was just one of those Jimmy things. For luck, I guess. Or maybe just out of habit. When we were girls, he used to take us out for ice cream sometimes. He made us splurge on triple-decker cones even if we weren't hungry. I always got butter brickle. I think he liked to impress the people at Moo'nGoo when he whipped out a hundred doll bill."

Glenn listened patiently.

"Sometimes though he'd just pull out the extra $20 he always kept in his wallet. Oh my gosh, where's his wallet?"

"Easy now, easy. It's right here." Glenn handed over Jimmy's worn leather wallet.

"Oh, thank goodness," Jasper said. She opened it and ran her fingers over the plastic covered driver's license, foggy in the near dark of the light from Glenn's flashlight. Jasper slipped her fingers under the license. Nothing.

"I didn't find a $20 anywhere in there either," Glenn said.

"Funny," Jasper said. "It was his emergency plan. He always told us we should tuck $20 away for emergencies. That's kind of odd." She looked to Glenn for confirmation.

"True that," he said. "It is odd." He opened his palm to her. "I found this too."

The flashlight revealed a small silver figurine with some kind of sparkly stone in the center. Jasper brought her face in close. "It's from a necklace, I guess. What is that – a crab or a lobster?"

"So it's not familiar to you? "

Jasper shook her head. "Where did you find it?"

"Next to him on the floor."

"Oh-h-h. Were you cherry-picking, Jimmy?" she whispered.

Glenn asked, "Cherry picking?"

"Sorry. That's auction speak for picking out the most valuable items ahead of time. Before the regular auction crew comes over for the pickup."

"To protect the good stuff, so to speak."

"Uh-huh. So to speak." She got slowly to her feet. Glenn held out his ringless left hand to help her up. "That's okay, detective. I can manage on my own."

"Jasper," Glenn said.

"Now that we know that he fell in the line of duty, more or less, I guess we should get back upstairs to the others," Jasper said. She stumbled forward. Glenn caught her in his muscled arms. Jasper began to cry, and Glenn drew her in closely.

"It's okay, baby, it's okay," he said. "I'm really sorry. But it'll be okay."

It felt good to rest for a moment in Glenn's protective hold, but the rest of her life was waiting for her and she had to get on with it. If only Glenn wasn't married and she had moved ahead with her own divorce. Jasper forced herself to return to the present moment. She eased away from Glenn who released her without question. "Let's go," she said to him.

"It's your world," he said. He kissed her palm gently, then guided her to the stairs.

Upstairs in the living room, the Austrings were standing talking in hushed tones with Officer Sheila. She closed her notepad. "Detective," she said to Glenn, "I have their statements and I know how to get in touch with them."

"Fine. You're free to go," Glenn said to the couple.

"Sorry for your loss," they mumbled to Jasper as they brushed by her on their way to the door.

"Dedicated guy – your stepfather," Kiefer said.

"He loved his work," Jasper said.

A woman's voice bellowed out from the front porch. She sounded demanding, belligerent. Jasper recognized that voice. Mary Clippert, trying to barge in. Officer Sheila hurried over. "Well, why the doubly-do not?" Mary Clippert's voice sounded, louder and angrier.

"What am I going to do without you, Daddy?" Jasper whispered. She went to the porch. "I'll handle this." She steeled herself

Mary Clippert barreled past her into the house.

"Jasper Biggs!" Mary was nearly panting. She grabbed Jasper's hands.

Jasper drew back from the damp heat.

Mary asked, "Is it true?"

The police officers moved in closer. Whether or not this crazy woman would be allowed to stay a second longer was up to Jasper who felt suddenly transformed into some kind of gate keeper.

"It's all right. It's all right." Jasper said to Mary. She turned to the police. "This lady is an auction client."

"You tell them. That's right. This is my house. My father's house."

So many auction clients were big babies, Jasper thought. This brought to mind Pastor Tim. Well, of course it wasn't just auction clients.

"You poor thing!" Mary Clippert was going on. "Tell me what happened. I must know!"

"I'll be okay," Jasper said. "Oh, my sister!" She dug her cell phone out of her pocket. Her hands shook and she stared at the phone as if it were a moon rock.

Mary reached for the cell phone. "I can help!"

Glenn held up the pendant.

Mary grabbed for it. "Wherever did you find it?" she asked with obvious excitement.

Glenn held it out of her reach. He gestured her to a place on the sofa. He eased the phone from Jasper's hand and spoke to her in a slow, reassuring way. "I expect she's in your favorites. Cookie with a C or a K?"

"C. Just plain Cookie, she always says. Doesn't she?" Jasper looked inquiringly into Glenn's face.

He said, "You better sit down." He gestured with his head toward Mary who shoved over begrudgingly to make a narrow sit-down spot for Jasper

"It's my jewelry," Mary grumbled. She hissed at Jasper, "These policemen don't know that I have every right to be here. It IS my house, my father's house, that is."

Jasper shrugged. She couldn't seem to match Mary's energy so she said nothing.

Mary said, "So what happened? Is it true that it's your father? That he died here. I mean, passed away right in this house, in my house, in my father's house?"

Glenn turned away. Jasper wondered if it was up to him, would he kick this nosy bitch out in the rain? Even in her shock and grief, Jasper was horrified at the language her own brain had just constructed. *Oh please throw her* out, she thought. But he was probably used to very bad behavior. Glenn got Cookie on the cell phone and told her briefly what happened. He handed the phone back to Jasper. "Your sister will be here right away," he said.

Officer Sheila crouched in front of Jasper, the way she had earlier with the Earnest Young Couple. "You've had a terrible shock. If you don't want to talk, you don't have to."

Jasper shook her head to clear it. "No, it's okay. This lady is a client of ours and she needs to know." She turned to Mary. "Yes, it's Jimmy. He's in the basement. He fell and hit his head."

"Are you sure he's…gone?"

Glenn and Sheila exchanged looks of incredulity. *Is she kidding?*

"I didn't check his pulse, did you?" Jasper struggled dizzily to her feet.

Glenn captured her with his arm around her shoulder. "He's gone, sweetheart. Your dad is gone."

"My daddy?" Jasper whispered. She sank back onto the sofa. She heard Officer Sheila rummaging through kitchen cupboards and running the faucet.

She returned and handed Jasper a Styrofoam cup of water. "It was the only clean one I could find," she said. "I rinsed off the dust."

Mary grew to her full height and lifted her chin. "I'd like to see the scene."

The police closed rank. Glenn stood silently. Mary towered over the female officer. But the officer knew how to handle bullies. "No need," Sheila pronounced.

"Maybe when Cookie gets here?" Jasper said. In times of crisis, Jasper's politeness loomed large.

Mary began to rearrange items on the cluttered coffee table.

"Leave it," Glenn said. "You heard what the lady said. Now just sit."

"I'm not accustomed to being ordered around in my own house," Mary said.

"Your father's house," Officer Sheila said.

Mary glared down at her for a long moment. "And I'd like my charm back."

"Sit," Glenn said. He dangled the small jewelry item in front of Mary. "How did this wind up with the auctioneer?" he asked.

Mary snorted. "That's a good question. I never did trust that guy."

Glenn raised an eyebrow at Jasper who said, "If she says it's hers, it's hers. Jimmy must have found it somewhere in this house after all."

"You'll get it back later," Glenn told Mary.

She reached for Jasper's hand. Jasper ignored her and clasped her own hands to her face. The house settled back into its shabby silence.

Later, cocooned next to Cookie in her twin's car, Jasper slumped with the exhaustion that was quickly overtaking her. "How're you holding up, Sis?" Cookie asked her.

"I feel weird," Jasper said

"Me too," Cookie said. "Sudden death will do that to you."

Jasper giggled. She couldn't help herself. "I suppose you're right. How are you doing?"

"About the same," Cookie said. "Shaken up. It's a lot different than helping other people with their dead relatives."

"Yeah, I suppose."

"We haven't had one of our own since Mom," Cookie said.

"You're right."

The twins drove along, warmed by the car heater cranked up high and the strong sisterly connection between them.

Jasper said. "You know, Mom's probably over on the other side trying to coax him into the light,"

"She already has," Cookie said.

"Just like that? Even somebody like Jimmy has an easy time of it?"

Cookie drove with one hand and reached for her sister's with the other. "Jimmy was a rascal, and maybe even a bit of a crook," she said. "But he wasn't an evil person."

"Nope, not a serial killer or anything."

"Nope," Cookie agreed. "And I'm pretty sure he paid all his property taxes."

"After he argued the city clerk to death."

They both laughed weakly and drove on, accompanied by the rain on the windshield and a carful of silent memories.

Chapter 13

The indifferent sun rose Thursday morning in its usual place as if Jasper's world had not just shifted. She'd spent her REMs on dreams of houses with unending cluttered rooms. Dancing cobras, hugging pythons, and harmless garters were alive and well, at home in the hoarder's jungle. Jimmy had walk-on parts like Alfred Hitchcock's cameos in his own movies. *One-Jimmy, two-two-two, two Jimmies, now three, got three Jimmies? Anyone go 'four'?* There he was again! But how did he avoid all the snakes?

Jasper woke with a headache.

She washed away the To Be Continued feeling with a big mug of instant coffee and a cold water splash in the bathroom sink. She took a fast glance in the mirror and shuddered. She looked like Alfred Hitchcock himself. At least Jimmy's face did not show up, the way Cookie said ghosts sometimes did. A shiver slithered up her spine. No more mirrors for her. Not for a good long while. She voiced a prayer for the repose of Jimmy's soul. If he was resting, he wouldn't be haunting.

She tugged on jeans, a navy blue sweatshirt, and sneakers. She eased her apartment door closed and tiptoed downstairs. It wasn't until she reached her locked car that she realized she had forgotten something. She ignored the note on the windshield and slouched back up the sidewalk.

Mrs. O'Neil opened the door on the first ring.

"Forgot my keys," Jasper told her.

"I'm so very very sorry. Come in and we'll talk about it."

"About my keys?"

"Tisk, tisk. You're in a bad way." Mrs. O'Neil tossed a spent cigarette past Jasper's head into a juniper bush. "I was there, you know, at the auction. Until the bitter end."

Jasper stepped in to a low-lying cloud of smoke.

"Would you like a cigarette?" Mrs. O'Neil asked.

Jasper had never taken up the habit, but she was probably already addicted, thanks to her housemates.

"Maybe just a teensy puff to ease your heartache?"

"I'm thinking about it," Jasper said.

Mrs. O'Neil pulled a fresh fag from her apron pocket. "See how it's helping me? My love is undying." She snapped the cigarette in two and handed the filtered half to Jasper. She burst into tears. She rushed back into her apartment. The door slammed behind her.

"We could tape it back together!"

Jasper heard no answer from inside. Just the keening of her mournful neighbor. Jasper placed the cigarette half outside the O'Neil's door. She hurried upstairs to fetch her keys. All was quiet on her way out.

On her drive to Biggs Auction, Jasper pushed the button to wash the bird poop off the windshield. The unread note under the washer blades blew away. Some nestling's parents were doing a good job cleaning up at home. Jasper was an orphan now. She had no parents left to help her clean up the mess of her life.

At the auction house, she parked next to Ted's pickup. He had taken Jimmy's old spot. Inside, Jasper found the crew cleaning up after last night's auction just the way they had last Thursday.

Ted strutted around giving unnecessary orders, yelling louder than ever.

Tony and Esteban worked at the back, rearranging items, grouping them closer together, making room for new stuff that sellers would drop off, unloading the truck from a pick-up Wednesday morning, rushing, rushing, rushing, working steadily.

"Put that box over here!" Ted yelled at Esteban and Tony.

The men's steps slowed way down. "Where did you want it, boss?" Tony asked.

"I don't need none of your lip today. You know where to put it," Ted said.

The guys exchanged a smirk. "You're the boss," Tony said. "I guess."

"Keep your fucking sarcasm to yourself," Ted said.

Jasper helped Grace and Kelly in the office, cashing out successful bidders who'd come in to pick up their items.

"Who made him the frigging pope?" Kelly tossed her red curls.

"Nobody. That's the trouble." Grace sighed. "I was hoping for a lighter day today myself. All things considered." She seemed to be moving in slow motion, going through the steps of her job by memory alone.

"Yeah. We haven't had one of those light days for a long time. Not since Jimmy got off the booze and stopped having mornings after."

"Kelly!" Grace scolded her.

"Simple truth," Kelly mumbled.

Jasper pulled a small butterfly box of costume jewelry out of the display case. "You think there were a lot of sunny days growing up under his roof?"

"Sorry 'bout your step-dad," the customer on the other side of the counter said. Absentee Bidder Number 116.

"Thanks." Jasper clutched the jewelry box.

"Here, I'll do that." Kelly reached for the flat. The nouveau amber necklace glowed like the real thing.

"I can do it." Jasper held on tight.

Kelly tugged.

Grace interceded. She pulled the straight pins out of the lid and lifted the necklace free of the case. She stepped over to the calculator. "Let's see. Buyer's fee, state tax. You owe us $23.10."

"Why don't you get out of here?" Kelly whispered. "You gotta be mourning, right?"

A chubby customer in jeans and an "Uff-Da" sweatshirt was moving up to the counter and from the look on his face, was about to offer Jasper another round of concern and condolences over Jimmy's death. "I could go help with set up," Jasper said.

"You could take a cigarette break," Grace said.

"Why does everybody want me to start smoking? "

"Get out of here already!" Kelly said gruffly, then added more kindly, "We've got it covered." She turned back to help the next customer at the counter. "Mr. Parker! Let's see. You won the box lot of puzzles and item number three from the showcase. The salt and pepper cows!"

Good," the plump man with the red face said. "Mother will be very happy."

"Estie!" Kelly yelled at her husband. "Mr. Parker needs his stuff from the back room!"

Jasper approached Ted Phillips who was sorting through boxfuls at the back table. "It's just like the Rose Bowl Parade, isn't it?" she asked conversationally. "As soon as one auction's done, we get started on the next one."

"Right," Ted grunted. His arm snaked around Jasper's shoulders even as he continued rummaging, with one hand only, through one of the boxes piled on a cart near the table. "Sorry for your loss." He squeezed her into her side.

Jasper pulled away.

"Tony!" Ted bellowed. "What lot is this?"

"It's for Andy!" Kelly and Grace called out simultaneously.

"Looks like Andy's. So what is he – 101?"

"One-ten," Esteban said. He handed over the puzzle box and salt shakers at the office.

Jasper grabbed up a marker off the table and wrote #110 on the sides of the boxes Ted was re-sorting into. She knew the drill.

Grace sidled up alongside her. "Come with me," she said into Jasper's ear. "Break!" Grace yelled without turning around.

Jasper followed her lead.

Outside the auction house, the spring sun persisted. "Feels good." Grace lifted her worn face. The bright light made her look older and more weathered than Jasper usually saw her. Sadder. She struck a match with her fingernail. The smoke spiraled heavenwards.

Jasper shook her head. "Got my own." She reached into the pocket of her jeans and pulled out the remains of Mrs.

O'Neil's cigarette half. Crumbs. She dumped them in the outdoor ashtray.

"I want to give you something." Grace gestured with her lit cigarette.

"No, really. I have enough guilt. I don't need a new bad habit. No offense."

"Here." Grace reached for Jasper's hand and pushed a key into her palm. "For Jimmy's apartment. I won't need it anymore." She took one long drag, then pinched the end dead and dropped the cigarette back into her chest pocket. She headed for the door.

"I'll go back to work with you."

"No, no. You take a real break, honey. Go see what he left behind. Maybe there's something you or your sister could use."

Jasper looked at the key to Jimmy's enclave. "There's plenty of time for going through his stuff," she said.

Grace paused. "I wouldn't be so sure about that. There are a few more keys floating around."

Ten minutes later, Jasper continued her meandering through Jimmy's deserted apartment. It had been cold, deathly quiet and dark when she first went in, but with all the lamps switched on, the blinds opened on the single window, and the thermostat kicked up a couple notches, it felt less like a tomb. It still smelled strongly of Jimmy – a blend of antacid tablets, cologne, bacon, and scented dryer sheets (Jimmy used to love doing laundry of all things; could it have been a compulsion aimed at washing away his sometimes dirty dealings, Jasper wondered) – and that was disconcerting. So was the stuffed moose head looking down from above the large TV.

Other taxidermied animals guarded the dead man's walls and tables. A coyote, wild ducks, a goose, and a very large fish with teeth that was scary even in death. Jimmy had not been a sportsman. In fact as far as Jasper knew, he had no hobbies. Everything probably came from the auction. Weren't some of those animals endangered species? Her auctioneering CD had warned about that. What did Wisconsin auction law say?

Jasper didn't recognize the furniture either. An extra-long leather sofa took up one whole wall of the living room. In front of it sat a polished driftwood table. On either side were oak end tables with shelves and drawers. The shelves held small figurines that might or might not have been made of ivory. The miniature monkeys and robed Asian figures had the look of age. Jasper tried the drawers but they were locked tight. Who had *this* key?

None of this had been here last time Jasper visited. That was several years ago, thanks to Tim's dictum about avoiding her money grubbing stepfather. At least Jimmy was honest that way. His passion was making money. At least Jimmy owned up to his life goals.

Jasper couldn't decide where to settle. Even though Jimmy's king-size bed was neatly made up, the comforter with bears ambling across a blood-red background spooked her.

She took her shivery self into the small bathroom. Avoiding the mirror, Jasper opened the medicine cabinet. Antacid tablets. Toothbrushes. Half a dozen, with most still in their store packaging. Two different kinds of toothpaste. Dental floss cases neatly stacked: strings, ribbons, waxed, unwaxed, mint, plain and cinnamon. Acetaminophen. Aspirin. Menstrual pain reliever. Condoms.

"He was well prepared," Jasper said to herself. She tried to think of that as a good thing.

On the bottom stood six bottles of cologne arranged by name. "Adventure, Boss, Curve, Desire, Envy and Old Spice," she read. She picked up the white glass bottle and sniffed in the familiar scents of orange, cinnamon and vanilla musk.

Her cell phone buzzed in her pocket. Jasper jumped. The bottle fell into the sink and shattered. Jimmy's signature scent filled the air. She exited the bathroom and closed the door behind her. Caller ID said it was Jimmy phoning.

"It was an accident!" Jasper shrieked into the phone.

"Miss Biggs?" a deep voice asked.

"Who is this?" Jasper backed onto the bed and sat down on some cotton grizzlies.

"Sergeant Relerford."

"Glenn? My neighbor?"

"Forest Grove Police." His tone was more officious than neighborly, although it still held that sexy dark chocolate quality. "I'm sorry about your father, he said." *Hot fudge.*

"Stepfather. But it's okay." Jasper lay down on top of the bear-decorated comforter. If you forgot that wild animals stalked beneath you, it was actually quite comfortable. She stretched out kitty-corner with her shoes hanging over. Maybe a short nap was just what she needed. Maybe she would drive through the frozen custard shop later and get herself a turtle sundae.

"Miss Biggs?"

Ooey, gooey chocolate topped with salty pecans. Maybe Glenn Relerford would like to share a sundae. She sat up abruptly. *Maybe she was totally warped sexually and could get turned on only when she was grieving.* She patted back the loose tendrils of her hair. "Hmm?"

"I'd like to get your father's phone back to you."

"I'd like that."

"Oh? Yes, well. It fell out of his pocket – last night."

"I know he fell." Jasper sniffed back some sudden tears.

"Look. This doesn't sound like a good time for you."

Jasper took a deep breath. "I'm just tired and hungry. I think I forgot to eat breakfast."

"I was going to have you come by the station. But why don't I meet you downtown for lunch?"

"Well." Dream come true or guilty pleasure? So far she had taken no steps toward her divorce from Tim. Maybe she was giving herself a safety net in case her new life didn't work out. She scrunched a poor bear up in her fist. "I don't know if I should."

"I understand," Glenn Relerford said. His voice had gotten all stern again.

Jasper pictured his handsome dark face. Kind of like a younger version of that African American actor who won the Oscar for that movie she didn't like very much but he was still good. "Oh, oh no! You don't understand. I would love to have lunch with you but the truth is, I've already made plans to meet my sister."

"Your sister. Mrs. Swanson."

"Cookie."

"Pardon me?"

"Cookie. That's her name."

No response this time.

Jasper said, "Why don't you join us?"

"Miss Biggs, are you there? This phone's beeping. Battery's going."

"Forester!" Jasper shouted. "Eleven o'clock!"

The phone garbled something at her.

"And call me Jasper!" she yelled. "Hello?"

Jasper got to her feet and smoothed the bears back into place. She quickly placed a call to Cookie. "Sis, I hope you're hungry," Jasper said. "I need you to be hungry."

Chapter 14

Inside the restaurant Jasper and Cookie hugged each other so tightly that their twin tummies growled hello. Jasper sniffled. Cookie too.

"Table for two?" a young man in black shirt and slacks asked.

The sisters pulled apart. Cookie followed the host; Jasper followed her. Today Cookie wore a turquoise cashmere sweater belted over a purple top and dark leggings. Jasper thought her sister was ruffle-less for a change, until Cookie's sweater fell open to reveal a pleated frill running down one side of the top. Jasper smoothed the plain front of her own dust-colored sweatshirt. She licked her finger and rubbed away some kind of food spot on one sleeve.

They took their seats at a semi-private table near the plate glass window. The Forester backed on the Honey River, and the view at the back could be pretty spectacular. But that was at night and for diners and fancy martini drinkers. The less formal section looked out on the downtown. Not a big city. Not a lot of people-watching to be done. But lots of late morning light. Brightly colored abstract art on the walls.

"I'm glad we're here early. It's not busy," Cookie said. "Sunshine! That makes one day in a row."

"It's weird, isn't it, how last night Jimmy…" Jasper's voice trailed away and she gripped the small laminated menu.

Cookie took Jasper's cold hands into hers. "We're in this together, Sis."

Jasper began to cry. "It's so much all at once."

"Life and death and rain and sunshine. I know."

Jasper squeezed her sister's hands. "It's more than that, I think. I feel afraid and I don't understand."

"It's the body that fears its mortality. You know that the spirit lives on." She picked up the discarded menu. "I don't know about your body but mine's pretty hungry."

A woman in black waitress garb approached their table.

"Do you know what you want?" Cookie asked.

Jasper looked up past the waitress' pregnant belly.

"Molly!" It was Ted Phillips' ex, the waitress of the broken down car. Jasper introduced her to Cookie.

"Are you hoping for a girl?" Cookie asked.

"W-e-l-l, as a matter of fact," Molly began.

"You get your wish! It's a girl." Cookie lifted her water glass. "Cheers!"

Jasper studied her menu.

"Ready to order?" Molly asked. Her voice had iced over.

"I'll have the chicken salad. Cookie, you want the crow?" Jasper asked

"What? I'll have the same as my sister," Cookie told Molly.

Molly scrawled ferociously on her pad.

"With extra cashews," Cookie said. "If you don't mind. Please."

"Me, too, Molly. Thanks. And diet soda for both of us."

After the waitress had stomped off, Cookie asked, "Did I say something wrong?"

"She already has a daughter. She wants a little boy."

"She'll forgive me after her little girl gets here. She's gonna love this child!"

"Cookie!"

"What? I don't make this stuff up, you know. I just call 'em as I hear 'em. And that's what the guides are telling me. I wonder if she wants to know the baby's name."

A breeze from the front door blew their way.

"Cookie, you can't go around telling people what they maybe don't want to hear," Jasper said. "Trust me on this. I've had a lot of practice with selective truth-telling."

"Candace Jasper Biggs! I am here to help you stop messing with your karma."

"My karma is just fine, thank you." Jasper stuck her tongue out.

"Is not."

"Is too!"

Cookie pointed over Jasper's shoulder. "Sis, isn't that the policeman from last night?"

Jasper turned to see Glenn Relerford. He wore civilian clothes, a deep blue shirt, patterned tie, and gray dress slacks. Jasper waved and he started toward them. She leaned toward her sister. "Cookie, listen up. No matter what the little voices in your head tell you about this guy, don't say anything."

"Oh-h, I see!" Cookie said. "Well, Officer. Fancy meeting you here. Have you had lunch?"

"Thanks." Relerford set Jimmy's cell on the table and took a seat between them. "Detective," he said. "Call me Glenn." He and Cookie shook hands.

Jasper smelled just a hint of sandalwood emanating from his wrists and neck. She liked the look of that neck, its muscles showing beneath his coppery skin, set off nicely against his royal blue shirt. She'd liked to see him without a shirt. Something hot and bothersome was stirring in her and she had not felt anything close to it in much too long a time.

"It's too bad about your dad," he said.

Blood rushed back up to Jasper's brain. "Step-dad," she and Cookie said in unison.

The detective's eyes cut from Cookie to Jasper and back again. "Twins, huh? I don't see it."

"That's what they all say," Cookie said. She tilted her head sideways and batted her lively green eyes.

Jasper sent her telepathic *tone-it-down* messages. "Thanks for bringing the phone." She reached for it, but Cookie beat her to it.

"I'll clear it," Cookie said and dropped it in her purple hobo bag.

"Once you get it recharged, you might want to save his contacts. For business. Or his funeral," Glenn said.

"What I meant was – "Cookie began.

Jasper interrupted her. "That's a great idea, isn't it, Cookie?"

Molly delivered their salads, setting down Cookie's with a clatter. "Hiya, Glenn," she said sweetly. "The usual?"

"Molly, maybe I oughta get what these ladies are having. Those salads look loaded with vitamins."

"Naw, take the advice of a mother-to-be and get what you want," Molly said. She patted her tummy and shot Cookie a look. She said, "Not another word, Glenn. You're getting the A-B-and C burger. Medium-well, right?"

"Mama knows best. Thanks, Moll."

"A-B-and C?" Jasper asked.

"All Beef and Cheddar." This time Glenn and Cookie spoke as one.

"Bread and butter!" Cookie said. She laughed and raised her glass.

"Bread and butter, yes ma'am!" Glenn clinked glasses with Cookie, then Jasper. She found herself crying. "We shouldn't be so happy with Jimmy so – "

"Dead?" Cookie asked. "I've told you, Sis, every time you mention him he shows up."

"What?" Glenn swiveled to look over his shoulder.

"Not there. There." Cookie pointed with her fork.

Glenn looked to Jasper who shrugged. "She sees dead people."

"Uh-huh." I guess I've heard that," Glenn said.

Welcome to my world, Jasper thought. *So much for fantasy boyfriends.*

Glenn took a big swig of water. "I've seen a few in my time too," he said.

That broke the ice. They chatted, sipped and chewed until they were all three well into their lunches.

Jasper pushed aside her salad bowl.

"You're not eating enough to keep a baby bunny alive, Sis!" Cookie waved her fork toward the window. A small hare hopped across the parking lot.

"I can't stop thinking," Jasper said.

"It's a family trait," Cookie said.

"I can see that." Relerford took another big bite of his burger. "Brains and beauty. You two ladies got it goin' on."

Jasper giggled. She had always been a giggler. She hoped one day to be a stronger woman who could either laugh graciously or smile like the Mona Lisa. Strong women didn't giggle.

Cookie snorted.

Jasper relaxed. "No, listen. I know it was an accident and all – last night. Jimmy. You know."

"Right. A really unfortunate accident. No signs of foul play. We're not investigating this as a criminal matter." Relerford spoke with burger in his mouth. A drop of mustard wormed down his chin.

Jasper stared.

"What? You think there's something hinky?"

"Hinky?" Jasper fixated on the bright yellow glob. Somebody ought to warn him before he stained his nice blue shirt. She didn't want to be the one. She switched her gaze to Cookie and tapped her own chin. Cookie automatically brought her napkin to her face. Jasper nodded her head slightly toward Relerford.

He laughed and wiped his chin clean. "You two crack me up." Then he went back to stern cop. "Hinky –odd, funny, suspicious."

"I'm kind of wondering why Jimmy tumbled down those stairs," Jasper said.

Relerford's spine straightened. "You have serious suspicions?"

Weren't his dark eyes more toffee than black coffee a moment ago? Jasper switched her gaze to his necktie. "Oh not hinky that way. Oh no."

Molly approached the table and refilled their water glasses. "You guys want anything else?" She directed her question mostly to Relerford.

He smiled and waved her off. "Clarify," he said to Jasper.

"Yes, Sis, clarify. *Now* please." Cookie's perfectly applied makeup suddenly looked a shade too pale.

"All I meant was that maybe if I had gone with him, I could have been the one to walk downstairs and Jimmy would still be here." Jasper started blubbering again.

"Oh, honey, no. It wasn't your time. It was his." Cookie went to her sister and wrapped her up in a hug. She held a napkin over her sister's nose. "Now blow."

Jasper honked into the cloth.

Molly hurried back to their table. "What is it, sweetie?" she asked Jasper. She pulled a chair up to the table and scooted in close.

"It's our stepfather."

"Jimmy."

"Yeah? The auctioneer," Molly said.

Jasper blew her nose again. "I'll wash it," she said.

"Naw. We have industrial machines. Your step-dad, huh? Jeez. What happened?"

Jasper's voice was all phlegmy. She tilted her head heavenward and pointed up.

Customers coming in the front door drew Molly's attention. "Dammit. Must be noon."

"Torry," Jasper blubbered.

"He got sent up?" Molly asked. She turned to Relerford.

His trouser pocket buzzed. He pulled out his phone. "Retail theft," he said. "Just around the corner. Small towns, you gotta love 'em," he grumbled. He pulled his wallet out and handed Molly some bills. "Ladies," he said. He headed for the door.

"Your stepfather got arrested for shoplifting?" Molly yelled to be heard above the gathering lunch hour crowd. People stared their direction.

"He went to that big auction house in the sky," Cookie said.

"Yeah. He's really taking ghost bids now!" Jasper said. She felt the giggles returning. Cookie joined in. This kind of hysteria was a lot easier to take than the waves of sorrow and guilt that had been washing over her since the discovery of Jimmy's body. Laughter was good for the soul.

Molly looked from one sister to the other. "I guess it's a pretty good deal to have each other at a time like this, huh?"

"You work here?" a man yelled to Molly.

"Only on Tuesdays," Molly said low. "Be right with you." She struggled to get up from her chair.

Cookie hurried around and hoisted her upright. "Been there myself," she said.

"Oh yeah? You're a mom?"

"Got two of my own," Cookie said.

Jasper, still seated, took a nice deep breath and sipped some cold water. She noticed a familiar-looking man adjusting the angle of one of the pictures near the bar. Sandy colored hair, medium height, nice shoulders. He turned her direction. She had seen him at the auction. He held up both hands in a questioning gesture and pointed back at the picture. Jasper gave him a thumbs- up. The handsome man made a little bow. Above her head, Cookie and Molly were chatting away about the joys and difficulties of motherhood.

Jasper had to get out of here soon. She couldn't handle the guilt of close proximity to two attractive men in one afternoon. She was supposed to be in mourning. She was supposed to be married. Both were true, more or less.

"Hey," Molly said to Cookie. "Before you had your kids, did you know whether they were girls or boys?"

Cookie said, "I was wrong – both times. The only thing I knew for sure was that I was going to love both of them no matter who they turned out to be."

"Food for thought," Molly said. "Hugs."

She and Cookie leaned in and included Jasper's head in a group hug. When she broke free, Jasper asked, "Do we owe you for lunch?"

"Nope. If Glenn didn't leave enough, it's on me. If he left enough, then I owe *you*. See ya." She waved bye-bye.

"This was fun," Cookie said. "We'll have to come here more often."

"Yeah, fun," Jasper said. Tears streamed down her face.

"Jasper? Miss Biggs?" the artist called to her. His artwork was avant garde but he had a voice like velvet.

Jasper headed for the door. Cookie said, "That man wants to speak to you."

Jasper, her head lowered, kept going. Fresh air. She utterly longed for escape from the restaurant, her hormones, her grief, her confusing new life. Cookie hurried after her and they left the restaurant one then the other.

Chapter 15

The rest of Jasper's Thursday moved along like an old clock; the minute hand stuck and stuck and stuck and suddenly jerked ahead. Everybody was scrambling to get the auction room ready earlier than usual for next week's sale. Jimmy's memorial service would take place there in two days. So most of the organizing and floor washing had to get done right away. The back table, the side displays, and the showcase would all be set up, locked and roped off before the service started Saturday afternoon. Jasper struggled to keep pace. She had to keep taking crying and nose-blowing breaks.

Jasper dropped a boxful of miscellaneous kitchen items and broke two of the fruit-shaped canisters inside.

"You just wiped out the strawberry and the big banana, so don't worry about it," Esteban said. "

"I want to pay for it. It's not fair to the consigner."

"If you start doing that, we're all gonna be in deep shit. I don't make enough money to pay for everything that breaks around here. Shit happens. Let it go."

Jasper tried to let it go. She tried to concentrate, but her mind wasn't on her work. Ted told her a consigner number to mark on a lot-tag for a bunch of push brooms. As soon as she found the marker, her memory misplaced the number.

Ted said, "Come here." He draped an arm around her shoulder and pulled her in close. She could see the individual whiskers that made up his afternoon facial haze. He smelled like mothballs and sweat. "Don't get me wrong. I liked Jimmy. He was my goddamn mentor, for chrissake. But in this business, he always told me, you gotta be tough. Even though you're a girl, you gotta carry on. You gotta toughen up, sweetie, or you ain't gonna make it."

"I'm tougher than I look," Jasper said. She backed away from Ted and tripped over a vintage toy robot.

"Hand it to me," said Ted. He didn't turn around. "Give the guys a hand. Estie! Tell her what to do."

After a near collision between two planters shaped like ducks set on wheels that she and Tony were each rolling toward the Antiques in the Rough display, Jasper retreated to the relative safety of the office.

"Just sit there," Kelly said. She was busy double-checking a list of winning absentee bidders against the people who hadn't yet shown up to claim their items.

"But I don't want to just take up space."

Kelly said, "Don't matter."

"You can spell us when we take our breaks," Grace said.

"Yeah. That'll be real useful," Kelly said.

"I just don't know what my job is supposed to be," Jasper said.

"It'll come to you," Kelly said.

Jasper blew. All the tensions and worries of the past two weeks rushed like red flood waters from her brain to her gut. She grabbed Kelly by the shoulders of her oversize sweatshirt. Jasper shook her. "You – don't – know - anything – about - me –or – my – life!" Her voice trembled.

Grace called, "Ted, get over here."

Ted pulled Jasper off Kelly. "Girls! Whoa, girls!" He pulled them apart.

Jasper was panting. "I – I'm sorry." She stuck out her hand.

Kelly crossed her arms. "Maybe I was right about you in the first place."

Jasper shook her head. "I just flipped out."

"Like father like daughter! Don't you come near me again. Try to be friendly…jeez. If you're not careful, you're gonna end up like your greedy old man. Never mind. I'm taking my break now." Kelly tramped away.

"Why don't you take a break too?" Grace asked. "You could go out the front door."

"But the auction," Jasper said.

"We've got it under control," Grace said.

"But Jimmy's memorial service. I haven't called about food. What about a notice in the newspaper? Don't we need somebody to recite a few fond memories about him?"

"We know how to do things in a hurry."

"But – "

Grace ticked off items on her fingers. "Food. – check. The Forester is bringing its basic funeral buffet. Lasagna. Salad. Chocolate cake. Newspaper obit - check. Speakers – check. Your sister's been in touch. Go home, honey."

"Get outa here," Ted said.

"Are you letting me go?" Jasper's legs trembled with the aftermath of adrenalin.

"I wish," Kelly said, brushing past Jasper. "Forgot my smokes."

"Go," Grace said.

"See you tomorrow," Ted said.

♦

As she fiddled with the front door lock at the house on Hickory Lane, Jasper could already smell cigarette smoke. She wondered how long it would take her hair and her clothes to absorb the odor full-time. And what if she ever wanted to have company upstairs? A date, heaven forbid, or maybe just a pet. Her nice neighbor next-door had given her the toy stuffed cat. But she longed for more. Maybe a goldfish. Maybe fish were sensitive to tar and nicotine. Smoked fish. Yeck. It wasn't the right time to think about bringing a new loved one, even a very small one-to-love, into her life. A pet would have to wait. Friends? Real life human visitors. Men? Jasper shuddered at the thought. Not ready, not ready, not ready.

She stepped inside. Her entrance had been noisier than she wanted. And sure enough, the Smoky O'Neils' door opened.

"Hi there!" Margie O'Neil stepped into the foyer. She fanned her hands in front of her face. "So did you bring the air freshener? I left you a note."

"Oh." That explained the note on the windshield that had blown away. "I think I forgot."

"It's your turn. After all, I spent my good money on the last two cans."

Jasper nodded. She knew how to be patient with unreasonable people. Usually. She tried to sidestep the bigger woman so she could head upstairs to the privacy of her own apartment, but Mrs. O'Neil blocked her way.

"Listen, can you take just a moment for an old woman who needs to talk to someone. I mean anyone. I know you're mourning and all. But I mean, I'm desperate."

"I'll try to help." Jasper sat down on a step. People used to say she was good at helping. Maybe she could turn this day around by being useful. The smoke was thicker the lower you went. She choked back a cough.

Mrs. O'Neil squeezed in next to her.

Up close the smell of unwashed clothes was stronger than that of cigarettes. Jasper breathed into her hands.

"See it's like this. I don't know how long he – "She tilted her head toward her own apartment door. "How long he will go on like this."

Maybe Jasper *could* help. Except for her own situation, she had always been pretty good with death and dying. One thing about helping other people, Jasper had learned long ago, it took your mind off your own troubles. "You're worried about Mr. O'Neil?" Jasper used her active listening skills. She had taken a day-long class in it once at a women's circle in one of the churches, a class in which she discovered that she was already a very active listener.

"He's never been this bad before. Day and night. Night and day."

"That's tough. It takes a toll on you."

"You betcha."

"What do the doctors say?"

"The doctor? He's the one who started this in the first place."

"Pardon me?" Jasper removed her hands from her mouth. Mrs. O'Neil's smell had grown benign. At least it had blended into the background. "You blame the doctor?"

"And Jimmy."

"My Jimmy?"

"Well, he wasn't mine, was he?"

"I didn't think so."

"Ha! The doctor's the main one. He wrote the prescription, right? You can't waltz into any old drugstore and buy these, these, elevator drugs unless you got a note from the doctor."

"Elevator drugs?"

"Sure. You got a soft little diddler that's stuck in the basement? All you need is a note from the doctor and, zoom, it's up to the penthouse with your wing-wang and your wife's never gonna get any more rest! I don't know how much more of this I can take."

Jasper wriggled to her feet. For a moment, she couldn't speak. "Can't you just hide his pills?" she finally asked.

Margie O'Neil lumbered up. "Tried it. He's tricky, that one. Finds 'em every time. That's why I was wondering - " She reached into her apron pocket and pulled out a prescription bottle. She held it out to Jasper. "Come on. If it hadn't been for your father – "

"Stepfather."

"Whatever. I watched him week after week up there auctioneering, chanting. He would look right at me. My, oh, my, I get flushed just thinking about him."

Jasper's stomach flip-flopped.

"Whenever my own husband would approach me, you know, my thoughts ran back to the auction. After I said 'No' a few too many times, Mr. O'Neil sort of lost his spunk."

Oh, Lord, Jasper prayed silently. *What did I ever do to you?* She hoped she could make it up to her bathroom. She accepted the bottle of pills and ran for her own door.

"Don't worry. He never climbs steps," Mrs. O'Neil called after her.

Chapter 16

Friday morning was business as usual inside Biggs Auction House. Never mind spring threatening to erupt at any moment. Outdoors robins, wrens and cardinals competed for mates, seeds, and nesting space. Not to mention the squirrels. It was a regular Disney movie of love and war. Jasper felt weary of family life. Philandering husband left behind not so very long ago. A week-and-a-half to be exact. Dead stepfather. Two days ago. Food. She was forgetting to eat more and more often. Her easy-fit jeans were fitting easier by the day. Soon they would look sloppy. No matter. One of these days, she would probably turn to chocolate, her favorite comfort food. Then watch out, world! Her waistline would soon expand to normal and beyond. And home. Her own new nest remained less than the retreat she had hoped it would be. Better, Jasper thought, to be indoors in the season-less place of the auction house. Better she should just continue on as auctioneer in training.

The morning zoomed by in a rush of sorting – bells, whistles, rusted old wrenches, setting aside the saleable, and tossing out the just plain junk, with customers dropping in to pick up, pay and haul away. Just the assorted busyness of an established auction house nearing the end of an unusual week. No Jimmy meant less yelling than usual. Although Ted broke out now and then in a fit of swearing. He seemed determined to fill the shoes of the angry, dead auctioneer.

Once an hour Ted pronounced, "It's what Jimmy would have wanted."

Jasper wanted to smack him but she had started avoiding violent confrontations much too long ago to change now.

She felt so embarrassed about her outburst the day before with Kelly that she avoided her all morning. Kelly seemed happy to do the same. *What a shame*, Jasper thought. It had looked like they might have become friends, but resentments kept bubbling up between them.

Tomorrow would be Jimmy's memorial service. But in the meantime Biggs Auction House carried on with business as usual.

At noon, Jasper had a couple pizzas delivered for everyone. She paid for them out of the till. "It's what Jimmy would have wanted," she told an annoyed Ted.

"Yeah, sure he would. Just don't get carried away," he said. "I'll be back in half an hour. Then we're going on a call."

"We're calling on someone?" Jasper asked.

Esteban and Tony exchanged a look of interest as they brought folding chairs over to the table for this impromptu pizza picnic. Kelly smirked. Grace studied the paper plates.

Ted remained standing. He told Jasper, "You and me. We're going to take a drive in the country." He quirked up half a smile.

Esteban said, "It's that artist guy. He's been to a couple auctions. He's got a studio east of town."

Jasper helped herself to a slice of pizza from the veggie side. She ate meat, just not on pizza. Maybe she was hungry after all. "Appraisal or look-at?" she called to Ted's back as he strode toward the front of the auction house.

"What's the difference?"

"So I know what to bring," Jasper called after him.

Ted shrugged and headed for the front. His truck started up and he roared out of the parking lot.

"Like father, like son," Esteban said. "Oh, sorry, Jasper."

Jasper plucked a piece of something resembling cabbage off her pizza and studied it. "You mean the 'Ready Teddy' bit?"

Kelly gagged on pizza.

Tony spurted Mountain Dew out his nose. "Man, that hurts!"

Kelly said something incoherent; only pepperoni emerged from her mouth. Esteban handed her a paper napkin.

He asked, "Where'd you hear that?"

"I met his ex," Jasper said.

"Is it true she's got a bun in the oven?" Kelly asked.

"That's not any of our business," Jasper said.

Grace patted her hand. "Everything is everybody's business around here. You might as well get used to it. And yes – "She addressed everyone at the table. "Molly's pregnant."

"When's she gonna pop?" Kelly asked.

Esteban shook his head at his red-headed wife.

"I don't know her that well," Jasper said, doing her best to emerge from the conversation with her fundamental niceness in place – without coming across in front of the roughhouse auction crew like a totally self-righteous prig.

"I heard it might not be Ted's."

"K-e-l-l-y," Grace murmured.

"Well, who is the father then?" Jasper asked.

"She sure was spending a lot of time here about seven, eight months ago," Kelly said.

"But you said – "Jasper stopped herself.

"Just like my dear, darling husband art-ick-u-la-ted, 'Like father, like son.'"

"Kelly! I have something I want to show you in the office," Grace said.

After she and Kelly had left the table, Jasper turned to Esteban. "Could it be true what she's implying?"

Esteban shrugged. "Who knows? No offense, but the old man liked the ladies. Whatever you do – don't say anything about this to Ted. He's got an ego 20 times larger than his dick. He wouldn't want to hear that somebody else knocked up his girlfriend."

"Molly's no longer his girlfriend. She told me so herself. Besides, Jimmy's not around anymore."

"Uh-huh." Estie pushed the pizza box toward her. "You want the rest of this?" he asked.

"Naw. I'm not so hungry anymore."

♦

An hour later, Jasper and Ted turned off the blacktopped country road. Jasper patted the hair around her face back into place. Although Ted didn't insist on driving with the radio blaring the way Jimmy had, he absolutely had to have the windows opened wide. At least the wind blasting through the pickup made conversation impossible. Jasper snuck a quick glance at the man behind the wheel. The set of his jaw didn't give anything away. Maybe Ted was as happy about the no-talking as she was.

There was no house visible. A long Tootsie Roll of land paralleled the road. Scruffy looking plants trying to decide whether to go out with the winter or join the new season of growth covered the berm. Attached to a rural mailbox was a large circle of wood painted black. No number or name announced the location.

"How do you know this place?" Jasper asked.

"He used to give big parties," Ted said.

"How come 'used to?'" she asked.

"There are a lot of stories."

"Hmm."

"People have their secrets. I don't pry and I don't lie. That's my policy."

"You don't say?" Jasper said.

A white stucco farmhouse appeared on their left. The glossy white pebbledash reminded Jasper of divinity candy at Christmas. Just past the house, the gravel expanded into a big parking area bordered on the west by a white barn. Like the house it looked old and young at the same time. Old-fashioned and cared for.

Ted parked right in the middle.

The artist sat outside at a metal table with a book in hand. He tucked a piece of paper in the book and got to his feet.

"Welcome to New Light Studios," he said.

"How are you, Solberg?" Ted stuck his hand out and slapped the artist's into a manly slapshake.

"Phillips."

Ted withdrew his hand. He winced.

"You can call me Sean." The artist extended his hand to Jasper.

"Nice to meet you, Sean. Studios plural?" She hesitated, then let him take her hand.

His large hand encased her much smaller one, and he gently raised and lowered it up and down one-two-three times. "Three times, then release," he said. "Like this."

Jasper giggled as he shook her hand again. "By Jove, I think I've got it," she said.

"And yes, it is studios with an "s." The friend who set up my website couldn't get the rights to 'studio.' I don't know. I don't get things like that. But he told me and I believed him."

Jasper smiled. This man was refreshingly off-beat. "I've seen you before. You were looking at pictures at the auction. And then, down at the Forester."

"That's my work. Hangs in New York and little old Forest Grove. Who says important art doesn't come out of the Midwest? "

"Grant Wood was from Iowa, wasn't he?" Jasper asked. She could easily see Wood's famous painting, "American Gothic," in her mind's eye. "That was really supposed to be a farmer and his daughter, not a husband and wife, I think."

"That's right, momma."

"We – we better look around now," Jasper said. She had pretty much used up her entire knowledge of 20th Century American art.

Sean Solberg was good for looking at. His gemstone eyes shone like moonstones. He was handsome to boot with his light brown hair, tousled by the wind, and his cleft chin. He wasn't as tall as Ted Phillips but six-feet-something was not an attractiveness requirement in a man, Jasper felt. Reverend Ted was tall and that had done nothing for his personality. Or his soul. Jasper liked Mr. Sean Solberg of New Light Studios plural.

And dammit, or rather darn it, the warm flame of lust had invaded her body again.

"What do you think of my art?" he asked.

Ted said, "I'm not an artiste like you. I wouldn't know a Picasso if it bit me in the ass."

"From what I've seen of it, it's pretty interesting," Jasper said.

"Interesting! What else?" Sean asked.

"Dynamic."

"OK. And?"

"Colorful? Inventive?" Jasper felt as if she was failing this test. At least his persnicketiness dampened her fire down below to a very low smolder.

Sean laughed. "It's all right. I have my artistic license. It lets me be a little pushy sometimes. Come on. I'll show you around."

He led the way across the graveled farmyard.

Ted picked up a homemade iron tool lying near a fire pit. "You make this too?" he asked.

"Creativity knows no bounds," Sean said. "I've got a collection of handmade tools made by me and other folks around this area. Want to take a look?"

"Oh, yes," Jasper said.

"Only if you want to sell them on auction," Ted said. "I don't want to be the bad guy here, Solberg, but we've got a couple other places to visit this afternoon."

"We do?" Jasper filled her lungs with the fresh country air. Okay, the ripe smell of early spring field fertilizing floated on the breeze, but anyway, it was outside and away from the tensions of the auction house – and the rest of her life. She was learning to grab her moments of relative freedom wherever she found them.

"Bet your bottom dollar," Ted said.

"Another time, I hope," Sean said to Jasper.

Jasper smiled and let her eyes linger on his for a moment.

"This way!" Sean led the way to the barn. "Painted it all myself," he said.

"Knew you were a painter, but I didn't know you specialized in barns," Ted said.

"I don't mind getting my hands dirty, Phillips." He turned to Jasper. "Here. Hold yours up next to mine."

Jasper glanced at Ted who seemed to be studying the sky for hidden rain clouds. She held her small hand next to Sean's paw. The contrast was mighty. "I bet you have a hard time doing embroidery," she said.

"I'm no good at typing either." Sean unhooked the white planked door and took them inside.

"I've never seen a barn like this." Under Jasper's feet stretched a polished wood floor, and on the north and south sides, rows of picture windows. Oak posts and beams added to the interior's golden glow. A basketball hoop hung high on the back wall. A big metal sign showed a woman in an up-do sipping a cocktail. Next to it hung an unplugged neon sign that said, "Dance!"

Jasper said, "This must be where you used to hold your parties."

"X marks the spot," Sean said. He drew a big X in the dust on a black tarp draped over a table with thick wooden legs.

"You don't like parties anymore?"

"It was a phase," Sean said.

He sounds sad. "I bet you got really busy with your art," Jasper said, trying to salvage the moment.

"Oh, yeah. Art is forever. M'lady. Sir. Come this way." Sean led Jasper and Ted across the floor, past a weight bench, and onto a graveled area where blue plastic topped a small mountain range of hidden objects.

Jasper followed the men. She had to admit that the view from the rear was not half bad. She liked one of their personalities more than the other but in the scenery department, they measured up nicely one against the other. *Oh, God, my stepfather's funeral is tomorrow and I'm thinking about men's tushes?* Jasper reddened with guilt. And with that emotion, came a wash of sadness. She wiped her eyes and joined the artist and the auctioneer.

They stood admiring a heap of assorted metal. Junk, Jasper thought at first glance. But the careful way Ted was picking through the pile told her there were auctionable items present. She let her eyes focus on individual items. She could make out a huge bell like the kind hung in a church belfry. She noticed an old Singer sewing machine, the kind with the foot treadle. And there were several old bicycles that looked like they had been ridden by boys and girls in flat caps and bloomers. Maybe they had been. "You guys need some help?" she asked.

"Thanks. We're okay," Sean said.

"Go out to the truck and grab a contract," Ted said.

"What do you think it's going to bring?" Sean was asking Ted.

Jasper slowed her steps to hear Ted's answer. "Not as much as you're hoping, but more than you'll get if you leave it where it is," he said.

"I guess I'm okay with that."

On the way back to the auction house, Jasper ventured a comment to Ted. She raised her voice to be heard over the rushing wind. "There's something profoundly sad about that man," she said.

Ted swerved the truck over to the gravel shoulder of the road.

Jasper braced herself against the dash and her door.

Ted said, "Hold on there, little lady."

"What do you think I'm doing? Jeesh! You didn't give me any choice."

Ted gave her a stern look. "Listen. I'll say this just once and you listen to me. Don't mess with our clients."

"*Our* clients, Ted? Do you mean *your* clients?" Jasper crossed her arms. "And I'm not messing with anybody, by the way. Unlike some people I know."

"What's that supposed to mean?"

Jasper glared out her window at another empty field.

Ted jerked her arm back toward him. "Listen. You're new in this business. You get involved with customers and clients, and things can get sticky before you know it."

An evil feeling passed over Jasper. "Sticky, Ted? How sticky can they get?" Jasper was trembling. Sarcasm did that to her. Even her own.

"If you know what's good for you, you'll stay away from that artiste and anybody else along the way."

"You're the boss," Jasper said.

"Watch your mouth." Ted pulled back onto the road and sent up a cloud of gravel dust that sent Jasper into a sneezing fit.

Chapter 17

"Why don't you girls just kick back in Jimmy's place, and I'll handle things up front." Ted Phillips spoke to Jasper and Cookie who were standing near the entryway to the auction house, receiving hugs and handshakes from the motley mourners arriving for Jimmy's memorial service. Although the funeral goers did not adhere to any unwritten dress code, some in overalls, others in their simple Sunday best of a variety of colors, they expressed sincere sympathy and exuded genuine grief over Jimmy's death. Mary Clippert and her father Ray came through the line. They wore matching daughter and father funeral outfits: black slacks and blazers. Mary had added a hat decorated with red plastic cherries. She kept a firm hand on the small of her father's back and nudged him along in line. She nodded at the twins, then said as if to Cookie alone, "Sorry for your loss."

"It's my sister's loss too," Cookie said loyally. She wore a deep purple caftan over a simple black dress. A bracelet of amethyst lilies fulfilled her daily ruffle requirement. Jasper swore she could see flames shooting out of Cookie's bracelet.

"Of course," Mary Clippert said with a nod toward Jasper. She moved off with her father shuffling along in front of her.

Cookie raised her eyebrows at Jasper who just shrugged.

Ted cut into line and said firmly, "Go on back. Let me handle things here." He put a hand on each of their arms and pushed. Just a little.

"Is he kidding?" Cookie said directly into Jasper's ear. "That sounded like an order."

"We're okay. But thank you very much." Jasper said. She could feel the strength in those hands. But today she didn't feel like taking orders. She stayed put, and after a moment, Ted walked away, slapping backs, shaking hands and greeting auction house customers as he went.

Jasper had chosen black everything: jewel-neck sweater, A-line skirt, and her best pumps with the practical heel height. Shopping in her semi-unpacked boxes for an outfit suitable for the memorial service proved easy since attending funerals had been a frequent duty throughout her time as a minister's wife. Cookie had offered to loan her a strand of amethyst beads said to help her tune in. She declined the necklace but agreed to wear the small purple earrings. Tuning in was Cookie's thing. Jasper would prefer to tune out.

"Oh, darling, what a tough time!" Edith and Ardith, the jewelry-buying sisters, surrounded Jasper with hugs. Even though they reeked of collectible My Sin perfume, they radiated real concern. "Your mother must have been a looker! You both look so nice." Ardith said.

"And so attuned," Edith added.

"We do what we can," Jasper said. "You know my sister Cookie."

"Indeed we do. The beautiful blonde fortune teller," Ardith said.

Jasper expected her sister to object, but Cookie said only, "You are really kind."

"We were just shocked to hear about J - your stepdad. And your sister here has been such a dear. She's getting to be our favorite auctioneer. And you will be our favorite...psychic person, is that right?" The older ladies held looks of genuine interest on their similar friendly faces. "What do you call yourself again? The work you do."

"Psychic medium," Cookie said. "And when I say you are kind, trust me, you are really kind."

'Tell us more."

Cookie reached into the pocket of her tunic and extracted a business card.

Jasper held onto her tense smile. "It's a funeral," she said.

Cookie hissed back, "This *is* an auction house."

The line of mourners progressed. Red-faced Mr. Parker arrived with his arm tucked through an older woman's. "I just loved the bovine salt shakers that Rodney brought home from last week's auction," she enthused. "It's too bad such a nice auction had to be ruined the way it was."

"Sorry for your loss," Rodney Parker said hurriedly. "Come on, Mother. Let's find a good seat."

"Near the lasagna."

"Yes, Mother."

Then came Glenn Relerford, dressed in a gray dress shirt and black slacks. He took her hand and, to her surprise, Jasper found that she was trembling. "You'll be all right," he said then turned to her sister. "Miss Cookie. My condolences."

And more mourners. And more. They were mostly auction-goers since Jasper and Cookie had no other relatives, and Jimmy's closest kin was some distant cousin out in North Platte. The Austrings were there, looking nervous and strained. Probably wondering whether they would still be able to get the Clippert house for their own, Jasper thought cynically. But they shook hands politely with the sisters and expressed their condolences, then moved on toward the back of the auction house. Cookie's compatriots in the professional psychic world also came to show their support. They looked like everyday people and Jasper wouldn't have realized who they were if

Cookie hadn't introduced them as members of her paranormal group.

When there was a lull, Jasper asked. "Aren't Will and the kids coming?"

"Will's away on business – Ohio again. Cody's still in Mexico, and Kayla's down in St. Louis with her boyfriend. I told them all they didn't have to come."

"Oh." Jasper felt gloom descend upon her. She had been looking forward to being surrounded today by family, and right now Cookie's was all she had.

"They send their love. You'll see them all at Easter.

"That's nice," Jasper said. Cookie squeezed her into a cozy side hug, and Jasper snuffled up her suddenly runny nose.

A short while later, the twins made their way with arms around each other's waists toward the main auction room where the service would be held.

"Ghost busters and auction types – such a combo," Jasper said to Cookie.

"Not to mention some interested parties from the other side," Cookie said.

"No more ghost talk, please."

"If you can't talk ghosts at a funeral, where can you then?" Country western music blared from the speakers. "Whose idea was this?" Cookie asked.

"Grace, I guess." Jasper recognized "Your Cheatin' Heart." The girls paused to listen. A more traditional song of mourning, "Amazing Grace" followed. Maybe Grace had let out all her steam with just the one mocking melody.

People reached out to pat them as they strolled by. Jasper shivered. "Is it all this touching? I'm all goose bumpy."

"*They* are touching us, too," Cookie said.

"They?"

"You know – other-siders."

"Cut out the psychic-ier than thou stuff," Jasper said.

"You're as psychic as I am. You just don't want to admit it. You know we have the same horoscope."

"Horrorscope," Jasper whispered back. The sisters giggled duplicate giggles then helped calm each other down.

They reached the front row of seats and took the places there that had been reserved for them by bidder numbers taped to the backs of the chairs, as was the custom of the auction house. Kelly and Grace sat on either side. Jasper looked around and waved. Cookie followed her example. "They're bidding to *us*!" one man joked. A few people tittered nervously. Then the crowd quieted down.

Ted Phillips, up on the auction block, turned on the microphone. "Folks, I want to welcome you all here today," he began. "Usually when I'm up here and you're down there, we've got a sale going on. So I hope you'll kind of excuse me if I get a little tongue tied." He cleared his throat and mopped his forehead with a tissue they always kept stocked next to the clerk's station.

Down front, Cookie gripped Jasper's hand. "He's here."

"He who? "

"Jimmy."

"Cookie, honey, you know we didn't bring him here. He wouldn't want to be seen helpless in a casket. I think he sold one once." Jasper's thoughts trailed off.

Ted droned on in the background while Cookie whispered urgently in Jasper's ear. "I'm talking about his spirit, of course. Try closing your eyes. You might be able to tune in better."

When Jasper blinked shut, all she got was a fuzzy screen like a TV when cable service gets interrupted. Maybe she had forgotten to pay her paranormal bill.

"You see him?" Cookie hissed.

"I got nothin.'"

Cookie stifled a laugh.

A woman sitting nearby said, "What's the joke? I could use a good one. Ted's a better auctioneer than he is a preacher."

A man joined in, "And he's not very good at auctioneering!" Random nervous laughter broke out.

Ted said from up on the auction block, "You just wait until next Wednesday, Carl. I'll show you how this works."

"What? You gonna kill me too?"

The laughter changed to gasps and shushes.

"Not funny, Carl," Ted said. "Now getting back to the VIP of the day, Jimmy Biggs." The crowd settled back into respectful languor.

Jasper whispered to Cookie, "So what *is* so funny?"

"You don't want to know."

"I do want to know, Cookie. What? Is Jimmy talking about me?"

"It's not always about you."

"I never think it's about me. You're not saying *what*, so I bet it *is* about me."

"Later, Sis! You're the one who didn't want any ghost talk."

"Now!"

"Later!"

Jasper slid her hand under Cookie's thigh and pinched her.

"That hurt! Now you're never going to find out."

Jasper rested her head lightly against her sister's shoulder. She knew how to beg like a soulful Labrador, a breed of which Cookie had always been fond. Cookie was smiling again. "All right, already. Jimmy said we ought to go up there behind Ted and goose him! Jimmy said it would liven up this party."

"I goosed you sort of. And you sort of got mad at me."

"That's different. I'm your sister and you love me. What do you think?"

"What do I think? I work for the man. Well, okay, *with* the man. But it's a lot like working for the man, and I think…" Jasper suddenly felt like throwing off the week's trauma and tension. She clapped her hand over her mouth like a cork in a bottle of shaken champagne. She took Cookie's hand and led her on a fast trot across the auction floor and out the swinging doors as if they were making a mad dash for the ladies' room.

Ted broke off in mid-drone. "Folks, should I wait for the girls?"

Assorted voices in the crowd shouted out "No!" And, "Get on with it! You're gonna be at this all day!"

"Amen!" a man said.

Ted resumed his monotone about Jimmy's long but not long enough life as an auctioneer.

Jasper and Cookie hurried through the back storage room and eased open the door behind the auction block. With Jasper crouched in the lead and Cookie following close behind, they crept silently up the carpeted steps like two cops moving up on a suspect. They reached Ted's khakis. Each one grabbed a pinchful of ass. "Goddammit!" Ted roared on mike. He whirled around. His face was scarlet. "You little devils! Like father, like daughters! Jesus H. Christ!" He tore off his headset and tripped down the steps. "Oh, man."

The auction-memorial crowd broke into applause.

Jasper grabbed Cookie's hand and they pushed themselves back out of Ted's hurtling way. "You okay?" Jasper asked him.

"Hrrrmm," he growled. "You're in charge now, brat. Gonna get some ice." He hobbled away.

Up on the auction block, Cookie whispered, "Speaking of Jesus Christ, here comes his worst disciple."

A familiar man hurried toward the front. The Rev. Tim Rowe, dressed in a blue blazer, a black knit shirt, and his usual bulge-emphasizing jeans, strode toward the front. A small contingent of familiar-looking parishioners followed on his heels.

Jasper spoke quickly into the microphone. "We're here today to say good-bye to our step-dad Jimmy Biggs. He was bigger than life." She held the business end of the headset to Cookie's mouth.

"Absolutely," Cookie said.

"We all have a lot of memories about him – both good and not so good," Jasper said.

Cookie snatched the microphone back. "We're not here to judge. It's all relative, isn't it?"

"Amen, Sister!" shouted someone in the crowd.

"So, uh," Jasper said, "let's all remember the good things about Jimmy. His – help me here."

Cookie said, "His bid-calling, his business acumen…"

"He had acumen up the wazoo," said old Mrs. Parker. "When do we eat, kids?"

"So in conclusion," Jasper said. "Let's bid a fond farewell to Jimmy Biggs – "

"Who is here anyway," Cookie said.

"We'll never get rid of him," Mrs. Parker said.

Jasper announced a few moments of silence. She hurried down to confront Rev. Tim.

"What the hell do you think you're doing?" she asked him.

"This is a religious event so I came to offer you religious support," Tim said.

"This is more like an auction event, and I don't need your support."

"Keep your voice down, Candy."

"Don't call me Candy. My name's Jasper."

"Be that as it may, I'm still married to Candace Jasper Biggs Rowe. How would it look if I didn't attend my own father-in-law's memorial?"

"Ah ha! I knew you would be worrying about appearances at a time like this."

"Somebody's gotta think about the look of things at a formal affair."

"Affair, Tim? *Affair?*"

The parishioners crowded in close. This was a field trip for them.

"Down front!" yelled Mr. Peters from the auction gallery. "We can't see what's going on!"

"Settle down, folks," Ted said back on mike. "I don't think they're going to come to blows. You're not going to hit him, are you, Jasper?"

"Don't let them anywhere near that lasagna!" old Mrs. Peters yelled.

"Get him good, Jasper!" another of the regular auction-goers shouted.

Tim bent in close. "Can I talk to you alone for a second?"

His eyebrows were doing that caterpillars-traveling-uphill-thing against all odds. Jasper relented. She drew him back behind the auction block.

"Look," Tim said. "You don't really owe me anything even though it's taken all I have to hold my head high in front of my congregation."

"If this is what you wanted to say, you can leave now."

"No, no look. Wrong approach. I just want to be able to take a moment to speak about Jimmy, to say something, you know, religious."

"Why should I? Jimmy wasn't exactly religious. And I'm not sure you're the best spokesman for the benevolent universe."

"I can't stand any more public humiliation."

"Why did you bring that mob along with you then?"

"They followed me."

"Huh."

Tim dropped to his knees. "Please."

"Get up, get up. Jeepers." Jasper felt that old familiar tug of wanting to save this pitiful man from himself. "All right already."

He got to his feet.

"One prayer. One quick prayer. And not too much Jesus. Got it?"

"Thank you, thank you. I owe you."

"You ain't kiddin.'"

From up on the auction block, Rev. Tim intoned, "Oh, Lord, cast your gaze down upon those gathered today as we commemorate the life of your son, James Biggs…" It was actually respectful, Jasper thought, appreciating Tim's decorum. Maybe Jimmy deserved something closer to a traditional memorial service after all. Many people in the audience bowed their heads in prayer.

As Tim continued, another figure entered the back of the auction house. Sean Solberg the artist made his way toward Jasper and Cookie. Handsome as ever, he looked casual but respectful in dark gray slacks and a navy blue shirt. With an irreverent twinkle in his eye, he whispered, "So when do we eat?"

Jasper shushed him with a smile, but her stomach gave a loud gurgle of anticipation.

"Amen," Tim intoned.

The relieved crowd rushed the buffet. Old Mrs. Parker brandished her cane to keep the rival eaters at bay.

Chapter 18

Standing behind the food table at the back, Jasper felt somewhat buffered from the attentions of Pastor Tim who helped himself liberally to the lasagna and garlic bread. "What I don't get," he mumbled through a mouth full of food. Jasper had often found that one of his less than endearing traits. "What I don't get is how you can let yourself come down in the world like this."

Jasper decided to take the high road. "Thank you for the prayer," she said.

Tim wiped his mouth on his sleeve and belched.

Jasper winced. So much for good intentions. "You missed a spot, Mr. High and Mighty," she said. "And your breath stinks."

"Excuse me, father," Jerry Murphy, one of the auction house regulars said. He focused his attentions on the salad. "Got to lose a few pounds. Good a time as any to start. Afternoon, Jasper. Holding up okay? Good, good." He shuffled down the line.

"It's Reverend, just plain Reverend," Pastor Tim shouted toward Jerry Murphy.

"Let it go!" Jasper said.

Tim opened his mouth in surprise and treated Jasper to a look into a gooey white and pink cavern.

Cookie left the conversation she was having with a group of ladies near the auction block. She joined Jasper. "Ted," she said solemnly.

"Courtney."

"Cookie," she automatically corrected him.

"I was just telling Candy here," Ted went on, oblivious.

Cookie elbowed Jasper lightly. Jasper said, "Jasper."

Tim shoveled more food into his already full mouth. "Any rate, what I wonder is if Jimmy didn't just bring this upon himself."

Cookie grimaced. "I'm afraid to ask but – "

"Yes, what's your point, Tim?" Jasper asked.

"And it had better be a good one," Cookie added.

Pastor Tim retreated half a step. He gestured at the sisters with his fork. "Any rate, he was not exactly the most Christian man I've ever known.""

"God bless the twits of the world." Cookie turned to her sister. "Can you handle this okay? I feel a trip to the lady's room coming on."

"No problem." She folded her arms and faced her soon-to-be ex-husband. "If you're trying to say that your wrathful God conked Jimmy on the head and shoved him down the stairs because maybe he wasn't such a good person, not as great a person as someone like you for instance, then you can just pack up some spare meatballs – and maybe some of those cookies down there if you want – and, and –"

A small group of auction goers had gathered behind Pastor Tim and were standing at the ready. "Everything all right here, Jasper?" Jerry Murphy asked.

"I'm fine," Jasper said.

From the desk area came a familiar voice. "I know he's here somewhere! What do you mean you don't know where he is? Pastor Tim, oh Pastor Tim!" the man's voice called.

Pastor Tim whirled around. Some of the salad spilled off his plate. Tim took a step and slid on the Italian dressing slick. He landed on his knees. People rushed to help. Jerry Murphy tugged him to his feet.

"Can you hand me over some napkins, Ardith?"

"Here you go, honey," a man in a Green Bay Packers t-shirt said.

Jerry Murphy said, "There you go, father. Good as new."

"I tell you –" Pastor Tim started to say.

The choir director from Truman Free Church hurried into the scene.

"Better go before it gets really messy," Jasper said.

"It's okay, Ryan, it's okay," Pastor Tim said. "Let's go. My work here is done." He turned to Jasper. "Back door?"

She nodded to the corridor.

Pastor Tim put his hand on Ryan's shoulder and the two walked away. Ryan looked back over his shoulder and shot Jasper a baleful look. "You're so hard on him," he yelled back at her.

"Hard is as hard does," Jasper said.

Tim and Ryan pushed their way out through the swinging door. The church folks trailed after, some of them waving backwards at Jasper. Their heads were down. They not only missed Jasper, they were now missing a nice funeral buffet, she had to think.

"Who are those characters?" asked a familiar voice. Sean the artist stood at the buffet table just out of arms' reach from Jasper. His plain blue shirt fit him well across his wide-enough shoulders and want-to-stroke chest. Jasper admired his strong forearms, revealed below his rolled up sleeves and his large hands, not manicured and sort of grungy looking with hard-work dirt making them look like works of art in progress. One of them waved in front of Jasper's face. "Did I say something?" Sean asked.

Jasper came back, well halfway back, to reality. "Did you say something?" My, his eyes were the color of Lake Superior even under the unflattering fluorescent lighting. Maybe it was the shirt. Had she always been a sucker for blue eyes? Was it Sean or the fluorescents giving off all that heat? Jasper patted her forehead. Sean daubed it with a napkin. Jasper swayed.

"You need to sit down," he said. He led her to the back of the auction block and eased her down beside him on the carpeted stairs that led up to the auctioneer-clerking platform. He extracted a silver flask from his side pocket. "Here. My own special blend."

Jasper discovered that her hands were shaking. Sean placed one of his own over hers and helped her tip the flask up. She swallowed down the bittersweet liquid. She smiled weakly at Sean and handed back the flask.

"More?"

"This is my breakfast. I better not."

Sean pocketed the flask. "Nothing like beer and lemonade, I always say."

Oh, jeez, not another addict. Alcohol this time instead of sex. "Well, that's that," she said.

"I didn't mean always *always*. I don't like words that claim to know it all," he said. His wide grin crooked up on one side.

"Best? Worst? Saddest?"

"You got it. I'm not crazy about funerals. I thought maybe I should bring something along in case anybody needed it," Sean said.

"I don't need alcohol," Jasper said. Jimmy used to drink and the memories were bad ones. She scooted away the four inches that the step would allow.

"Of course not," Sean said.

The noise of the milling crowd grew louder in Jasper's ears. "I just meant - "

"Whoa."

Jasper felt Sean's gentle hand on the back of her neck, guiding her head downward to rest on her arms crossed over her lap. "Thank you," she mumbled into her knees.

"What's going on back here?"

The warm hand deserted her neck.

Jasper sat up too fast. "Aw, Ted." Her stomach lurched. She had to get to the ladies' room. Fast.

Ted and Sean stood facing each other. "You need help, Jazz?" Ted asked. He took one of her elbows.

"I'm helping her," Sean said. He reached for her.

Jasper sidestepped both of them. "Nobody has to help me," she said. She exited the room through the swinging doors and nearly took down Cookie in the process. Her twin took one look at her, then grabbed her hand and hurried her out of the storage room toward the restroom at the back of the auction house. She tried to say thanks but Cookie shushed her.

In the hall Ted hurried up alongside the women. "Can I do anything for you girls?"

Jasper's stomach heaved and she threw up right next to Ted's cowboy boots.

"Nice of you to offer," Cookie said.

"Yeah, thanks Ted." Jasper with Cookie alongside disappeared into the ladies' room, leaving behind the mighty Ted to deal with the mess on the floor.

"Estie, get back here!" they heard him roar.

By the time Jasper had rinsed out her mouth with soapy water and Cookie had helped her comb her hair and apply some lipstick to her mouth and cheeks, the twins found that most of the memorial service guests had left. A few strays hung around the nearly empty buffet dishes, but Grace and Ted were strongly encouraging them to leave. The other auction workers had already gone home. Sean Solberg was still there talking in a desultory way with Glenn Relerford. Neither one looked like he was enjoying the other's company.

"We'll be right back," Ted said over his shoulder as he and Grace herded the last of the stragglers toward the front door of the auction.

"I won't. G'night, all," Grace said.

Jasper and Cookie stood with Glenn and Sean, watching the crew from the Forester break down the buffet. Molly wasn't with them. "That's it then," the supervisor said.

"What're those?" Jasper asked. She pointed at five aluminum containers, covered and stacked.

"Food. It's yours. You paid for it." The man shifted from one foot to another. "Or I guess you will be paying for it. Boss said he's sending you the bill."

"That's right," Cookie said.

"Uh – "

"Oh, right. The tip," Jasper said.

Cookie whispered in her ear, "Sorry, Sis. Didn't bring any cash."

Glenn fished out his wallet. "Can you take a credit card?"

Sean dug into his pocket. "I've got a five."

"Never mind. There's money back in my purse. Now where did I put my bag?" Jasper gave the auction house a dizzy full circle.

Cookie reminded her that she had left it in Jimmy's apartment at the back of the auction house. "That's right. I'll go get it," Jasper said.

Cookie said, "I'll go with you."

"Me too," Glenn and Sean said at the same time.

Everyone including the Forester man picked up a container and followed Jasper out the back door and through the parking lot to Jimmy's door. Jasper wiggled the key into the lock, turned it, and then discovered that the turn of the key had locked the door. "It must've been opened," she said. "I guess I forgot to lock it before the service."

"I'll go first," Glenn said. He told everyone to wait while he stepped into the dark apartment, switching on the overhead light.

Sean stepped forward to follow Glenn but the detective ordered him to wait with the women. "Mr. Authority," Sean mumbled.

Cookie elbowed Jasper lightly in the side.

The rustling of paper from the dumpster a few yards away caught her attention. "Did you hear that?" Jasper asked.

"Rat?" Cookie wrapped her shawl tightly around her shoulders.

"I think I'll get going. You can add the gratuity to the bill," the restaurant man said. He handed off his aluminum container to Sean and left.

The sound of paper and cardboard being walked on, crushed, came louder along with a single low note.

"Maybe a raccoon," Sean said. He and Jasper slippered over to the dumpster. "If it's a raccoon, you don't want to corner it."

"Shhh," Jasper said. "Let's listen."

The low note sounded again but with more articulation.

"Kitty!" Jasper said. "Please take this." She added her aluminum container to Sean's armful. He set them on the ground near Cookie and helped Jasper lift the dumpster lid. Two round eyes blinked at them from the furthest corner. "How'd you get in there, sweetie?" Jasper asked.

"Good question. There's no food in there."

Cookie joined them, setting her leftovers container on the ground. "You think someone put her in there? Or him?"

"Could be. Let's find out what we have here. I'm going in," Sean said. He clambered over the side of the dumpster. His work boots scrunched the paper beneath them. The little cat let out a loud "Mow" and leapt onto a cardboard box, then up toward the edge of its temporary prison.

Without stopping to think, Jasper grabbed the cat in mid-air. She clutched it to her chest and its tiny but keen claws dug into her skin through her sweater. "Ouch," she whispered so as not to scare the cat. The cat purred loudly and nuzzled its head under her chin. It climbed onto Jasper's shoulder looking backwards so its tail end faced front. Its front legs and paws draped over her shoulder. The cat was small-boned, sleek and the color of dark chocolate. "It's heavier than it looks," Jasper said. "You're a heavy little baby, aren't you?"

"More like a motor boat," Sean said, climbing out of the dumpster. He scratched the cat between its ears. The purr was never-ending.

"Good kitty," Cookie said, joining in with some petting of her own.

"Is it a girl?" Jasper asked.

Sean lifted its tail to check. "Nope, a boy.

"How can you be sure - ?" Jasper asked.

"Full package. He's fully equipped," Sean said.

"Balls," Cookie whispered in Jasper's ear.

"Oh-h-h," Jasper said.

"Everything's safe inside. Just make sure you lock up next time," Glenn said, rejoining the group.

"I'm certain I locked the door," Jasper whispered.

"Looks like you cooked up a little trouble out here. What's this?" Glenn asked.

"It's a cat," Sean said.

"I can see it's a cat, Solberg."

"Want to pet him?" Jasper asked. The cat's warmth and its continual hum of contentment made Jasper feel like a little girl, and that was a happy feeling she had not enjoyed for quite some time.

"I'm more of a dog man," Glenn said.

"You are a dawg, man, but you're not my dawg," Sean mumbled.

"Cats carry disease. Kitty-mouth is a real hazard," Glenn said.

"Kitty-mouth!" Sean snickered.

Cookie shot him a look. "It's okay. This cat's okay."

"Maybe it was chipped. I'll take it to Animal Control and see if they can find the owner." Glenn reached for the cat and it dug its claws deeper into Jasper's back and chest.

"Big ouch," she murmured. She turned away from Glenn. "Somebody put the kitty in the dumpster," she said. "I don't think his owner was taking very good care of him."

"He looks healthy enough," Glenn said.

"Then you don't think kitty-mouth is a real hazard here, is that right, officer?" Sean asked.

"Detective." Glenn glowered.

Cookie linked her arm through Sean's and led him away.

"Look, I know you think you're doing the animal a favor, but what if its owner is searching for it? And if it has been on its own for a while, it may have picked up something that doesn't show," Glenn said.

"Fleas?"

"Ticks. Worms. Distemper. Look, Jasper. Miss Biggs."

"Jasper's fine. I don't know what to call this little guy though. Not yet."

"If you're not gonna let me take it to Animal Control, then promise me you'll get it to a vet first thing tomorrow," Glenn said.

"Tomorrow's Sunday."

"First thing Monday."

Jasper stroked the cat's sleek fur. "Mama's gotta work to earn some cat food. Very soon, okay?"

"Mama's gotta take care of herself first," Glenn said.

Jasper looked at him wonderingly. Was this some kind of flirting? She was way out of practice.

Glenn cleared his throat. "Just keep safe is what I'm saying. I've gotta go. Call me if you need anything."

"At the police station?" Jasper pried the cat's nails out one by one and cradled it like a baby. This was one flexible little animal. It stared wide-eyed up into Jasper's face. Without thinking, she kissed it on the forehead and it snuggled in closer.

"Wherever and whenever you need me," Glenn said. He hesitated as if about to say something else. Then he turned and walked away. He passed Sean without a word. "Miss Cookie," he said.

Jasper led the way to the apartment. Sean and Cookie carried all the aluminum food containers inside to Jimmy's kitchen. Jasper hadn't eaten much at the buffet after the memorial service but she wasn't feeling at all hungry. The little cat had all her attention. Sean and Cookie busied themselves in the kitchen while Jasper played with the cat on the sofa. It seemed to like hand under blanket, hand behind pillow and pouncing hand. Jasper didn't mind the minor scratches she was accumulating.

Soon Cookie announced she was leaving. She gave Jasper a questioning look which Jasper understood to mean, *Are you okay alone with Sean?* Jasper said aloud, "It's okay, Sis, the cat is here too."

"Okay then," Cookie said. She gave Jasper a hug and a kiss and said she would call her later. Jasper told her to take home a couple cartons of food.

Sean settled himself on the opposite end of the sofa. He was adept at cat games and showed Jasper how to play shoestring-pretending-to-be-a-small-snake and how much felines enjoyed a rough and tumble wrestling match with a human hand. Jasper had a sudden small sense of what it might be like to have a baby with a man she loved. They would sit like this in the evenings and play with their child. She settled in with Sean and the cat, and encouraged Sean to tell her all about his art work. She had to admit, even at a time like this, the man had definite appeal. She loved the way he looked, and his velvet voice soothed her soul.

A sudden shrill sound interrupted them. The cat mrowed loudly and leapt off the sofa. It raced for the bedroom. Jasper and Sean got to their feet. "Is that a fire alarm?" Jasper asked.

"I don't know. Alarm for sure. Coming from the front of the building," Sean said. "Come on."

Jasper shook him off and hurried to the bedroom. "Kitty, kitty," she called frantically.

With a loud mrow, the cat jumped down from the top of the chest of drawers onto Jasper's shoulder. Jasper put one hand behind its neck and the other around its tail. Then she and Sean exited the apartment.

They found the parking lot a busy place with two police cars parked just outside the auction house's front door. Their red lights were whirling around on top. Glenn popped up from where he was crouching beside one of the cars. He and a uniformed officer had their guns drawn. "Get over here," Glenn ordered.

Jasper and Sean hurried over and ducked down behind the police car.

The other policeman spoke into a microphone and his voice bellowed out from the top of the squad car. "Come out now with your hands up," he ordered.

Ted Phillips walked out the front door of the auction house, his hands on top of his head.

Jasper eased to her feet. "Ted, what do you think you're doing?"

"Stand down," Glenn said. He sounded disgusted. "Phillips, what the hell are you doing?"

"I started driving away and remembered something I'd forgotten."

"Yeah, that's usually what I remember," Sean said.

"Shut up, Solberg," Glenn said.

Jasper focused on the cat which seemed content to be part of the excitement. Its purring vibrated reassuringly against her.

"So?" Glenn asked Ted.

"So I got to the door and found out it was unlocked."

"You left it unlocked?" Glenn asked.

"I always lock it," Ted said. "I don't know how it got that way. So I went inside to look around – "

"And get whatever it was you forgot," Sean said.

Jasper giggled into the cat's fur. It purred all the louder.

Ted said that he stepped inside and was switching on lights when the alarm went off.

"How'd the alarm get on?" Glenn asked.

"I armed it before I left the first time like I always do," Ted said.

"What the hell is going on around here?" Glenn signaled to the other cop and they went into the auction house. They emerged a few minutes later. "All clear," Glenn said. "Why don't you turn on the alarm, lock up and we'll all get out of here." He turned to Jasper. "You and I are going to get whatever you need from the apartment. Then we are going to lock that door and I am going to watch you get in your car and drive away."

"But Sean's here," Jasper started to say.

"Come on," Glenn ordered.

Sean said to Jasper, "I can follow you home if you want."

"She lives down the street from me, Solberg. I'll follow her home," Glenn said.

"What about me?" Ted asked.

The day was catching up with Jasper. She started walking toward the back of the auction. She turned back and unpeeled the cat from her shoulder. She handed it over to Sean.

"What am I supposed to do with it?" he asked.

Cookie spoke. "Just take it home for the weekend and we'll figure something out on Monday."

Sean agreed. Jasper was tired of talk. Of conversation and argument. Glenn followed her to her car. She didn't say good-bye. She pulled out of the parking lot and headed home to Hickory Lane. She ached for a hot bath and bed. The only thing she would miss would be the little cat

Chapter 19

"Hand me that whatchamacallit, will you," Cookie asked.

It was Monday morning, and she and Jasper were going through things in Jimmy's apartment at the back of the auction house. It smelled of oil, dust and those flowery dryer sheets Jimmy had been so fond of.

"Hear you go." Jasper handed over the old weight scale that sat on top of Jimmy's bookshelf.

The living room looked taken apart, as if the occupant was just moving in or just moving out. The twins had been working for two hours now and the mess seemed to be getting worse instead of better.

Something might have gone missing, she supposed. Someone could have snuck in Saturday night while Sean and Jasper were out in the parking lot with the police since they had left the door unlocked, but why would someone want to steal something from the apartment of the dead auctioneer? And why did the stray kitty turn up that night in the dumpster? Could the same unknown person be responsible for both?

Cookie took the scale and examined it like a blind person - eyes closed, sensitive hands. "He hadn't had this very long had he?" Jasper started to speak but Cookie hushed her.

"Somebody focused a lot of attention on this. That's funny. I'm seeing a young woman in some kind of red smock holding this."

Jasper smiled. "I got that for him at a flea market last Christmas. It took me awhile to make up my mind."

"Okay." Cookie opened her eyes and put down the scales. She dusted her palms off and shook them in the air. She frowned. But she instantly brightened. "So I was right about the red smock!"

Jasper smiled over at her. "Yes, Sis. You're pretty much always right."

"Pretty much!" Cookie put on a pretend pout. The cell phone she wore at her side sounded three bell tones – bum, bum, bum. "Psychic Medium Rare, Courtney speaking," Cookie answered automatically. "Oh, it's you. Well, I don't know, honey. Have you tried looking under the bed? Uh-huh. Okay. So maybe it was in the refrigerator last time. That was an honest mistake. You'd left it in the laundry basket. Huh? Well, never mind. Okay. Me too. Bye, honey." Cookie replaced the phone in her pocket.

Jasper looked at her sister with wonder. "I don't get it."

"Easy to explain," Cookie said. "Will left his favorite household hammer in the laundry room. I was doing laundry and then I remembered I'd left the groceries in the car. So I grabbed the hammer and – "

Jasper held her elbows and rocked her body back and forth in laughter. "That's not what I didn't get!"

"But – "

"Explaining how your husband's hammer – his household hammer?"

"Yes. One of his household hammers. Never to be confused with those for professional use. Those are locked up safe from my reach."

"Right. So that's the easy part of it all," Jasper continued. "What I don't understand is how you managed to find the right man when you were only 17." She flopped down on the leather sofa, and Cookie settled in next to her. The sisters kicked off their shoes, Jasper flinging her stinky sneakers over to one corner, Cookie tidily arranging her blue ballet flats side by side. They sat cross-legged.

Cookie pushed a strand of stray blonde hair off her face. Although she had started out a medium brunette, and her sister a dark, almost black brunette, Cookie's hair color changed season to season. "Actually, Sis, I was only 16 when I met Will."

"See – my point is just that! You were so young. And you met and fell in love, and now it's two great kids and lots of years later, and you guys are still going strong."

Cookie examined her manicure. "Now don't you go kicking yourself." Neither of the twins relished the other one feeling badly especially by way of comparison to each other. They'd put up with enough of that when they were back in high school. When Jasper went off to college and Cookie got married and had kids, they were both relieved at first to have people stop comparing them. Their names and appearances had gone through so much change since then that people didn't believe them when they said they were twins.

Jasper touched her sister's arm. "You're not making me feel bad, Cookie. It's just that I wonder, I really do, how you managed. Maybe I can learn something from you."

"Whatever could I teach you? I've always wanted to go to college."

"You could still do that. You think I could still have kids?" Jasper asked.

"Everything gets harder when you get older."

"We're not old ladies yet. Maybe you could start with community college."

"Maybe you could start with a pet," Cookie said.

The door buzzer sounded.

"Will you drink more coffee if I make another pot?" Cookie, asked, heading out to the kitchenette.

"Sure," Jasper called back. She peeped through the spyhole on the otherwise solid door. As usual, she saw only a blur. How did other people use these things? she wondered. She opened the door and there stood Sean Solberg holding the dark cat from the dumpster.

"Somebody misses you," Sean said. His wide blue eyes looked into her own. She was such a sucker for blue eyes in a guy. But come to think of it, Glenn Relerford's dark eyes held their own kind of fascination. "I'm standing here holding a cat," Sean said. And that voice…

"So you are." Jasper forced her gaze down to the cat. In the morning sunlight, its fur appeared more brown than black. More like dark chocolate than licorice. Its little dark face was shaped like a wedge, wide at the forehead and narrow at the chin. Jasper found it quite beautiful and exotic looking. She leaned in and kissed its dark brown nose. She had never tasted cat before. Sort of like freshly ironed scarves.

Its purr motor went into high gear. It gazed on Jasper with huge eyes. It blinked at her. Instinctively, Jasper blinked back. The cat opened its little mouth and bellowed forth a huge "Mrow." Sean eased his hold and the cat leaped over to Jasper's shoulder. It felt surprisingly heavy for such a small animal. It purred in close against her chest, with its front paws resting on her shoulder. "Well, hello yourself," Jasper whispered. "Come on in, both of you."

Cookie appeared with a tray holding three coffee mugs, a bowl, and a carton of half and half. "Looks like you're in love," she said. "Ask and you shall receive."

"W-h-a-t?" Jasper and Sean asked in unison.

Cookie laughed. Sean took the tray from her and set it on the coffee table. Cookie stroked the little cat's head between its large, translucent ears. "She – whoop's, he - is a little beauty. Wasn't I just saying you needed a pet?"

Jasper sighed. She leaned her cheek gently against the cat's face. How could one little animal emit such a soothing deep noise? Jasper thought she felt her heart slow in response to the loud, rhythmic purr. She cuddled the cat in closer. She gave him a hug, then pried his claws free and handed him over to Sean. The cat opened its mouth wide and yowled. Sean pushed him gently back into Jasper's arms.

"I tell you – he's been asking for you. I've hardly gotten any sleep since I took him home Saturday," Sean said.

"But – "

"He looks good on you," Cookie said. "Anyway, treats for everyone."

Everyone - twins, artist, cat – settled in for coffee and cream. Although the cat made its rounds from person to person after lapping up its treat, it took only a few minutes before settling in next to Jasper with a satisfied sigh.

"But I tell you, I can't keep it," Jasper said. "I don't know how to take care of a cat. What if I'm not a good cat mother?"

Sean and Cookie laughed. "You'll be fine," Cookie said.

"Cats take care of themselves," Sean said.

"And you don't want him *why*?" Jasper asked.

"He's like a huge operatic bass in the body of a tenor," Sean said.

The little cat let out another major meow as if he were joining in the conversation. Jasper stroked the glossy fur.

Sean covered his ears. "I love cats. I love their independence. This one is more like a dog. A noisy dog. Not only does it show up wherever I am, it has to comment on its life all day long. 'I got up. I laid down. I fell in the toilet. Again.' It's been trying to tell me how to run my life."

"You fell in the toilet? It fell in the toilet?" Jasper asked.

"More than once? Why didn't you just close the lid?" Cookie asked.

The cat looked up, yawned, and let out another loud meow.

Two of the three people present laughed. Sean groaned. "You think it's funny now. Try living with this little loud mouth following you around. Look, you women can understand. I live alone. I make art. I love my privacy."

"Oh-h-h," Cookie said. "You're playing the privacy card."

"Oh." Jasper felt rather sad all of a sudden.

"I'm not playing," Sean said miserably. "I can't work. I can't sleep. I have a headache."

"That's too bad," Jasper said although she didn't really mean it. What she felt mainly was disappointment. Strong handsome artist man too selfish to share his life even with one small cat. He probably would not be good father material. She blushed. With an effort, she brought herself back to the conversation at hand. "So you thought you would just bring the poor orphan over here and dump him off on me?"

"Atta girl," Cookie whispered.

"Guilty," Sean said. "But I've also begun to wonder if Little Bugle Breath here might belong to someone."

Jasper smiled at the affectionate nickname. Maybe Sean Solberg was not so bad after all

"Just look at him. He's more than an average alley cat. He might be some sort of purebred that wandered away from home."

"He's certainly beautiful," Jasper agreed. The cat stretched out in a full-length arch as if inviting further admiration. "But how did he get into the dumpster?"

"This cat leaps before he looks. He's like a ballet dancer in shoes that are too big for him."

The kitty purred alongside Jasper. It didn't seem to disagree.

"You could ask people at the next auction."

"Wait." Cookie closed her eyes and held her hands above the cat. "He's right, Sis. This kitty has a chip."

"Poor kitty," Jasper said.

"No. To ID it in case it gets lost," Cookie said.

"You can tell that with your hands?" Sean asked.

"I can tell a lot even with no hands." Cookie focused her gaze on Sean who slurped down some coffee and got to his feet in a hurry.

"Can you tell who the owner is?" Jasper asked.

"No. Just that they don't want the cat. But I could just be picking up the vibes in this room."

Sean looked at his shoes. "I don't want to shirk responsibility here," he said. He brought out his wallet and held out two twenties to Jasper. "Is that okay?"

"You're buying me off?" she asked, her disappointment in Sean plodding around her stomach like a good meal gone bad.

"Expenses. For the cat. Food. Advertising. Vet."

Cookie took the money from Sean and handed it to Jasper. "What about a cat box and kitty litter?"

"I just used a shoe box and some old newspapers," Sean said.

"I'm glad *you* can't read *my* mind," Cookie said.

"Mine either." Jasper scratched the cat between its ears. It gave out one of its basso profundo meows.

"Three of you," Sean said. He handed over an additional ten.

"Thanks for caring," Jasper said. "See you at the auction."

"Can I call you?"

"Sure," Jasper said, but she kept her attention on the cat.

Sean backed toward the door. "Will you answer? Jasper?"

Jasper didn't look up until the door opened and shut with a lonely clunk.

"Oh, Sis," Cookie said.

"I am in love with a cat." Jasper lifted the cat up and cradled it like she had once cradled Cookie's children when they were small. The dark kitten opened his eyes and gave her one wise, trusting blink, then settled in with a sigh and a satisfied rumble.

♦

Instead of leaving Jimmy's apartment, as she and Cookie continued to call it, when her sister did, Jasper lay on the sofa cuddling the sturdy dark cat. He purred away and Jasper relaxed under his warmth. It felt nourishing to have some time away from the hustle and bustle of the auction house proper and the too-closeness of her smoky neighbors at home. Soon she would have to re-enter the world and face her worries. How had Jimmy really died? Had there been someone else present in the house? Was it really an accident? Or could it have been a deliberate accident? A murder. Jasper felt unexpected anger. Here she was, newly relocated, newly freed from a marriage haunted by deceit, newly arrived in her new life. Why couldn't she be free to enjoy this peaceful nap with an innocent little being purring against her heart? Jasper felt that she had the potential to be a happy and carefree person although she was enough of a grown-up to realize that no one's life was really picture perfect.

Even this cat came to her with a trunkload of trouble. Jasper would have to take it to the veterinarian and perhaps give it back to its original owner if what Cookie had said about the owner not wanting it turned out to be false.

Maybe she just wouldn't take it to the vet. Maybe she would just keep it here with her and care for it and nobody but her sister oh and Sean would ever have to know…Jasper held up the furry little body and the cat stared down on her with benevolent eyes. "No, that would be catnapping," Jasper said. She lowered him down to her chest and resettled. "I'll be good and responsible, kitty," she said. "I'll take you to the vet. Maybe you can stay with me after that. Would you like that?" The cat licked her hand. "You sure are a little love. You're standing in for what I don't have too much of right now," Jasper whispered. "Proxy would be a good name for you."

Her cell phone rang. It was Cookie inviting her down to the Forester to talk about the Austrings. They wanted to schedule a house-clearing before they closed the deal on the Clippert place, Cookie told her. Jasper set the cat down gently and got up from the sofa. The cat followed her out to the kitchen where she set out bowls of food and water. Then, with the cat still trailing behind, she fetched a boot box from Jimmy's bedroom, took it into the bathroom and crumbled up a bunch of toilet paper inside. The cat immediately climbed into the box, crouched and took a pee. "This is just for temporary. Good Proxy," Jasper said. She lured the cat back to the kitchen and, when it was fully engaged with its food bowl, hurried out of the apartment, locking the door behind her.

Chapter 20

At the Forester Jasper pointed out Sean's new art work on the wall. The photographs in their simple silver frames were dazzling in their color range and abstract shapes. Jasper's eyes mirrored their sparkle. The pictures took up one entire wall of the restaurant, midway between the coffee shop and the more formal dining area. "You sure he didn't take these with a super power telescope?" Cookie asked. "They look like distant galaxies."

"Nope. They're really all of his head. Self-portraits. He uses stencils and gels to change the color of the sunlight and the shapes of the shadows. Oh, and mirrors to bounce the sunlight. See here, if you look really closely, you can see his eye."

Cookie studied one of the pictures close up. "I see it!" she marveled. "Crazy! Watch out for him, Sis."

"What?"

"The man's infatuated with himself. He seems to have deep blue eyes – or at least one of them. And he must have at least four hands."

"Ha! That doesn't sound so bad," Jasper said.

"Two tall lattes, one skinny, one caramel mocha!" the coffee barista called.

They got their coffees and took them to their favorite table near the front window. For a Monday mid-morning the place was busy with lap-toppers and people reading newspapers or just gazing out into the sunny day. Jasper wondered how all these people could get away from work. Didn't any of them have regular jobs? Being an auctioneer and a professional psychic medium had their perks, she guessed. Although Jasper knew that once a few more days had gone by, people would expect her to put aside whatever grief she was experiencing in the wake of Jimmy's death and get back on track. She wished she could get all these nameless, faceless people out of her head, but they were always there cajoling and criticizing. She sighed.

"Drink up, Sis," Cookie said, reading her thoughts. "We have all the time in the world here. So let's just relax and savor."

Jasper sipped her skinny and Cookie sighed as she took a small but pleasurable slurp of her caramel mocha. Cookie asked, "Sean seems like a nice guy. But his work is really…well, wild."

"You said 'crazy.'"

"I mean, Sis, I've never seen anything like it before."

Jasper smiled with pride. "Yay! That's great. I'll tell Sean you said so. I mean if I see him again." She leaned across the table, intent on conveying Sean's intensity. "That's what he's striving for. Super originality. He says, 'Why bother making something if somebody else can do the same thing.'"

"Hmm, that's a thought," Cookie said. She traced her finger around the rim of her mug. Hers was sunny yellow today. Jasper had requested blue.

"Something bothering you?"

"I've never known an artist before. I mean not up close and personal," Cookie said.

"So. Me either. He's just a guy who happens to make art for a living." Jasper shrugged. She felt her shoulders rising defensively.

"Hey, you know I'm on your side, Sis. It's just that how can he afford that big place he has in the country – what did you say, 20 acres? Does he really sell enough art to be able to live better than a lot of us?"

"Well, there are his inventions," Jasper said. She drank down some more latte.

"What? Toys for cats and dogs? That's not like a cure for cancer – "

"I'm not sure you can patent that."

"Are you sure? Ask your boyfriend."

"He's not my boyfriend."

"Not yet."

"Hush."

"But that's not the point." Cookie sipped more of her rich latte. She laughed and shook a finger at her sister. "You're trying to change the subject! Okay, okay, I'll lay off. But I just want to look after my little sister."

"Born two minutes before me does not a big sister make!" Jasper protested. "Two lousy minutes and you're going to hold that against me the rest of my life. Or our lives. Or whatever. Not fair, not fair, not fair."

"You're a nut," Cookie said fondly. "Maybe you and that crazy artist deserve each other." Her tone was kind and Jasper didn't take offense.

"Maybe," she said. "Too soon to tell. Here's to the future and whatever it holds."

They clinked mugs. Jasper added, "And just don't tell me what that is, okay? I'd rather find out on my own."

"I keep telling you. I'm not Ms. Psychic Predictions. Especially when it comes to family matters." Cookie and Jasper exchanged a somber look. Cookie looked down at the table.

Jasper reached for her hand. "Hey, it wasn't your fault. Jimmy lived his own life. He made his own decisions."

Cookie slumped, deep furrows between her brows. "But, Sis, why didn't I get anything before it happened? No chills, no foreboding, no dreams. And worst of all, no Mom. Wouldn't you think she'd care enough to speak up ahead of time?"

"Now you're being silly. You're always telling me that sometimes things happen because they're meant to happen. Maybe if you had gotten some hint that Jimmy might be heading for a fall, you would've stepped in. But who's to say he would have listened to you anyway? Did he ever take advice from anybody – especially us?"

"You've got a point there, girlfriend." The sisters double clinked their mugs. "I've got to get a to-go cup," Cookie said, standing and picking up her oversize and highly fashionable purse.

"What happened to sit and savor?" Jasper felt separation anxiety kick up inside like a cat in a cage on its way to the vet. She reached for her sister's hand. Cookie leaned down to kiss Jasper on the cheek.

"Family matters."

"Yeah it does," Jasper said.

"Don't try guilting me. I'm better at it than you are."

"Am not."

"Am too." Cookie smiled fondly. "See you at three." She made her way to the counter.

Jasper turned her attention to her mug, studying the foam as if somebody's life depended on it, as if she could catch any glimpse of wisdom in the cloudy coffee.

♦

Cookie's afternoon appointment with Emily and Kiefer Austring was already underway when Jasper walked into the waiting room of Psychic Medium Rare. She'd waited too long before leaving the auction house, fearful of raising Ted's ire for ducking out twice in one day. It didn't matter that he wasn't the real boss. His maleness and his booming voice made it hard for her to step out of line.

A placard hanging by a decorative brass nail on the door to Cookie's consultation room proclaimed:

SESSION IN PROGRESS. SHHHH PLEASE!

There was a second message scribbled on a post-it note and stuck below.

Jasper, this means You!

No doubt about it – Cookie didn't want her in on the meeting with the Austrings. Who knows what all they wanted to go into without a nosy auctioneer intruding. Maybe checking on the fingers and toes of their unborn baby and whether or not they were expecting the future president of the United States or at least a member of Congress.

Knowing that Cookie would invite her in when it came to talking about the house where Jimmy had died, Jasper picked out a magazine, choosing between Psychic Phenom and a stack of others, chose Traditional Home, and perched on the Rococo revival settee Cookie had bought at the auction. Jasper had just begun to envision the perfect cottage garden she might one day make for herself if she ever had a home she could truly call her own, when the door to the inner office opened. Cookie stuck her head out and beckoned with a formal nod of the head.

"Hi!" she said and reached to hug her sister.

"Love you too," Cookie whispered. Her hug was light. Jasper surmised that Cookie's spirit was otherwise engaged. She stepped in to the office and admired the way the light filtered in through the lace curtains Cookie had chosen, one of her few brand new purchases.

The Austrings looked calmer than when Jasper had first met them the night of Stepfather Turned Body. In Cookie's deep red wingbacks, they sat holding hands across the small angled divide between them. The box of blue tissues on the piecrust table had been well used it appeared, since several crumpled tissues surrounded it. Jasper greeted Emily and Kiefer and took the place Cookie nodded her to, on a folding chair brought in for this unusually large group reading. Consultation. Meeting. Cookie herself sat in the oak desk chair she had wheeled over from her roll-top desk, two more nice auction buys.

Jasper felt some pride in the appearance of her sister's office. It had a nice, rosy, comforting glow about it. Something very pink attracted her attention out of the corner of her eye. Then it was gone. Maybe Cookie's energy itself had something to do with the room's glow.

Cookie directed everyone to take a full, deep breath.

Jasper did her best but found that suddenly she had a tickle in her throat. She tried to fight it off but it erupted into a full-fledged cough. "Sorry, everyone." She headed for the tissue box. Kiefer grabbed it off the table and tossed it to her. "Well, thanks," Jasper said. She saw a brief look of annoyance cross Emily's face. *Jeez, these people are impatient.* She wondered to what lengths they would go to get into the Clippert house as soon as possible and make it their own. Jasper got back to her chair, kept her posture erect because she knew that was important for receiving good energy, and found her cough retreat as her breathing grew deep and regular.

Cookie announced that there was someone present.

Jasper squinched her eyes shut and clapped the tissue across her mouth. *I don't want to see anybody. I don't want to hear anybody. And nobody touch me. Please, God and angels and all good types.*

It was a frequent prayer for Jasper. Cookie often reminded her that their horoscopes matched and they had the same gifts they could choose to develop or not. "Not!" Jasper would always say.

"Just because you have a gift doesn't mean you have to develop it," Cookie would reassure her.

"Fine, fine, fine." And Jasper would change the subject.

"Shhh, I'm trying to tune in," Cookie said. Jasper wondered if she had spoken aloud. "It's a man standing in the position of father," Cookie said. Jasper's spine shivered suddenly like an unexpected chiropractic maneuver had just taken her by surprise. She sat up straighter. Cookie said, "He says he doesn't want you to name the baby for him."

The Austrings bent forward.

"I? E? E-E-E-E-E," Cookie said. "Ilky? Evil? "

Jasper shuddered.

Kiefer Austring put a hand lightly over Emily's mouth.

"Evelyn? Like that?" Cookie pronounced the name British style with a long "e."

"Evelyn." Kiefer said. "My dad. People called him 'Inky.'"

"I told you he stood in the father's position," Cookie said, a bit more sharply than Jasper might have expected.

Jasper swallowed down a giggle. She could understand not wanting to name a baby boy Evelyn. It just didn't sound modern enough. Maybe not for a girl either. Although Evie or Evvie weren't such bad nicknames. And how about 'Inky'? Jasper would smile with delight if she were ever introduced to anyone in the flesh named Inky, man, woman, girl, boy, dog, cat.

"Why – why is he here?" Emily asked.

"Because you wanted to talk to someone and he's ready to talk. Yes, yes," Cookie said. She touched a hand to her ear as if she were adjusting a headset. "Slow down a bit. "He says he has to hurry because someone's trying to shove him out of the way. He wants you to return the baby car seat you bought and get a better one for his grandchild. He says go to Milwaukee or Chicago. Don't order on-line. He doesn't trust the Internet."

Emily shook her head from side to side. "That's Inky. He never approved of me," she whispered.

"He's holding out a pink rose. He's saying he's sorry. I think. The other man is really pushy. Let him finish!"

Kiefer grabbed Cookie's shoulders. "Let him finish!" he shouted in his sister's face.

Jasper gripped him by the back of his well-pressed shirt. "You leave her alone! She can't help what they're doing on the other side."

"You leave him alone!" Emily said. From behind, she seized Jasper's wrists and tried to pry them off her husband.

Suddenly, Jasper felt herself diving forward, following Cookie's backward fall with the Austrings sandwiching her between them. The four of them landed in a heap on the floor.

"Everybody off," Cookie muttered.

They all untangled and got slowly to their feet. Several hands reached down to help Cookie but she managed on her own. Kiefer picked up her chair. He apologized. "I think I got a little carried away there," he said.

"His father always has that effect," Emily said. Kiefer shot her a look that, Jasper thought, did not bode well for a happy evening ahead. They were about to resume their seats, but Cookie announced that the session was finished.

"But we didn't get our full hour," Kiefer said.

"No, we didn't get our money's worth," Emily said.

"You haven't paid me anything," Cookie said.

"But we planned to." Kiefer brought out his wallet. He whispered in his wife's ear and she whispered back. He dug out two ten dollar bills and flared them out toward Cookie.

Jasper opened her mouth to protest, but Cookie stood silently, arms folded.

"Alright," Kiefer grumbled. He dug out an additional ten and handed the 30 to Cookie who accepted the half-payment. "Thank you," she said. She escorted them to the door of her consultation room. "You know," she said quietly, "you did get to hear from your dad, dad-in-law."

The Austrings paused. "You're right," Kiefer said. He shook hands with Cookie and with Jasper.

"If only that awful other man hadn't interrupted," Emily said. "I wonder who that was."

Cookie smiled and shook her head. Jasper knew that Cookie knew but was not sharing with the Austrings who now headed toward the stairs, talking to each other. They paused and Kiefer turned back toward Cookie and Jasper. "So you'll still be coming over to the new house to do the clearing?"

"Oh yes," Cookie said. "The current owner's paying for that."

"Well, thanks. Thanks again," Kiefer said. He hurried his wife away.

Behind the closed door of Cookie's office, Jasper asked, "Okay, Sis. Who was the interloper?"

Cookie smiled in that annoying older twin kind of way she had sometimes. "You tell me."

"Oh, come on," Jasper began to complain. Then it came to her. A clear picture in her head. Short man. Sturdy stance. Pushy. Dressed in a suit jacket and tie – just like he was getting ready to conduct a fund-raising auction. "Jimmy! It was Jimmy, wasn't it?"

"Uh-huh. You got it."

"Oh, blessed cheese-head," Jasper said.

"That just about sums it up," Cookie said.

Chapter 21

"Bid and buy at Biggs!" Grace recited into the phone so quickly that she could've been an auctioneer herself. It came out sounding like BiddenbuyitBiggs. "Yeah, yeah. Right, right. We never buy things. You wouldn't want us to. We take stuff on consignment.

"Now listen, you big bag of wind! What if we paid you 50 bucks and we coulda got you a hundred on auction? Well, if you do find another auctioneer who'll buy your stuff outright, just remember – he's a crook! Thanks for calling," she added in a super sweet voice.

She slammed the phone down on the marble countertop. "Another worthless windbag," "Seems like they're asking to be cheated. What's up with you?" she asked Jasper who stood waiting just inside the office.

"I mean, you've been here a lot longer than I have – "

"Don't go pullin' the age card on me, baby girl," Grace said. She pinched Jasper's cheek affectionately.

"But, Grace, don't you think there's something to that old saying, 'The customer's always right?'"

"You've spent too much time in church, honey. The auction draws a tough crowd. You gotta hold your own with this bunch or they'll eat you alive."

"I'm tough," Jasper said.

Kelly snorted. She was busy magic-marking numbers on a stack of fresh bidder cards. "Tough as chicken skin," she mumbled.

"I heard that." Jasper lifted her chin.

"You were supposed to!" Kelly said. "You think I say these things to amuse myself?"

"Well, what the heck — what the hell do I say to that?" Jasper held her hands palms up.

Kelly snorted again and Grace gave Jasper a light elbow to the ribs.

Kelly said, "You can't pull that off, lady. You shouldn't even try."

Jasper couldn't think of a single smart-alecky retort.

Grace reached an arm around her shoulders. "She's right, honey. Just be yourself. You'll do just fine."

A man on the other side of the counter cleared his throat. "Can't anybody get waited on around here?" he asked. There was no smile in his voice.

"Who's not getting waited on?" Grace said.

Another bidder had come up to the counter and Jasper turned to help. "Number 67," the large mahogany-skinned man said.

"Oh, you're a regular," Jasper said. She found his number on the list of permanent bidders, faithful auction-goers who got to claim the same number as their own by dint of visiting the auction week after week, some of them for many years. "Mr. Johnson." Jasper marked a line across the plastic sheet cover through his name and number. Grace would register him in the computer program later so he was on record as a bidder that evening.

"Call me Ernie," the big man said.

"Jasper."

"Got a joke for you, Jasper. Why did the Auctioneer cross the block? To sell something of course!"

"That's just ….. kind of groan-worthy. I don't know what to say, Ernie."

Ernie held a big grin on his face. "Just say it's bad. Big Bad Ernie. I got my reputation to keep up."

"Well, it's nice to know you, Mr. Big Bad Ernie Johnson."

He saluted her with a two-finger wave, took his card with the big 67 written in red across the top, and headed purposefully into the main auction room to preview items that would be auctioned that night. If he found something he liked, Jasper knew he would scrawl the item description and his top bid on the back of his card so that Kelly could proxy-bid up to that amount for him.

Grace was still on the phone, rat-a-tat-tatting her fingers against the marble that topped the counter underneath the phone and the charge card reader. It was auction day! She had plenty to do! Jasper admired her friendliness under pressure even if it was just a polite veneer half the time. "Grace clicked down the receiver. "Some people just don't get it. What's up, Jasper?"

Jasper explained that she had to leave the building for a while. She had two last minute look-ats that Ted had handed off to her, and a 1:30 meeting with Ray Clippert to get a new contract signed. She didn't tell Grace that she also wanted to secure Mr. Clippert's permission for the house clearing Cookie had scheduled on the Austrings' behalf for Friday evening. She loved her sister and respected her work but she didn't like to rub her beliefs in someone else's face. Grace was a good-natured person and, from what she'd seen so far, pretty accepting about other people's peccadilloes but maybe ghost hunting and house clearing were beyond her ken.

Grace's reaction startled her. "What is that jackass doing sending you off alone. You've only been here two weeks. Take one of the guys with you. Tony!"

Tony, busy out on the floor, demonstrating how easily the drawers of a bureau opened and closed to a customer, looked up, waved, and kept going with his demonstration.

"Why, that lazy little toad! I swear they can read my mind when there's extra work to do."

"Grace, Grace. That's not necessary." Jasper put a calming hand on Grace's arm. "Ted said these were really simple. Somebody's Precious Moments collection and an apartment with a few furniture pieces. I can handle it."

"Well, you know what your father the philosopher used to say? Have your precious moments now. Don't hold on to the things."

"Jimmy said that? Maybe there were things I didn't know about him."

"Most of it you wouldn't want to know," Grace said. Some customers approached the counter. "Just a minute, you guys. I'll be right with you." She took Jasper's elbow and walked her away from the people. "You say you're going on that appointment to Ray Clippert's? Doesn't that sort of give you the willies? I mean, you gotta remember that it was just about this time of day when Jimmy god rest his goddamned soul went to the Clippert house. And you know what happened to him."

"Grace! Don't be silly. Ray Clippert is at Forest Park Nursing Center now. Nothing can happen to me at a nursing home. I'll be back way before it's time for the auction."

"W-e-l-l. Just a goddamn minute, Bobby! I said I'd be right there."

"Come on, Gracie," the man at the counter wheedled.

"Jasper, keep your cell phone with you at all times."

"Great. I'm fine. I'll do good," Jasper said, edging out of the office.

"You'll do great!" Grace called after her. "Now what are you fellas chafin' at the bit for? Go get 'em, Jasper!"

"Go get 'em, Jasper!" the men echoed.

Jasper waved and marched briskly away, shooting out brief "hi's," "just fines," to customers entering the building as she left. Even in the rough world of auctioneering, mutual respect helped soften the edges of human interaction.

Jasper's two auction look-ats went just as planned. The first one, at a small apartment in a rent-controlled building for seniors, wrenched her heart a bit. A woman no taller than five feet showed her in to her place. It smelled of cauliflower and cabbage and, indeed, there was a pot of soup simmering on the gas range in the kitchenette. The 80ish woman led Jasper into a bedroom piled up with dolls and teddy bears. The Precious Moments collection of black-eyed girl and boy figurines took up the wide windowsill.

Jasper pretended to scrawl on her notepad but there wasn't anything noteworthy. She broke it to the woman as gently as she could without patronizing her. "Brand name collectibles like this just aren't bringing much on the auction block. Right now. Uh - Mrs. Sperling."

The woman's hunched shoulders straightened a bit. "Then I'll just have to wait," she said.

"I'm glad you took this so well," Jasper said as Mrs. Sperling escorted her to the door.

"Just as well. If I die before the price comes up, they go to my lousy excuse for a daughter-in-law."

"Well, all righty then."

Jasper's next look-at took her to the home of two professors from Forest Grove College. Theirs was a red brick ranch house a few blocks west of campus. It had the appearance of upper middle class respectability. Jasper knew better than to judge by appearances. Inside, the two female professors walked her through the sparsely furnished living room to show her the furniture they wanted to auction. Maybe they had had to sell other things. One woman kept her arm draped over the other's shoulders while Jasper examined their dining room set. *Oh God*, she thought, *another chance to break people's hearts*. Aloud she said, "Nice Windsor set. Maple. Six chairs."

"The hutch goes too," one of the professors said.

"The server, dear."

"We have the expert right here," the first professor, the taller one said. "Hutch or server?" she asked.

Jasper hesitated. She took a deep breath and said, "Hutch, server, buffet, or sideboard. See the thing is, it may not matter what you call it. It's not part of the original set. See – look really close at the finish. It's different."

"Maybe the family who had it before used the wrong finish," the shorter professor said.

"That would be your family, dear."

"There she goes again – always about my family. I'm sociology. She's art. They always told me to watch out."

Jasper stepped between them. "And the chairs – they don't really match the table," she said.

The woman turned their mutual glower upon Jasper. They were not pleased.

She backed toward the door. "What's more important than any of that is that formal dining room sets are not selling so well right now. Not at our auction house."

"I knew we should've tried that new guy I saw in the shopping news," the art professor said.

"He auctions on line," the sociologist said.

Jasper's hand reached found the doorknob behind her. "Good, good idea. Well, ladies, wish I could've helped." She edged out the door. Her cell phone went off with Ella Fitzgerald's rendition of the Cole Porter song, "Love for Sale." The auction house was calling.

"Jasper here," she said.

"Everything okay out there, baby girl?" Grace asked.

"Ladies! Bosh. Did you hear that?" Jasper heard from inside the half-opened door.

"Peachy," she told Grace.

Jasper hurried down the front sidewalk and escaped into her car. Grace wanted to know where she was and whether she had found anything auctionable. "Nope. Just as predicted," Jasper said. The professors emerged onto their front porch. Jasper waved cheerfully at their angry faces and accelerated away. "Whew!"

"You sure you're okay?" Grace asked.

"Oh, you bet. I'm off now to the nursing home."

"Guess you can't get into any trouble there."

"Trouble and I are not even on speaking terms," Jasper said with a pseudo laugh.

"Be right there. Gotta go, Jasper. Hurry back," Grace said. The phone went silent in Jasper's hand. She laid it on the seat next to her and focused on driving across town to the Forest Park Nursing Center. All she had to do was head west to the river and then turn right. Ten minutes max

A half hour later, Jasper finally pulled into a parking stall at the nursing home. "Love for Sale" was coming from her cell phone again. She didn't want to explain that her lousy sense of direction had reared its awkward head again. She left the cell phone singing away on the passenger seat, grabbed her clipboard with the auction contract clamped to the front, and headed into the one-story blond brick building.

The resident directory posted inside the front door said that R. Clippert was in SE 3. Jasper had to ask only three uniformed assistants for help before arriving at SE 3. She used the brass knocker to tap out Shave and a Haircut.

"Nobody's home!" a gruff voice shouted from inside

"Mr. Clippert! It's me, Jasper Biggs from the auction house."

"Don't want any. Go away"

An older woman using a cane to make her way slowly down the hall paused next to Jasper. She rapped on the door with the curved head of her cane. "Ray Clippert? There's a nice young lady out here wants to talk to you." To Jasper she said, "You look okay." The woman opened the door. "Go on in," she told Jasper. "He won't bite."

"You interfering old biddy!" the man inside shouted. He was lying down on the sofa, a brown and orange afghan draped over his legs. "Well, get yourself in here, girly. You want to give me a deathly chill?"

Jasper stepped inside. The air smelled of urine and moth balls. "This won't take long, Mr. Clippert," she said. She hoped that was true.

Ray Clippert struggled up to a seated position. Jasper hurried over so he wouldn't grow any gruffer.

Jasper perched atop a short stack of newspapers on a stepstool. "I brought the auction contract for you to sign."

"Oh, talk to my daughter. She's another busybody. She'll know what to tell you to do with your paperwork."

"It's not much. She doesn't have Power of Attorney, so you have to sign this yourself or we can't go ahead with the auction."

"Who says I want to go ahead with the auction?"

"Why, don't you want to make some money for yourself? This can't be cheap living here and keeping your house too."

"Money, money, money. It's all you females think about. Fee Males. Get it?"

Don't take it personally, don't take it personally, don't take it personally, Jasper told herself. "The idea is to make money for you."

"You're not doing this from the Godness of your heart, missy."

"What?"

"Bear in mind that I've still got my balls and my bearings. Ball bearings. Get it?"

Jasper rose from her uncomfortable perch. "Well, I'll see you this afternoon. I guess we can sign the paperwork at your old house."

"Old house. Old man." Ray Clippert chuckled and shook his head. "Where do you think you're going? Ain't got much of a sense of humor, do you?"

"I'll laugh later," Jasper said.

"Hah. You got a funny bone after all. Hand over that contract, why don't you, and we'll get 'er signed. Got a pencil?"

"How 'bout this pen?"

♦

As she pulled out of the nursing home's parking lot, Jasper's mind pondered the strangeness of her new life. Ever since she had left Rev. Tim back in the church basement, her determination to change into a stronger woman who no longer bowed to goofball authority figures had been challenged. Jimmy. Dead now. Ready Teddy, always willing to win over women whenever they were foolish enough to agree. Mary Clippert. *Her* father Ray.

A red car pulling into the parking lot nearly clipped her left fender. The dark-haired woman behind the wheel gave her the finger. Speak of the devil! Mary Clippert herself. The woman had her gaze focused straight ahead so Jasper tucked her chin and drove away. Safely out of view, Jasper headed south on Riverside Road and pulled into the empty parking lot that faced the walking path. She tossed her purse into the back seat and covered it with an empty trash bag, left the auction contract on the front seat, then got out and admired the river and a flock of grazing geese. Maybe a nice long walk would clear her head. She headed down the path. A little voice in her head nagged her about leaving the car unlocked. *Come on. It's safe. I'm safe*, she told it. The voice ordered her back to the car.

Jasper stomped her foot like a little girl. Some strong woman, she chided herself. She couldn't even stand up to herself. She returned to the car and had just opened the door to push the lock button, the electronic locks having quit working long ago, when a cherry-colored car pulled into the lot, then raced on by. Jasper stared after it. It was going too fast for her to make out the driver. A shiver went up her spine. She climbed inside her car and when her shaking subsided, drove with concentration back to the auction house.

Chapter 22

When Cookie saw the red car parked in front of the alley garage behind the Clippert house, she scowled. "Is someone else going to be here?" she asked Jasper.

"Shouldn't you have sensed that?"

"I knew you'd say that."

Jasper drummed her fingers on the steering wheel. She drove slowly by, the twins together in Jasper's serviceable clunker which for once was cooperating and did nothing more than squeal mildly whenever they made a right turn.

"So?"

"It's like this," Jasper said. "The Clipperts are our clients and I had a responsibility to tell them when we'd be doing this clearing. They have a vested interest, after all."

"You're too responsible. You're like, responsible to a fault."

Jasper said, "Am not." She headed the car down the gravel alley. She made a right squeal turn, then another, so that they pulled up in front of the Clippert place and stopped the car with a jerk.

"I don't need whiplash today, thank you very much," Cookie said. She rubbed the back of her neck. "And you are too too responsible for your own good. It's like you're trying to make up for Jimmy's irresponsibilities."

"Yeah, well, sorry I'm such a compensator or whatever. But it's tough enough finding my way through all the auctioneering stuff and putting up with Ready Teddy and everybody without my own sister turning against me." She glanced sideways at Cookie. Sure enough, she could see a smile break out on her sister's face. Overstating things generally broke through any temporary frostiness between them.

Cookie snorted. "Oh, p-l-e-a-s-e." She reached over and took Jasper's right hand. "You look just right today, by the way. I like that rosy colored top on you. It brings out the pink in your cheeks." She squeezed Jasper's hand, then let go and guided her through a deep breathing routine. "Let's do some chakra clearing too – especially since it might get a little complicated inside with them in there."

Jasper glanced toward the house. She saw the front curtains twitch. Let them wait. We're early anyway.

Cookie went into professional pre-clearing mode. "Surround yourself with the white and gold light of universal love and divine protection. Know that you and the universe are one." Cookie opened her eyes and glanced toward Jasper.

Jasper nodded and took a deep breath.

"I think we should go in after all," Cookie said. "I'd better save the rest for the Clipperts."

Lord knows they need it, thought Jasper.

The twins got out of the car and eased their doors shut. Jasper's door squealed, Cookie's merely squeaked.

They paused on the front porch. Jasper had been back since Jimmy's death, helping clear out the physical clutter. Cookie hadn't. Jasper vowed to be extra sensitive to her sister's sensitivities about their stepfather's death now while it was Cookie's turn to clear away any psychic remnants – Jimmy's or any of the generations of working class families who had lived here in the house's hundred year old history. A haunted house? Disembodied entities? Ghosts? That kind of thing. Or, rather, those kind of people and that kind of place.

"Ready?" Jasper asked.

"Always."

Suddenly the door flung open. Jasper jumped. Cookie didn't move. Mary Clippert stood there. Today she wore a red suit with black cowl-neck silky blouse and a big costume jewelry daisy pinned to her lapel. Jasper thought it was an odd outfit for communing with the dead, imagining that people on the Other Side might be hyper sensitive to bright colors and overstated fashion but maybe Mary Clippert wasn't really a believer and just wanted to be there in an official capacity. "Come in, ladies."

Jasper and Cookie entered the living room. An old musty smell permeated the now bare space. Biggs Auction had paid their regular cleaning crew to come through after the pick-up and scrub the place down, but Jasper could tell they had just lazed through a hasty wash, dust and vacuum. She'd have to talk to Ted about that. Yeah, right, he wouldn't care. They were probably old drinking buddies he'd promised the work to.

Someone cleared her throat. "Miss Biggs?"

"Is your father here?" Jasper asked.

"He couldn't make it," Mary said. "The home said he had an incident earlier today."

I thought it best if we did this on our own."

"An incident? Gosh, I hope I didn't push him too hard. What kind of incident – did they say? "

"You pushed him?" Mary's voice had a slightly hysterical edge to it.

Cookie stepped between Mary and Jasper. "We're ready to get started now."

Jasper gave her sister a small, grateful smile. Cookie looked quite the professional psychic medium, Jasper thought proudly, in flowing purple slacks and a turquoise sweater that made her blonde hair glow like a halo. Or was that an actual halo? Her sister wore a silk scarf of lilac and teal and dangling silver and amethyst earrings. "Just stay relaxed and receptive," Cookie said. "Let me do the talking. If you have a question for anyone who shows up, tell me and I'll ask them."

Cookie continued on in the soothing tones of her profession, "First we'll focus on the lower chakra. Just breathe in a beautiful white gold light to the area between your sit bones."

Jasper knew what that meant. She had done yoga back in the basement hall of the Truman Free Church. The first chakra. Basic survival.

"Let the golden white light cleanse your root chakra. Breathe in. Breathe out. Now let a lovely rose-colored light, a red light, fill the area. "Then to the reproductive area."

Under Cookie's guidance, Jasper worked her way up the chakras, cleansing with the white and gold light, then filling each of the energy centers with its own particular color. Orange for the second chakra, yellow for the solar plexus, green and pink for the heart, turquoise for the throat chakra, bright blue for the third eye in the middle of the forehead, and finally violet for the crown chakra. Jasper was pretty much able to concentrate in spite of Mary Clippert's presence. That was the problem in tuning your own psyche: you started tuning in to other people's hidden energies. Jasper sensed a lot of heat coming from Mary's direction and she didn't want to get burned. She took a step closer to Cookie.

"Now let's picture a radiant fountain of white light cascading down from above your head all around you and pooling beneath your feet.

"We thank you for protection and clarity," Cookie intoned.

"Especially protection," Jasper whispered. "Amen."

"Can we get on with it?" Mary asked in a strained voice.

"Yes of course." Cookie stood in silence for a moment, then led the way carefully down the hall to the main bedroom. Jasper and Mary followed.

Devoid of much of the clutter of junk that had been in every room of the house, it was nothing but a sad little space. Jasper pitied both men connected to the place – Ray Clippert who had lived lonely here and Jimmy who dropped off into the Big Sleep while trying to mine the poor old house for any hidden gems.

"We are here in strength and peace," Cookie said.

Her voice was unnecessarily loud, Jasper thought, but maybe the passed-overs had a hard timing hearing the voices of the living. Mary Clippert hovered over Jasper's shoulder. Jasper could feel that additional heat that the overbearing woman continued to radiate. She could hear Mary's quick breathing. Jasper stepped closer to Cookie. Mary followed.

Cookie laughed. "They are a little nervous," she said. "There's a man here who wants to talk to all of us."

Jasper's palms went sweaty. Mary panted like a St. Bernard in the summer.

"Okay, okay. There are two men here actually. One at a time, gentleman. Let me talk to the first father figure. Jasper, it's Jimmy."

Jasper suppressed a sudden coughing fit. "Tell him everything's fine at work," she said.

"He hears you. He already knows that. He's not here to talk about work," Cookie said.

Jasper could now smell Mary whose bright red outfit would be sweat-soaked soon if she kept this up. Ugh, sour. At least the woman wasn't trying to boss them around. Fear of the dead was keeping her usual overbearingness in check.

"What's he saying already?" Mary demanded, but her voice lacked its usual domineering tone.

Cookie opened her eyes and looked directly at the taller woman. "He says you already know what he wants to say to you."

"He can damn well tell us all then!" Mary said. Her belligerence had returned.

"Enough!" Cookie said. "He's allowing the other man to step forward."

"Oh, please," Mary said. "I've had enough of this mumbo-jumbo. Let's shut down this magic show."

"You're the one who hired us," Jasper said.

"So I get to set the rules. This is my house – I mean, my father's house," Mary said as she backed toward the door.

A wind suddenly blew through the room. Jasper felt both cold and hot. Like a cold wind on a hot day or a hot wind in the winter. Jasper watched as Mary's neatly coiffed hair rose and fell, one dark lock bolting across her forehead. "Damn you all!" Mary shrieked. She began to cry. Jasper instinctively went to her and put an arm around her waist. Mary pushed her away. "You had a father who loved you!"

"Okay. We're almost through here," Cookie said. "All spirits of low energy must now leave. I call on Archangel Michael to complete the clearing. Bless this space and protect it now and always."

Jasper stood side by side with Cookie for a moment. Mary was nowhere to be seen. "She really freaked out," Jasper whispered in her sister's ear.

"I've seen it before," Cookie said. "People who aren't in touch with their own essence can get really disturbed when the outer realms are present. How 'bout you, Sis? How are you doing?"

"Surprisingly well." As she said it, Jasper realized how true it was. "Did you feel that wind too?

"Oh, yeah."

"It didn't scare me somehow. I felt surprised but not totally creeped out."

"You did really well," Cookie said.

"Yeah, I guess I did. The only thing I wish is that we would have more time to talk to Jimmy."

"Well, it just wasn't the right time for that. He's not stuck here by the way. He's moved on. He just came back for a visit," Cookie said.

"That's a relief. I was kind of afraid that he'd end up – you know."

"In hell?"

"Well, kind of yeah. No offense, Jimmy, if you're still listening in, but you were sort of a bastard in some ways," Jasper said.

Cookie took Jasper's hand in hers. "He's back. He says he's sorry for however he hurt us." Cookie spoke through her tears. "He just sends his love."

"Thanks, Jimmy." She gave her sister's hand a squeeze. "Thanks, Cookie."

"See you later, Jimmy. We'll talk another time," Cookie said. "And so it is." She spoke in Jasper's ear, "Now let's look for the nut case client and see if we can help her."

They found Mary in the kitchen, leaning against the sink, staring out the bare window toward the barren backyard.

"How're you doing?" Cookie asked in a calm, conversational tone.

Mary turned toward them. Her eyes were ringed with red to match her power outfit. "How do you think I'm doing?"

Cookie shrugged. "About as well as can be expected. Do you want to call it quits for the day? Jasper and I can finish the house on our own."

"Yeah, no problem," Jasper echoed, unable to look at Mary's disturbed eyes.

"I must go on. I must," Mary said, pounding her fist on the metal sink for emphasis.

That must hurt, Jasper thought, but Mary seemed impervious to the pain.

"All right," Cookie said gently. "We could do the kitchen right now while we're here."

Mary squared her shoulders. "Let's go to the basement. That place was so full of his squirrely mess that who knows what kind of demons are lurking there."

Cookie said, "I don't sense any demons in the house. Maybe just some unhappy souls."

"Well you didn't know my father," Mary said. "He was quite the devil."

Jasper thought over her visit to the man earlier in the day. Sure, he was gruff and messy, and probably housed a multitude of ugly thoughts, but Jasper hadn't sensed real evil in him.

Maybe he had tried to make up for earlier sins as he grew older. Jasper felt beyond her depth when it came to recognizing wickedness. She hoped that someday she would mature beyond her Innocent Orphan persona.

Cookie led the women in another prayer of protection, then they all trooped over to the basement door. Jasper had not noticed before now how scarred the door was. Its right hand

The Case of the Angry Auctioneer   211

edge looked chewed on as if large mice or small rats had been gnawing their way into the cellar for years- or maybe a dog once upon a time. Jasper turned the knob and felt around the corner for the light switch.

Mary shrieked. Cookie inhaled deeply. Jasper, her mouth opened in a silent *oh no*, stared downward.

Ray Clippert was lying at the foot of the stairs on the basement floor, his blank eyes looking like antique wooden buttons. Jasper forced herself to hurry down to the old man. Ray Clippert sure looked dead. She made herself check for a pulse, first the side of the neck, then the wrist. Nothing. She ran as fast as a cat back up to where Cookie and Mary Clippert waited. "Call 911. Don't go down there," she said.

Cookie put in the call on her cell phone.

"You can't tell me what to do!" Mary pushed Jasper aside and rushed down the stairs. She began yelling, "Oh my God!" Over and over and over again.

Chapter 23

"Oh my God, oh my God, oh my God." Mary Clippert staggered around the basement. Ray Clippert's body lay in a half circle near the stairs, reminding Jasper - of all the things that exist in this weird world - of a crescent roll. Not a croissant. For Ray, even in death, looked every inch the American. Red blood splatters decorated his blue jean overalls and white t-shirt. His face was that strange shade of the newly dead that Jasper had seen not too long ago on her own stepfather's visage. Dead Caucasians took on the hue of granite, not the deathly pale cliché color, Jasper thought, or at least dead Caucasian men of a certain age did.

Cookie and Jasper went down the stairs to Mary's side. "There, there, there, there," said Cookie. She and Jasper eased Mary to the floor. "No-o-o-," moaned Mary as she touched down on the cold concrete not far from her father's body. Mary paddled away with her feet, Cookie's and Jasper's hands hooked under her arms, until she had crab-walked herself backwards and resettled on a lower step.

"Why, why, why?" Mary held her head and continued moaning. Then she ceased her noise-making as abruptly as she had started. "Are you definitely, definitely, definitely certain that he's - " Her voice dropped to a whisper. "Dead? I have a feeling he's still here with us."

"You got that right," Cookie muttered.

Feeling somehow stronger by the moment, Jasper told her sister, "Stay with her." Then she re-approached the body. There was no movement. Jasper crouched near him to double check for a neck pulse just the same. Tragic death was an oft-used cliché, but it would really be tragic if Mr. Clippert was merely near death and might yet be saved. In spite of her outward calmness, Jasper's hands had gone icy. She took a deep breath and forced herself to touch the man lying so still. His skin was colder than her own, and unmoving under her touch, almost like a rubber chicken. Things under the skin were at a standstill. No pulse.

Jasper got to her feet and made a conscious effort to avoid wiping her hands down the side of her slacks. She turned back to the steps where Cookie sat near but not touching Mary Clippert.

"Is he really gone?" Mary asked.

Cookie gave her a look, then stared up at her sister. Jasper shrugged. Mary Clippert must have a hard time accepting the death of fathers. She'd said something like that the night Jimmy died.

Jasper spoke in consoling tones. "Yes, he's gone," she told Mary.

There was a pause in which it seemed as if all three women and the basement itself held their breaths. One big silent moment of shock. The house had killed again.

Mary lumbered to her feet. "I'd be obliged if you'd leave me alone with him for a minute," she said.

"I think we should wait together for the police," Jasper said.

"Not gonna happen, Miss Biggs Mouth," Mary said. "Know-it-all auctioneers," she mumbled.

Cookie waved Jasper to back up a couple feet. Further away, Jasper felt a little safer from the angry and confused Mary Clipper.

"I agree with my sister. I don't think you should be left alone," Cookie said.

"I won't be alone. He's here with me," Mary said. She held her hand to her heart.

Off on the other side of the basement, a pipe banged. Mary shrieked.

"You were saying?" Cookie asked.

"Maybe you are right. Shall we go wait for the police?" Mary led the way up the steep steps post-haste. Jasper waited with Cookie for just a moment longer while Cookie said a short prayer for the peace of Ray Clippert's soul. Then they walked more sedately upstairs.

Voices came from the living room. Jasper thought the police were getting better all the time at finding their way to the Clippert house. If this dead man theme continued, they could include the place in some kind of training video. Jasper was surprised to see the Austrings standing with Mary. No police yet.

Jasper glanced at Cookie. Her sister's face held its habitual look of amused acceptance which Jasper envied. Her own face tended to give away whatever she was feeling, and right now, that was a whole lot of confusion and fear. She hoped she could learn to grow calmer without having to follow in Cookie's footsteps and learn to commune with the dead. Not that there was anything wrong with dead people. Jasper just wanted to learn how to really live in the now before she started spending time in the later. "What are you doing here?" she blurted out.

Kiefer Austring said, "If this is going to be our house, we need to know what's going on."

His wife Emily put a restraining hand on his arm. She moved in front of him. "What my husband means is, 'What the hell is going on here?' We understand there's another dead man. Two bodies in two weeks. Our bank is going to cancel our pre-approval if this keeps up."

Cookie said, "These bodies belong to our fathers."

"Well, what are they doing dying here?" Emily asked.

"Couldn't this have been prevented?" Kiefer Austring demanded.

Jasper turned to Cookie. "Would you speak to them? I don't think I can."

Cookie said quietly, "I don't think rational or empathetic are in their makeup."

"Yes, couldn't this have been prevented?" Mary Clippert said. Her eyes were inflamed with a look that Jasper thought she had seen in a silent movie by that old Danish director. What was his name? Dwyer? Dyer? Dreiser!

Jasper was having a hard time keeping her mind on the moment. She stared silently at Mary Clippert and the Austrings.

"It's ridiculous that you are blaming my sister," Cookie said.

"Of course you would stand up for her," Mary said.

"Maybe it's the house. Maybe the house has something wrong with it," Emily Austring said.

"There is nothing wrong with my house, my father's house," Mary said.

"Nothing other than him falling down the basement stairs," Kiefer Austring said. "We might have to lower our offering price."

"How do you know he fell down the steps?" Jasper asked.

"You can't get away with that!" Mary told the Austrings.

"It's not as if you *ladies* were keeping your voices down," Kiefer said. "Wait and see what we're able to do. This house is losing value every day. It's blighted property."

Mary took a step toward him. Cookie blocked her - the way Jasper had seen her once jump in front of her children when they were little at a busy intersection.

Jasper forced herself to concentrate on the here and now. "So when did you get here?" she asked the Austrings.

"And who you let in?" Mary wanted to know.

"Jasper? Are you in here?" a man's voice asked. The front door pushed wide open and in walked Esteban and Tony. "Hey, the door was unlocked," Esteban said. "Grace sent us. She was worried about you."

Ted Phillips barged in, all big and sweaty. "What the hell is going on now?" he demanded.

Tony shrugged. Esteban said, "He brought us."

Glenn Relerford came in next. The room had gotten quite crowded. He looked right at Jasper and asked, "Who called 911?"

"I don't remember. One of them," Jasper said. Her sloppy mind must be due to delayed shock, she supposed.

"I did," Cookie said. "There's a body in the basement."

"Show me." Glenn's tone was sharp.

Jasper followed them.

Mary dogged her footsteps. "He's my father," she said.

The Austrings fell into step behind Mary. "It's our house," Kiefer Austring said.

The men from the auction house stayed put in the living room. They did not look eager to join the death parade.

Glenn stopped. Mary Clippert jammed into Jasper's backside. The Austrings nearly tripped over Mary. "Who found him?" Glenn asked.

Jasper raised her hand. "That would be me."

"Miss Biggs. Come."

"Officer, I refuse to be left out in the cold," Mary said.

"What about us?" the Austrings said in one voice.

Glenn raised his hands as if he were directing traffic at an accident scene. Jasper supposed that, in a way, he was. "You, you, you, you and you," he said, pointing at Mary, the Austrings, Esteban and Tony. "Stay here."

"Hey!" Ted Phillips shouted.

"And you," Glenn said. "Wait here." He ushered Cookie and Jasper ahead of him.

In the dank cellar, Ray Clippert was right where they had last seen him.

"He's definitely dead," Jasper mumbled. Dizziness hit her hard. She sank to the floor alongside the body.

When she woke up a short while later, attended to by her sister who held a wet cloth on her forehead, Jasper realized that she had been in what has been called a dead faint. "Am I dead?" she murmured.

"Not even close." Cookie planted a tender little kiss on her sister's forehead.

Chapter 24

"Just tell us exactly what happened," Glenn Relerford said to Jasper.

Jasper sat across from him at a simple metal table in an interview room downtown at the Forest Grove Police Department. When they'd arrived, Jasper, Cookie and Mary Clippert had been escorted to separate rooms to give their versions of what transpired before and after the discovery of Ray Clippert's body. Both Glenn and the uniformed officer appeared solemn.

"I know this is very serious," Jasper said. "So I want to be accurate."

Glenn nodded.

Jasper smiled weakly at his patience. "And I know maybe you think that because I'm an auctioneer and all that possibly I have a good memory for details under stress…" Jasper spoke using a lot of hand gestures, a sure sign of her nervousness. She caught herself and clasped her hands together atop the table. It felt sticky. She brought her hands back down to her lap. She wished for hand sanitizer but didn't see any in the room. "The thing is that I'm not sure I have it all straight in my head. And I don't want to do anything to steer you wrong." She paused. Took a deep breath. And started coughing.

"You want some water, Jasper?" Glenn asked. Everybody knew that Glenn was her neighbor and it was such a small town, no biggie to go by first names. "Sheila, would you?" he asked the officer. She left the room.

Glenn leaned closer to Jasper. "Listen, there's no way I think you had any kind of involvement in the old guy's death. This is just following protocol. You understand?"

Jasper nodded through her cough.

"It's not like I have anything but fond regards for you. You know what I'm saying?"

"I *–cough* – think so," Jasper said. There was something about the intensity of his gaze that was doing nothing to calm her cough. She shook her head. "You're confusing me."

Sheila returned. "Leave the woman alone," she told Glenn. "Here, honey. You've been through enough today without having to worry about this guy's intentions."

Jasper sipped some water. That and Sheila's presence seemed to do the trick. Jasper dribbled some of the water onto her hands, wiped them together, then down her slacks. Did Glenn have *intentions* toward her? Intentions was such an old-fashioned word.

"So you and your sister and Ms. Clippert were all inside the house conducting this séance, you were saying." Glenn crossed his arms over his solid toned abs. He was all business now.

What was going on here that she would notice his abs? At a time like this. Was she harboring intentions toward him? She took another sip. "Well not a séance exactly. More like a clearing, I think that's the right technical term when you're checking to see what if any or which of any ghost or disembodied spirits, I guess you could say, are still hanging around, so you can ask them, or in some cases, order them to leave. You could check with my sister."

Officer Sheila patted Jasper's shoulder.

"Whatever," Glenn said. "Go on. Where were you in the house?"

"Upstairs."

"On the ground floor?"

"Yes."

"All together. All three of you there together?"

"That's right." Jasper thought about it. "Mary met us there when Cookie and I arrived."

"On the first floor?"

"The front door's on the first floor," Jasper said. "Excuse me. I didn't mean to sound sarcastic."

"You're just overwrought," Sheila said.

"Yes, yes I am," Jasper said. "You're being very kind to me."

Glenn said, "You're fine. Just go on with your story."

But Jasper was having a hard time concentrating. That remark from Sheila about not worrying about Glenn's intentions had set her to worrying about his intentions. Why was he sitting so close to her with his knee nearly touching hers, for instance, while Sheila the other cop stood several feet away? Jasper adjusted her chair a few inches away from Glenn.

"Are you nervous, Miss Biggs?"

And why this "Miss Biggs" stuff all of a sudden? "You were crowding me a little bit, that's all," Jasper said.

"It's not a very large room," he said.

"I've been in tighter spots," Jasper said.

"Oh, yeah?" Glenn, it turned out, was one of those people who could raise a single eyebrow at a time.

"Oh, brother," Sheila said. "Jasper, Miss Biggs, I think the others are done. Why don't you and your sister get out of here and get some rest."

"What about Mary? She's my, our client, I guess," Jasper said.

"We'll look after Miss Clippert," Sheila said.

Jasper got wearily to her feet.

"Sorry to put you on overtime," Glenn said.

"Couldn't be helped," Jasper said. She turned to go. Cookie stood waiting in the now open doorway.

"Hey, Jasper," Glenn said in a softer tone. "You stay out of trouble now, okay? I don't want nothin' happening to my one and only lady auctioneer."

Jasper felt a quiver in her stomach. Was this flirting what he was doing?

"Enough is enough," Sheila said, giving Glenn a stern look. "You get out of here, hon," she told Jasper. "Take her home," she said to Cookie. "You've both had a long day."

Cookie and Jasper trailed out of the police station arm in arm. "You know, I'm pretty sure he likes you," Cookie said.

"I'm pretty sure he's not allowed to," Jasper responded.

"I thought he was separated."

"Separated is as separated does, I guess." Jasper yawned.

"What does that expression mean anyway? I've never understood that 'is as does' thing."

"I just like the way it sounds. Kind of cynical, you know. Worldly maybe?"

"Cute. That's what I have to say for you, Sis. You are cute."

"Thank you."

"Want me to drive?" Cookie asked. "I can drop you off and get you back your car tomorrow."

Jasper was tempted, but something inside her rallied. She slapped her cheeks to wake herself up. "Nope. You be the passenger. I'm tired of just going along for the ride."

"You made a little joke there." They climbed into the car. "Just as I said, you are a cutie, Jasper."

"You too, Sister Mine."

Chapter 25

The next morning at Cookie's office, Medium Rare, the twins relaxed as they went over the details of the aborted clearing the night before at the Clippert's house. The discovery of Ray Clippert's body had upset everything and everybody all over again.

Cookie sat with her feet tucked under her on one of her rose-colored wingback chairs. Jasper lay on the Oriental rug with her own bare feet propped up on the other wingback. It was a posture she'd learned in yoga classes in the church hall, and it definitely eased the tension out of her sore back.

"What I don't get," Cookie was saying, "is why I didn't catch on right away that it was Ray Clippert."

"You mean the other ghost."

"Spirit," Cookie corrected. "I mean, not enough to recognize him for who he was. Darn it. I hate it when I don't get it exact."

"Don't be silly. I mean, don't be so hard on yourself, Sis. You did say it wasn't just Jimmy who had showed up, right?"

"Mm-hmm."

"You said something about another father figure stepping forth, didn't you?" Jasper let go of her neck muscles so her head could loll back against the floor. Now that she was settled in near the person in the world with whom she could totally relax, her memories of the scene appeared vividly in her mind. "You knew that some other guy was waiting in line behind Jimmy."

"You're right." Cookie resettled herself in the chair. "I did see another somebody, another man, stepping forward. Keep going, keep going, Sis. The more you say aloud, the more it comes back to me. When I go into medium mode, sometimes I don't remember much of it afterward."

Jasper laughed. "I'm sure you and I were just about the best witnesses the police have ever interviewed."

Cookie groaned. "Yeah. They won't be calling on us anytime soon. At least I hope not. Anyway, I do remember another man. But why couldn't I tell who it was? You'd think that since he hadn't been dead all that long that he'd want to announce who he was right away."

"Wait a minute now," Jasper protested. "You only had long enough for that wind to blow through the room. That was just a few seconds. Besides, aren't you the one who told me that people who've just arrived on the other side can be pretty confused about what's going on?"

"Well, yes, that's true. Except we don't know for sure how long he'd been dead."

"I saw him a few hours before at the nursing home. And Mary saw him after that."

"Are you sure you trust her to tell us the truth?" Cookie asked.

"I saw her. At least I saw her car pull in. She didn't see me, I didn't think. And then, I think I saw her just a little bit later down at the river. She must've seen me then, but she didn't stop."

"Hmm."

"I don't think that means much," Jasper reflected. "She's not the friendliest person but that doesn't make her a liar."

"I need a manicure," Cookie said.

"So what did this guy look like? Or what was his personality like? Any clues?" Jasper asked.

Cookie picked the nail polish off one of her pink-edged toes. "And a pedicure." She closed her eyes. "He was kind of tall. And…" her voice trailed off. "Kind of basic, I guess you could say."

"Basic," Jasper repeated. She scooted her bottom closer to the chair and rolled her neck from side to side. This was almost like a do-it-yourself massage. More tension eased out of her body.

"Yeah, basic. I don't like to speak ill of the dead – "

"Not you!" Jasper teased.

Cookie laughed a little. "Not to say that he was stupid, but maybe someone not used to discussing the fine points of anything." She pursed her lips in concentration. "Not used to discussing his own psychology, that's for sure."

"That sounds like you're getting more information on him now. Are you tuned in to him right now?" When Cookie didn't respond, Jasper rolled onto her side and sat up.

Cookie's eyes were closed. Was it Jasper's imagination or was Cookie's blondish hair doing that halo shimmer thing again?

"He's here now. Yes, it is Ray Clippert."

"Where? Where exactly is he?" Jasper looked nervously around the room.

Cookie giggled. She opened her eyes. "He's standing right next to you," she said.

Jasper's arms goose-pimpled from wrists to shoulders. She didn't know if that was from the ghost, the spirit, of Ray Clippert or just her own nervousness. How did Cookie stay calm in the midst of talking to dead people?

"He says there's nothing to be afraid of. Uh-huh. But he still likes to scare women a little. Behave yourself, Ray, or I'll send you away!" Cookie said.

Jasper felt the everyday warmth of the room envelop her. The chills went away. "Ask him how he died," Jasper whispered.

"Now, now, it's okay," Cookie said. "We don't have to rush things, Mr. Clippert. Okay, Ray."

"Did I scare *him?*" Jasper asked.

Cookie kept her eyes closed. "You came to us. What is it you want to say?" She spoke soothingly in a way Jasper had heard her speak to her daughter and son when they were little. Cookie had transplanted skills from her old job of raising children to her new one of soothing spirits so that they could communicate with the living. "He's saying the word, *secret.* Or maybe *secrets.*"

"Secrets," Jasper repeated. "What secrets?"

Cookie's eyes flew open. "He's gone." She yawned. "He just kept saying the word. Then he left. Either he didn't have the energy to stay here any longer, or he wasn't ready to divulge." Cookie stretched and stood up. "Want some coffee or maybe tea?" She headed for the kitchenette at the back of her office.

Jasper followed. "What do you suppose he meant? Coffee for me please unless you have some Lady Grey."

"Fresh out of Mrs. Grey today. I'll make us some French roast. I need strong."

"Strong is good."

Cookie got a bag of ground coffee out of the small refrigerator and reached out a coffee filter from the cupboard.

Jasper leaned against the counter. "I just wish he had finished saying what he wanted to say."

"I guess he said all he could for today," Cookie said, pausing in mid-scoop. "I have a feeling we'll hear from him again."

As Jasper sat next to her sister a few minutes later sipping from a hot mug of strong coffee, she wondered just how and when they would hear from the dead Ray Clippert. And when they did, what exactly would he say? What secret or secrets was he going to share?

Chapter 26

That night at home in her apartment on Hickory Lane, Jasper felt restless. The cigarette smoke wafting upward from the O'Neils didn't help. At least she hadn't run into Mrs. O'Neil lately, and she still had not had the dubious pleasure of meeting the Mister. She got up from bed to pee, and narrowly avoided stepping on Proxy the kitten. The little guy was a small black shadow that Jasper wasn't used to having around. He had been with her now for three days ever since she brought him home from the vet where he had been neutered. The chip showed that he had been adopted from the county animal shelter which released the adoptive family's name and phone number to the vet. The family was moving and did not want the kitten back. "You're in your forever home now, little guy, so no worries." Proxy was such a tough little guy that he didn't seem to notice his missing equipment nor need any extra time off from his kittenish duties following the surgery.

Sitting on the toilet, Jasper scooped up the kitten and set him on her lap. She thought his purr sounded like a miniature power tool from the old Milwaukee Electric Tool Corp. "Good lord, I'm really getting into antiques, huh, kitty?" The little guy jumped onto the vanity. "Ouch. You're due for a toenail clipping, pal." She reached for the nail clippers she had put in a small basket by the sink. She pulled her nightgown down and set Proxy back on her lap. He rested on his rump so that all four paws were presented for clipping. She snipped off the sharp pointy end of each nail, avoiding getting too close to the sensitive quick, as the vet had instructed her. It was all over and done with in 30 seconds. Jasper kissed the top of Proxy's head. "I think you are an unusual cat," she said. He mrowed loudly in response.

She and Proxy were tucked back in bed, the kitten insisting on sleeping under the blanket between Jasper's ankles, when her cell phone sounded with Leroy Vandyke's "The Auctioneer Song." She felt glad she had substituted the new ringtone for the default Halleluiah Chorus of her past life. But still. She grabbed up the phone. 4:15 a.m! *Unknown number*, the phone said. Should she answer? The trouble with cell phones was that you had to make up your mind in a hurry. She hesitated too long. The song ceased. Jasper set the phone down on the 1960s TV tray she had gotten herself at the auction for use as a bedside table. She switched off the lamp, a garish candy red one from the 1950s that had made her laugh when she won the proxy bid for it. She wasn't laughing now. She lay in the dark for a couple minutes wondering who had called her in the middle of the night. Then she grabbed up her phone. The caller had left a message. She dialed voicemail and tapped in her password.

"Better keep yourself to yourself," a harsh voice said. And that was that.

Man, woman, boy, girl, machine? Jasper couldn't tell. Even under her soft blanket with the kitten nestled in, she shivered. "Here, Proxy," she said in a small shaky voice. "Come visit your mama. She needs you." She coaxed the cat up and snuggled it next to her chest. It was snoring lightly in just a few seconds. Jasper held it close as she lay awake wondering and worrying about the menacing call. Somebody else was awake and worried enough to go to the trouble of a phone call in the middle of the night. Someone who had her number.

The next morning Jasper still felt uneasy. She considered phoning that nice Ginny Gardener next door, who had offered to help her in any way she could, for cat-sitting services. But that would mean the older lady would have to climb the slopes of Mount Smoky to reach Jasper's apartment. Or Proxy would have to go next door. Jasper didn't trust the active kitten to stay out of trouble and avoid destroying her neighbor's house or getting himself hurt.

Jasper got out the harness and leash she had purchased for Proxy. "Let's give this a go, huh, buddy? Want to take a walk?" Twenty minutes later after several minor wrestling matches with the cat, interspersed with games of catch-me-if-you-can, the little black cat was safely secured in his red sequined harness and leash. He looked up at her with his huge green eyes as if to say, Now what? Jasper scooped him up and carried him down the stairs, tucking his head under her arm to protect him from the cigarette smoke. Stairs were too much for the first time anyway. He could learn to walk on his leash outside.

Proxy gave Jasper her first lesson in how to walk a cat. She learned how to go whatever direction the cat decided to go. She learned that she should wait patiently while the cat sat and sniffed the air. And she learned that walking a cat was no way for a human to get any exercise.

She was sitting on the sidewalk a couple feet behind Proxy who was studying a crack waiting for ants or other small prey to appear when a shadow momentarily blocked out the sunshine.

"Hey, neighbor. Taking Fido for a stroll I see." Glenn Relerford squatted down next to them. Proxy pounced on the handsome policeman's bare knee. He was wearing black running shorts and matching muscle shirt. He had the muscles for it. "Tough guy, eh?" He gently took the kitten by the scruff of his neck and flipped him over on his back. Proxy extended what little claws he had left and attacked the policeman's big hand. Their wrestling match was a delight to Jasper.

"Getting some exercise?" Jasper asked. "You look like you're dressed for it."

"Naw, this? I can do this in my sleep." Glenn's grin was infectious.

Jasper laughed. "I mean, you going for a run? Or something?" His stare was so straight-on from his chocolate eyes into her hazel ones that Jasper turned her attention back to the kitty. She said, "Quit beating up the neighbor. He's a cop. You can get in trouble." The kitten yowled mightily. Jasper picked him up by his harness, set him on his four feet, and patted his tail end. She and Glenn got to their feet. Maybe Glenn could give her some advice on how seriously to take the call from last night. Annoying, dangerous or somewhere in between?

"Never seen anyone walk a cat before," Glenn said. "You get dragged much?"

This guy really gave her a case of the giggles. "No-o-o. Not much."

"I'm just out enjoying the sun. Might take a walk myself. Care to join me?" He glanced behind him and at the windows of the neighbors.

"Must be tough, I mean being the only policeman in the neighborhood and all."

"And *all* is right, lady. You can say it, I know what color I am. Compared to all you *chalkcasians*, I'm more like the blackboard in this classroom of life."

"Wow, a philosopher too."

"I practice in my spare time. Come on, let's go over by the cemetery."

"But the cat…"

"Bring him along," Glenn said.

Jasper leaned down to pick up Proxy and he jumped onto her shoulder. "Wow, did you see that? This is one smart little kitty, yes he is." The kitten purred into her ear.

"Enough with the baby talk now. You two can do that when you're alone again. C'mon," Glenn said.

Soon they were walking through the lawn bordering the cemetery. "This is where we first met," Glenn said.

"Uh-huh." Jasper scratched the kitten's head. Having him along made the conversation with Glenn much easier. The cat gave them both a small diversion when they needed one.

"Yes, ma'am, the scene of your first crime in our fair village," Glenn said.

That remark stopped Jasper in her tracks. "My first crime?"

"Hey, I'm just joking. Cop humor. You know."

Jasper set Proxy on the ground and trotted after him as he chased after a loose leaf. Glenn walked over and took her by the arm. She shook him off. "There have been two deaths since I came to town. Are you saying I'm a…a person of interest or something?" She had seen a few police dramas on TV.

Glenn started to laugh, then stopped abruptly. "Of course not. Both deaths are considered accidental. Besides, if we wanted to we could have brought you in for questioning."

"You did bring me in for questioning."

"Right, along with the other two who were at the house the day Mr. Clippert died. C'mon, Jasper. It's a sunny day. We both have the afternoon off. You have your new cat. Let's relax for a little while here."

The kitten had keeled over on its side, worn out by two minutes of determined chasing. Jasper gathered him up and held him to her chest like a baby. "We are going home now," she announced. The cat mrowed.

"Can't take a joke, huh?" Glenn called after her.

"Insensitive much?" Jasper said so quietly that only the kitten heard. She was pretty sure.

♦

A short while later, Jasper and the cat were ensconced in Jimmy's apartment at the back of the auction house. She was glad her new pet was so portable. It made sneaking out of her apartment past the neighbors, including a certain confusing detective, that much easier.

The kitten was still such a cozy ball of fur that Jasper delighted in having him nearby doing just about anything. "Hey, Proxy," she said, touching her nose to his. He rubbed his little dark nose against hers, purring loudly. With just a little encouragement and a hand cupped gently under his backside, the kitten climbed up onto her shoulder and wrapped himself around her neck like a furry boa. "You're such a good boy," Jasper told him. Her gentle voice sent him into paroxysms of purring pleasure.

Jasper sat at the kitchen table. Her own apartment didn't feel private enough. She wanted some solid alone time. She'd gotten in the habit of keeping an extra litter box, cat foot, contact solution and lens case there for times like this. She was going over the latest issue of Auctioneer magazine, trying to focus on business for a change and get her mind off the two deaths. A to-go cup of coffee with cream from the closest drive-through sat nearby and she absently sipped from it every few pages. She sighed, and Proxy applied his baby teeth to her ear lobe.

"Ok, little buddy," Jasper said, lifting him off her shoulders and nestling him on her lap, "I know that's a love bite but don't get carried away." She scratched him between his ears and he resettled himself for a nap.

The kitten's gentle breathing and warmth blended with Jasper's own tiredness, and soon she rolled her torso forward over the sleeping kitten and cushioned her head atop her arms on the table.

She came awake with a start. Pounding. Door. Someone was knocking on the door. The noise startled Proxy too, and he jumped down to the floor. Jasper slapped her cheeks to bring herself to full alertness and hurried to the door. Through the peephole she saw a distorted Ted Phillips.

"Okay, okay." She opened the door. "What's going on?"

"Nothing special," Ted said. Without invitation, he stepped inside. "Just wanted to see how you're doin.'"

Jasper told him that all things considered she was doing fine. When he didn't move, she invited him in. "Want some coffee or water or something?"

"Got any Mountain Dew, Sierra Mist, Alpine Spray?"

"Sorry."

"S'okay." Ted sat down, again without invitation, and spread his jean clad legs wide in front of him.

Proxy jumped up on the sofa to check him out.

"Boo," Ted said. The kitten arched his back and hissed. Then he shot to the floor and sprinted to the other side of the room. Ted laughed. "She's a funny little character," he said.

"Yes. He is."

"Like you."

"You're really handing out the compliments today, Ted. What do you want?"

He cleared his throat in a way that said, *What's coming up next is real important. Get ready.* "It seems to me you and me ought to talk about Biggs' Auction. About what its future is with all these…changes going on around here."

"Changes. Right, Ted. Keep going."

"I mean, *our* future."

"Whoa, Nelly. There's no Our future."

"I happen to know that Jimmy was planning to give me a big chunk of the action."

"The action?" Jasper repeated.

"The auction. Biggs Auction House. The business. Jimmy told me I could expect a substantial cut. Maybe even full ownership. You know, auctioneering has been what I wanted to do all my life, Jazz."

"Good. Glad you got that figured out early." Jasper scratched the fabric of the sofa and the kitten trotted over to investigate.

"Pay attention, missy. I got something here to show you." Ted leaned down to Proxy's level. "Boo."

The kitten leapt into the air, then recovered and helicoptered up onto Jasper's lap. Ted handed over a piece of paper dense with typed words. Proxy batted at it.

Ted grabbed it and held it in front of Jasper's face. "Look about halfway down and tell me what you see. Right here."

"Here? Article the Fifth?"

"Yep."

Jasper read aloud, "I do hereby divide and bequeath my business holdings between my longtime business partner, Theodore Phillips and my step daughters, Courtney Jasper Biggs Sherman and Candace Jasper Biggs Rowe, with Mr.

Phillips to maintain controlling interest in Biggs Auction House."

She soothed the kitten onto her lap, where he curled his tail around his body and began purring. She said, "Where did you get this? I don't remember hearing anything about it."

Ted spread his jeaned legs further apart than Jasper would have thought possible. He leaned back and spread his arms out across the back of the sofa. "I guess Jimmy didn't think you needed to know."

"I changed my life to work at the auction house..." Jasper felt all sputtery. The idea of working under Ted Phillips with entitlement to greater power unnerved her. The kitten sensed her unease and fled to the kitchen in search of comfort food.

"Jimmy came up with a job to help you out," Ted said. "He knew your marriage was falling apart and he didn't want you to end up on the streets."

"What?" Jasper got to her feet.

"He didn't think you really had it in you to make it in the auction business. Or any business, I guess. But maybe if you worked alongside him and me. And you and me got to spend more time together. Maybe everything would work out. If you get my drift." Ted stood and looked down at Jasper. He decreased her personal space.

Jasper turned her back on him. Suddenly his arms wound around her. Jasper went into instinctive self-defense mode. She raised her right foot and brought it down hard on the top of Ted's foot.

"Crazy bitch," he yelled. "What are you playing at, lady?"

Jasper faced him and backed him toward the door. "This is not a game, Mister Phillips. The name on the sign says

Biggs Auction. And you and I – not *me*, Ted, *I* - are not drifting anywhere together."

Proxy gave one of his enormous meows from the kitchen.

"He needs me," Jasper said. "Maybe Jimmy didn't need me. But that little guy out there – he needs me. And I don't need you." Jasper stomped off to see about the cat. "Close the door so Proxy doesn't get out," she yelled back over her shoulder. In the kitchen, she stood panting heavily for a moment until she heard the apartment door slam shut. Then she lifted the kitten down from on top of the refrigerator. He licked her cheek. "I'd rather have a junior mountain climber like you instead of a good ol' boy bid-caller any day of the week," Jasper told him. She held her pet up in the air and turned in a slow circle so he could survey the upper realms. "You're new to the job," she said. "But you'll do all right." The kitten gave a mighty little roar in response.

Her cell phone buzzed at her to say a message had arrived. It was a text from Ted. It read: *M clip here come now office.*

Chapter 27

Feeling deeply curious, Jasper let herself in the auction house's side door and made her way to the front office. Mary Clippert was there, planted like somebody else's Rottweiler on the leather chesterfield. Her face held its usual dogged look with jowls dragging down her jaw line.

"Miss Clippert has some concerns," Ted boomed. He took a seat behind the executive mahogany desk that had once been Jimmy's.

Jasper stood for a moment not wanting to get any closer to the other woman's anger. But after a glare from Ted, she took a place at the other end of the couch down the way from Mary Clippert.

Ted asked, "What can we do for you?"

Mary Clippert glared at Jasper, then faced Ted. Jasper decided to act mature and avoid sticking out her tongue. She settled for rolling her eyes heavenward.

Mary Clippert sniffed like a bulldog rooting through garbage, "It's about my father's contract with this auction house."

"All perfectly legal, all fine," Ted said.

As if he's a lawyer. As if he really knows what he's doing. Jasper's resentment toward Ted bubbled back up. Didn't take much.

"Well it's not all right. It's not perfectly fine," Mary said.

"What's the matter with it?" Jasper asked bluntly. Some of her careful politeness had worn thin.

"Everything is the matter with it."

Jasper groaned. To hell with professionalism.

Ted jumped in hurriedly to smooth the waters. "I'm sure we can work this out to everyone's satisfaction. After all, we are in possession of your father's items and we want to get top dollar for everything in the estate."

"There may be some items I don't want to part with after all."

Jasper sat back with a smile on her face. If Ted wanted to be Top Dog, let him dig his way out of this one.

"I can tell you. And Miss Biggs here can tell you," Ted said, trying to share the sudden negative responsibility with Jasper, "we have already got the advertising out on your father's estate."

Mary lifted her chin. "On his Living estate," she said. "I've seen the ads and the flyers and your website. They all say the same thing: 'The Living Estate of Raymond Clippert.' In case you haven't noticed, my father is no longer living."

"Sorry about your loss," Ted said solemnly.

"He's not lost. He's dead," cranky Mary said.

Ted picked up a pen from the desk and twirled it around in his fingers. "But it is still an estate, and we will be going ahead with the auction." He leaned forward with that sly smile on his face that Jasper had seen him use with women, herself included. "We can't bring your father back, but we can do all we can to help you out. And if we change the auction bill at this late date, I guarantee there'll be a drop-off in attendance at the auction. Fewer people. Fewer bids. Fewer dollars. Guaranteed."

"Huh! Bad news for the auction house," Mary said. "You with your ten percent commission."

"It's standard," Ted said, probably about to launch into the usual spiel about how the ten percent that Biggs Auction collected might be more than some auction houses, but it was rapidly becoming an industry standard, and an amount that never got in the way of the highest bidding this side of the Mississippi…

Mary leaned in. "I don't want people paying 10 percent. That's my money," she said. "Besides that, I think she – "She paused to point an accusing red lacquered nail at Jasper. – killed him."

"What?!" Ted and Jasper said in the same second.

Mary hoisted herself up to her full height. She took a tango step toward the door and twirled back toward them with extra drama. "Furthermore, I'm going to tell the police about my suspicions."

Jasper lunged toward the bigger woman. Jasper had never before felt capable of murder, but for an instant she pictured the satisfaction of squeezing the smug smirk off Mary Clippert's face. Ted grabbed Jasper from behind, and gripped her in such a strong hold that this time there was no escaping him.

Mary tromped away. Ted did not release Jasper until the sound of the front door lock turning and the door opening and closing had stilled.

"That woman!" Jasper spluttered and fumed. She kicked one of the tree root legs of the Indonesian coffee table masquerading as a piece from the Northwoods.

"Don't hurt the table. You don't want to hurt the table. You want to boot the Clippert bitch."

"You're right." Even though Ted had just displayed insight that she wouldn't have ever thought him capable of, Jasper kicked the leg again.

Ted lifted her up and set her down on the sofa. Jasper was so surprised she just stayed seated.

"Now listen," he said. "We've gotta get her back on our side."

"We, Ted? Did you just say 'we?'"

"Cut it out. This is serious stuff here."

"Yeah! She's going to tell the police that I killed her father."

"They're gonna shrug that off. That is, unless you had something to do with it."

"Ted!"

"Can't you tell when a guy's kidding? You didn't kill him, did you?"

Jasper whimpered into her hands.

"Hey, just kidding! I've got an idea."

"Oh, lord," Jasper said. "It's come to this? What, Ted? What is your big brilliant idea?"

Ted squirmed in close to her. She scooted away. Good idea or not, he was still Ready Teddy. "It's pretty much common knowledge that I have a way with the ladies." He squirmed nearer, Jasper scooted further. "So I'm thinkin' we'll split up the chores that need to be done here."

"Chores?"

"I'll handle her – "

Jasper shuddered at the thought of how Ted's smarmy hands might handle Mary Clippert.

"And you can take care of your pal the cop."

Jasper had to forcibly close her wide open mouth. She couldn't speak.

"You know, Glenn Ruffledfur or whatever his name is."

"I know who you mean, Ted. And it's Relerford, by the way."

"So what do you say, Jazz? Ready to go to work for the cause?"

"You want me to seduce a policeman so that things go easier for the auction house?"

"You are such a little prude. Jimmy had your number all right." Ted shook his head and snorted. He wiped his nose with the back of his hand. "You don't have to marry him, for Pete's sake. And it's just as much for you as it is for the auction. You're the one whose ass is going to get hauled off to jail. Might as well put your sweet ass to better use."

Jasper slapped him hard across the face. "That's for pretending to be on my side," she said.

"Am I interrupting something?" another man's voice asked. Sean Solberg stood in the doorway.

Ted was rubbing his jaw. "What the hell are you doing in here? We're closed."

"The door was open – at least it was unlocked," Sean said in his wonderful velvet voice. His eyes shone satin-blue today, deepened in color by the chambray shirt he wore that fit him so well, Jasper thought, neither too loose nor too form fitting. He had a pretty nice build. She kept her gaze from straying down to his chinos.

"How are you?" Jasper asked.

He beamed. *And what nice teeth you have, not too white. Just right.* Jasper was beginning to feel like a wolf. "Everything fine here?" Sean asked.

Ted's face deepened to rose madder. He picked up an antique paperweight from the desk and tossed it from palm to palm.

Jasper linked her arm through Sean's. "How about we step outside?"

"Phillips," Sean said by way of good-bye.

"Solberg," said Ted, equally solemn.

Outside Jasper told Sean about the visit from Mary Clippert and her threat to go to the police.

"There's got to be a way to clear this up," Sean said.

"Not you too!"

"Did I say something wrong?"

"Sorry, Sean." It was the first time Jasper had used his name and she liked the way it felt on her tongue. "Ted was just presenting me with his brilliant plan." She shuddered.

"I take it it wasn't so brilliant. So?"

"Promise you won't laugh, okay? He plans to sweet-talk Mary Clippert," Jasper said.

"Sweet talk." Sean wasn't laughing but his smile had grown wider.

"You know – seduce her. Win her over in bed," Jasper said. If she had had freckles they would have lit up like shooting stars.

"Oh, you mean go all the way. Score a home run."

"Stop it," Jasper said, laughing.

"Put that little bat of his to good use."

"Stop, stop, stop. You're making my stomach hurt."

"It's good for you. You need more laughter in your life," Sean said. "So that's Phillips' not-so-brilliant plan."

"You haven't heard all of it," Jasper said, still laughing. "He wants me to go after Glenn Relerford."

Sean turned on his heel and headed back to the auction house. Jasper ran after him and grabbed his arm. "Now really stop," she said. "If I knew you were going to get mad, I wouldn't have said anything."

Sean took her hands in his. "Look. Jasper. That guy is an idiot. I know you work here. It's your legacy from your father –

"Stepfather."

"Stepfather. He brought you in to his roughshod business because you were in a fix and needed a job. But Phillips is a complete idiot and if you keep working with him, you're gonna lose IQ points on a daily basis. You're better than this place."

Jasper's heart hurt a little. "Thanks for caring," she said, meaning exactly the opposite.

"Now who's mad?"

"Let go of my hands so I can tell you what I really think." Jasper tugged but Sean held tight.

"Don't run away. That doesn't solve anything. I'm just saying that you're a talented lady. You can get a different job. You don't have to stay here and lose your soul."

Jasper tugged harder and this time Sean let her go. "You want to save my soul? I had too many years living with a man who wanted to save my soul! I don't need some crazy guy I just met trying to tell me how to manage my life."

"You think I'm crazy?" Sean's voice had wilted.

Jasper told herself she should count to ten. She counted to two and continued her rant. "You think your soul is doing well? You live alone out on a hilltop in the country making art that people don't get. You can't even take care of a little cat that needed a new home. You're selfish, Sean Solberg!" Jasper began to sob there in the parking lot of Biggs Auction House.

"Hey, hey now," Sean said. He tried to draw her in close for a hug but Jasper was having none of it. She pushed him away. Sean said, "Don't walk away now. We can talk this through. I am selfish. I know myself pretty well."

"You, you… You are an egomaniac." Jasper could barely get out the words. Her coughing and hiccupping were mixing in with her tears.

"Yes, you're right. I have a big ego. You're getting hysterical. Calm down."

Sean's very reasonableness only made matters worse. "I am not hysterical!" Jasper yelled at the top of her lungs.

"Quiet down now. Please. Somebody's going to call the police."

The police! How dare he remind her of the police! She was sick of the police. Jasper had had all she could take. She left Sean standing there and, dizzy and ailing from all the drama, stumbled back on her own two feet to Jimmy's apartment. Her feet might not be man-size but they'd been with her forever and right now she liked them better than any male in her life.

Except for Proxy cat. She opened the door to the apartment and the little guy trotted over to greet her. He stretched his paws up her calves, and she gathered him up and looked him right in the eyes. Jasper and Proxy exchanged a trusting blink.

Chapter 28

Monday morning Jasper worked hard alongside the rest of the auction crew, trying to winnow out saleable items from the glut of consignments clogging the back storage room. A certain order of progression was supposed to take place with items that had been consigned first sold first. But after Jimmy's death, things had grown disorganized. People were beginning to complain that that they had waited much too long for their stuff to be sold. While Grace and Kelly handled phone calls, paperwork, and customers stopping in to pay for their auction buys from the week before, Esteban and Tony brought out cart after endless cart filled with stuff from the far back of the giant storage room. There was particleboard furniture from consigner No. 7, dolls and dolls and more dolls from No. 99, and assorted art glass from 111.

It was going to be a junky sale, Jasper thought. People didn't realize that if they could be patient, the auctioneers would place their everyday stuff in sales seeded with other consignors' gems, and everything would bring more money. Ted told her they would just bow to the demands of the complainers and get some of the backlog out of the way. Jasper thought he was wrong. He was just being lazy.

To tell the truth, Jasper knew she was being lazy too. She wanted to avoid any more confrontations with Ted – at least until all the legal matters concerning Biggs Auction got sorted out. She was tired, so tired her neck and back ached and her head swam as if she'd been traveling for much too long. She would like for the last leg of her current journey to come to an end but she could not foresee when and how that would ever be.

So she kept sorting through boxfuls of items from storage, working robotically alongside Ted at the back table, and breaking away for a quick cup of bad coffee from the snack bar whenever she could. It was nearly dark by the time she and Ted had broken down the last consignment, tossed away the mildewed linens and broken china, and numbered the groups of stuff to be arranged on the auction tables the next day.

"Want to get a bite to eat?" Ted asked. He rubbed the back of his neck.

For once Jasper didn't feel any untoward vibrations emanating off her fellow auctioneer. He seemed just plain tired like herself.

"Sure, that sounds like a good idea," Jasper said. Then her heart sank and the hair on the back of her neck stood on end as Ted reached toward her and pulled her into a bear hug.

"Mmmm," he growled.

"Ted!" She pushed away from him. "Forget it!" She stomped toward the front office to retrieve her purse and keys.

"Oh, come on, Jazz, just kidding," Ted whined.

She kept going but flung back over her shoulder, "You wouldn't want to go where I'm going anyway. The Forester is a great place. Nice people working there too. Oh, especially that waitress named... Margo? Maggie? No, I know – Molly!"

"Bitch," Ted said.

At the Forester, Jasper took a seat near the window. Molly greeted her. "Hey, hon, you're looking pretty shitty."

"Thanks, Molly." She downed half a glass of the ice water the waitress had automatically set in front of her. Jasper ordered a bread bowl of lobster bisque and a glass of pinot grigio. She was mentally going through the cupboards and refrigerator in her Hickory Lane apartment, trying to decide whether she absolutely had to stop at the grocery store on the way home. Although she was out of milk so Proxy would be deprived the couple tablespoons full he got as a treat, the box of kitten food held plenty of dry kibble. The grocery store could wait. Jasper's shoulders sagged in relief.

She was nearly done with the creamy bisque and starting to work her way through the artisan bread when Molly plopped down on the chair across from her. She propped her feet up on the bench next to Jasper. "Don't mind me," she said.

"Your ankles are so swollen! Poor thing."

"Comes with the territory. Everything is kind of puffed out right now," Molly said.

"How much longer do you have?"

"I saw my doctor today. He tells me it could be anytime in the next week. "

"Wow." Jasper really did feel impressed. Having expected a child only once and with that pregnancy ending in a miscarriage early on, she always felt in awe of women about to bring full-term babies into the world. A little sad. But mostly amazed. "You ready for this?" she asked the younger woman.

Molly shrugged. "Yeah, I guess. Don't have any choice." She launched into a description of the room her mother was helping her set up for the baby at her apartment. Yellows, greens, pinks and blues with a circus theme.

"Colorful. Don't know yet if it's a girl or a boy?"

"Don't you trust your sister's psychic predictions?"

Jasper just smiled.

"Nope. I'm doing it the old-fashioned way," Molly said.

Jasper took a slug of wine. "What about the father?"

"What *about* the father? Wish I could have some of that wine right now. Oh well, soon enough."

Jasper hesitated. It really was none of her business. But still. "I mean, will the baby's father be there for the birth?"

"That jerk? Conception was all he cared about. Yeah. They all really like the conception part."

Jasper plunged in. "So you know for sure who the father is?"

"Oh, sure. And believe me, he's gonna cough up child care. I have an uncle – well, more like a good friend of my mom's – who's a lawyer and he's gonna make sure that sucker starts sending the checks."

Jasper downed her wine. It had been a long day. "Well just who is the dad? You never told me!"

Molly lowered her voice. "Well, actually, I've got it narrowed down to two guys I was dating at the time. Both of them heavy believers in sex without strings – or rubbers for that matter. Coupla jerks."

"You mean you're going to have to go through paternity testing and all that?"

"Shhh. Keep your voice down. The baby's gonna tell me when it comes out."

"I think I need another glass of wine," Jasper said.

Molly waved to the bartender and pointed at Jasper's empty goblet. "It's on me," she said. The two women waited until Jasper had taken one more sip from the refilled glass. Then Molly whispered earnestly, "See, the baby is gonna be either chocolate or vanilla. That way I'll know where to send the bill."

"Oh-h-h," Jasper said. "I get it. But what if it turns out to be butterscotch?"

Molly giggled. She heaved herself up to her feet and swiped away Jasper's glass before she could take another swallow. "You're gonna drive home real slow now, right, Jasper?"

Jasper sighed. "I'll be a good girl," she said. "I guess I don't have a choice."

"That's what friends are for," said Molly.

"You call me if you need anything," Jasper told her. "And let me know when that baby gets here."

"Watch my Facebook page. The kid's gonna be a superstar."

They exchanged cheek kisses and Jasper left for home.

Chapter 29

Jasper paid her bill at the bar, included three dollars for Molly, and then headed out the back of the restaurant through the doors that led to the patio. She made her way past two tables of early diners and exited through the iron gate that was merely latched, never locked. The Honey River reflected the ginger sunset as it ran from right to left just the other side of the path. Jasper headed upriver at a brisk clip. The meal had fortified her, the wine had relaxed her, and away from the repetitive sorting at the auction house, she felt livelier than she had in hours. She breathed in the cool early evening air. She could smell the water. It was a wet, neutral smell, more green than fishy. It interested her nose but didn't overwhelm her. Jasper strode with confidence.

The path led her past sea green benches positioned so that people could sit and stare across to the old millworks whose brick walls had been painted over into a mural of the working people. Old photographs and modern design blended to convey a sense of industry and history. There were even, Jasper noted a little cynically, a few faces of color shown. A big influx of African Americans from Southern states helped build up the Northern factory workforce in the early 20th Century, but it was only recently that their presence and their importance was acknowledged. She wondered whether Glenn cared much about local history.

As she went, Jasper felt the stresses of the past few weeks settling in her lungs and then moving out on her exhale. Except for her moments with her sister, her kitten, and a bit with Molly, life hadn't proved very relaxing of late.

Jasper passed behind the Angel Museum, the old church that had been reconverted into an unusual little tourist spot. Jimmy used to do benefit auctions for the Angel Museum. Maybe she could give them a hand one of these days – if things ever calmed down in her life. Just thinking about Her Life and about Jimmy brought tension back into Jasper's body, and she determined to make her mind go blank and just enjoy the fresh air and exercise.

When she walked behind the old power plant, however, she suddenly felt as if she were not alone. She glanced at the blocky brick structure on her right, then at the waterfall created by the dam on her left. Even now in early spring, and close to dusk, there were fishermen down in their boats on the Honey. What did they catch? Jasper wondered. There was movement in the shadows of the power plant. Then gone again. Was she so tired she was seeing things?

She hadn't met any other walkers yet. But, no worries, people had told her the river walk was perfectly safe even for a single woman striding along with a canvas purse strap slung across her chest. Glenn Relerford said there had never been any serious incidents at the river. Jasper paused for a second and gave a good hard stare in the direction of the power plant. There was nothing there. Just the lengthening shadows created by the tired sun.

Soon the sidewalk snaked out toward Riverside Drive and she hurried along. The traffic she faced just to her right was noisier than her mood craved, but there weren't many cars. Rush hour in Forest Grove didn't amount to much. Part of her felt grateful for the dozen or so cars that hurried by. She didn't feel so alone. It was so everyday, she couldn't get spooked by shadows out here.

Still, as she moved along at a rapid pace, Jasper felt as if she were being watched.

She reached the point where the sidewalk trailed down under the bridge supports. She could go that way and maintain her privacy or she could turn right and follow the sidewalk that lined the road.

Under the bridge, she would be lost to sight for a few yards. Cars passing over the bridge above would make too much noise for anyone to hear her if she shouted for help. *Help for what?* she asked herself. Jasper marched in place to use up some of the extra blood her heart was pumping into her system. *It's daylight, for Pete's sake.*

Rev. Tim used to tease her in a mean-spirited way about what a scaredy-cat she was. "You shriek when you see a mouse running across the floor," he had said when they talked about her leaving him. "You think you can make it out there in the big bad world by yourself?"

Jasper squared her shoulders. She grabbed hold of the strap on her shoulder bag, and headed for the shortcut beneath the bridge.

The roar of the river and the echoing traffic sounds combined into white noise that blocked out other sounds. Jasper could no longer hear her own breathing let alone her footfalls against the concrete. She leaned forward as if into a strong headwind and entered the tunnel.

The shove that struck her from behind sent her stumbling close to the river's edge. A teenage couple strolling hand in hand a few yards away dashed toward her. The red-haired boy raced in front of Jasper and braked her fall. His girlfriend grabbed hold of Jasper's purse strap and tugged backwards. Jasper landed on top of the girl with the boy piling atop the two of them. Heavy footsteps raced by them.

In the half minute it took to disentangle the human heap, the other person had run out of sight. "Everybody okay?" the young man asked. "Maddie? Madison? You okay?"

"Yeah, yeah," the dark-skinned girl with long mahogany curls said. "Sorry about your purse, lady." She handed back Jasper's bag, its strap broken. "Are you all right?"

"Sorry I kind of crushed you," the boy said.

"Yeah, he's sort of big." The girl giggled.

Jasper assured them that she was unhurt and then made sure the girl hadn't been injured. After all, she had been the one on the bottom of the pig pile. "You guys came along at just the right time," she said. "Did you see who pushed me?"

"Not exactly. They were wearing a hoody," the boy said. "Kind of gray or maybe brown. I don't know. How 'bout you, Maddie? Did you get a good look?"

The girl shook her head. "I was kind of focused on keeping everybody out of the river."

Jasper asked, "Did you see if it was a man or a woman?"

"Somebody tall, probably a guy," the boy said. He introduced himself as Jeremy Reagan and his friend as Madison Relerford.

"Relerford? Are you related to Glenn Relerford?'

"You know my uncle Glenn?" The girl shook her curls. "Ohhh, are you the lady auctioneer? My uncle's talked about you."

Jasper wanted to know what Glenn had said about her, but suddenly a wave of dizziness hit her hard and she wobbled on her feet. Jeremy and Madison got on either side and braced her up straight. Jeremy said they would walk her back to her car. Madison offered to call her uncle, but Jasper said she was okay and she would talk to him herself. Later.

Much later. After a hot bath, a cuddle with Proxy, and maybe a good long nap.

Chapter 30

Jasper arrived home to find a stunning scene unfolding outside her Hickory Lane home.

Instead of the O'Neils' black Sunfire, a large gray station wagon waited in the driveway with its tail end aimed at the house which had its storm and interior doors open. Jasper glanced back at the station wagon. In the power-saving glimmer of the porch light, she saw that it was actually a silver hearse.

More death. Numbness salted her down and her thoughts calcified. The house stood stark and tall and white as a monument to all death everywhere. It was early dark now and Jasper stood as the only outdoor witness when two men wheeled out a sheeted body strapped to a metal gurney. Grunting, the man on the lower steps hoisted the gurney high so that it was as level as possible. The two men worked with efficiency. Business as usual for them, Jasper supposed.

They opened the back of the hearse and slid the white draped figure on the now collapsed gurney into the back of the death wagon. One of them acknowledged Jasper with a two-finger salute before he and the other man got into the hearse and eased out of the driveway.

Jasper trudged toward the still open front door. The smell that had been building for days met her halfway up the walk. She had attributed it to all those cigarettes plus bags of garbage that must have accumulated in the lower apartment while Mrs. O'Neil tended to her sick husband. Jasper was glad she had scored an air cleaner for herself and Proxy at the last auction. She wondered how much good it could do against a stench this deep, dark and disgusting.

Just inside, the door to the O'Neils' was open for a change and Jasper peeked in with trepidation. A faded orange sofa covered with a tousled heap of random afghans faced her. Blue and white striped, orange and brown and red. Tedious and confusing. In her duties as minister's wife, Jasper had seen many a sickbed with many such an afghan. So far, so typical. Across from it was a circa 1970 coffee table covered with large type crossword puzzles and Sudoku paperbacks, Bibles, newspapers and books with titles like Peace and Prosperity: What's the Difference. Bed pillows and cushions littered the maroon shag rug along with discarded tissues.

"Mrs. O'Neil?" Jasper stepped tentatively past the mess into the dining room. There, with her back to the entrance, sat Mrs. O'Neil in a rocking chair. A cloud of cigarette smoke had attached itself to her head. The old lady turned and registered Jasper's presence with a tiny nod.

"Cigarette?" she offered.

Jasper crouched in front of her. "What happened?"

"Didn't you see the meat wagon out front?"

"I mean, when, uh, how did Mr. O'Neil pass? What exactly happened?"

"You know he's been at death's door for a while. Just recently, he seemed more dead than alive."

"Worn out, huh?" Jasper asked in her kindest voice.

"I mean, not breathing. I said 'more dead than alive,' didn't I?"

"Yes, yes you did," Jasper said, wondering how she could get away from this addled woman and at the same time how she could possibly leave her alone. "When did you notice him not breathing?" This was a whacked-out conversation but

Jasper could think of nothing to do but keep Mrs. O'Neil talking.

Mrs. O'Neil lit a new cigarette from the end of her current one, then dropped the live inch to the floor. Jasper ground it into the wood floor which she saw already carried multiple cigarette scars. Mrs. O'Neil said, "I tried praying. I didn't want to give up hope. But I guess when the hubby gave up the ghost, he went all the way. That would be just like him. He was kind of a radical in his own way."

"Uh-huh." Jasper was looking around the dining room for random phone numbers or names of next of kin, someone she could phone in to take care of Mrs. O'Neil. She asked if there was someone she could call but Mrs. O'Neil rocked and puffed in silence. Just as Jasper was giving up hope that there was anyone who could step in, a familiar voice said, "Ladies? Mrs. O'Neil? Ms. Biggs?" Glenn Relerford walked into the room.

Jasper reached up automatically and tugged her hair behind her ears. Tim used to tell her that her ears were her prettiest feature and she should always pull her hair back so they showed to their full advantage. Jasper shook her head and freed her hair to fall back over her ears. If Glenn registered anything odd about Jasper's sudden head movements, his cop mask of inscrutability kept it hidden. She was glad for that.

"I'm here to help get you to the ambulance, Mrs. O'Neil. They'll take you over to the hospital and get you all settled in." His voice was low and soothing.

"The hospital's not going to do any good," Mrs. O'Neil said. "He's way beyond that point."

"Well now, my concern is with you, ma'am. People sometimes forget that the caretakers need help too."

"Yes, maybe. I suppose that's true," Mrs. O'Neil said. "I'll have to pack a few things though." She looked around the messy room unfocusedly. Then, she shambled to her feet. Glenn moved closer to support her.

"Ms. Biggs can bring you whatever you need," he said.

"Of course I can. You name it, I'll bring it."

Mrs. O'Neil looked alarmed. "Let me see. This may take me a little while."

"No worries, no worries," Glenn said encouragingly. He coaxed her toward the front door, steering her expertly around piles of pillows, blankets and magazines.

"Got it all under control," Jasper called after her.

"Who is she?" she heard Mrs. O'Neil say as Glenn escorted her out the doors. Jasper watched from the front window as a paramedic stepped in to assist Mrs. O'Neil into the back of an ambulance. Ginny Gardner from next door, with her cat Alice standing alongside, waved and gave a gentle smile. The ambulance pulled away and Glenn climbed up the porch.

Jasper closed the apartment door behind her and joined him. She took in a lungful of cleansing fresh air. She sniffed at the sleeve of her sweater. "Whew. It's going to take a good long soak to get rid of the smell," she said.

Glenn said, "The whole house is gonna take some powerful forces to overpower the stink in there."

Jasper felt a little insulted. After all, it was her home.

"You have a place you can stay while the house gets fumigated?"

Jasper scowled. After all, she had only barely gotten settled.

"Aired out as it were. Freshened up if you get my drift." Glenn chuckled at his own bad joke.

"Ha ha ha. Not funny," Jasper grumped. "My apartment is not bad at all."

"Are you sure?"

"I have an air cleaner."

Jasper could see Glenn fighting off a smile. "Jasper – "

"Ms. Biggs, if you don't mind."

"You don't think the landlord's gonna let you stay in there under these circumstances, do you? "

Jasper stomped her foot. "I'm staying."

"The city's not going to let you, that's for sure."

Jasper didn't answer. There had been too many changes lately. Her new home was her new home, no matter what.

"What I don't get," Glenn said, shaking his head, "is how you managed to live above a ripe body for as long as you have."

Jasper's eyes opened wide. "I thought he just passed away – I mean, maybe last night?'

Glenn shook his head.

"Yesterday morning?"

"No, ma'am. How long you been living here now?"

Jasper sat down heavily on one of the steps. "I never did meet him. This whole time I thought he was just sick."

"She was the sick one," Glenn said. "He was dead."

Chapter 31

Jasper and Proxy resettled into Jimmy's apartment. Fulltime living at the back of the auction house placed her and her pet too close to the work place as far as Jasper was concerned. But she felt grateful that she had a place to go after her Hickory Lane home was shut down until further notice. She put a Do Not Disturb sign on the apartment door and, for the most part, the auction-goers and the staff respected her privacy. Ted Phillips had persisted in tapping and rapping for the first couple days but Jasper stayed firm and refused to respond. He seemed to have gotten the message.

So when a gentle knock sounded one afternoon, Jasper at first felt irritated. Proxy waited for his owner's cue before jumping off her chest where he had settled in for a noontime nap. Jasper tiptoed to the door and Proxy trotted after. Jasper gazed through the peephole. A friendly wave greeted her.

"Cookie!" Jasper opened the door immediately. "To what do I owe this honor? Are you doing some previewing up front at the auction?"

"I've got more than enough stuff," her sister said, stepping inside. "Oh, here's the new man of the house." Proxy stood up on his hind legs and kneaded his front paws on the leg of Cookie's jeans.

"He likes you."

"Animals always do," Cookie said.

"Uh-huh. You probably remind him of me." Jasper lifted him up and the twins passed him back and forth between them. He purred like a small motorboat. "This is your Aunt Cookie," Jasper told him. "I am Mama. Repeat after me. Auntie Cookie. Mama."

"Who's going to be the most spoiled pet in town?" Cookie asked even as she scratched Proxy between his ears. "How about spoiling your sister here a little bit, Sis, and fixing me some coffee? That is, if you have anything besides Brand X."

Jasper plumped Proxy all the way into Cookie's arms. "It just so happens that I am becoming a woman of the world," she said from the kitchen. "I bought a bag of beans from the Forester and a grinder. I even have organic half and half."

"Pretty impressive," Cookie said. She and Proxy followed her. This time of day the galley kitchen took on a bright golden glow with light coming in the clerestory window Jimmy had installed high over the sink. The apartment did not get much natural light since their stepfather had emphasized privacy and security over attractiveness. He wasn't much of a home decorator. As far as the twins knew, he had spent most of his time out in the auction house proper, or up front in the office where he kept his computer, or tooling around town dredging up new business.

Proxy leapt from Cookie's shoulder onto the top of the refrigerator. "Your kitty is pretty impressive too. Is he allowed up there?"

"It gives him a different perspective. I think it's good for him," Jasper said.

"Spoiled, spoiled, spoiled."

"Did you come over to comment on how I'm raising my cat?"

"I'm here with an invitation," Cookie said. "Just get me my cup of joe and I'll explain.

"Gotcha." Jasper whirred the beans in the grinder, added them to a filter in the coffee machine, poured in water from the filter pitcher she had purchased, and flipped the on-switch. Cookie fetched mugs from the cupboard and cream from the fridge. Proxy kept an eye on the operation from his perch. Cookie poured a little half and half into a saucer and set it on the floor. Proxy was on it immediately. The sisters took their mugs of whitened coffee out to the living room and got comfy on the well-worn leather sofa.

Cookie got right to the point. "I'm going to do another house-clearing at the Clippert place," she said.

"How'd you get talked into that? Was Mary after you? Or was it Ted? He's really eager to calm her down."

"I don't take orders from them," Cookie said. "But I tend to listen when souls on the other side ask for my help."

"Oh, boy. Jimmy? Mr. Clippert? Somebody I haven't met yet?"

"Could be a combination thereof," Cookie said.

Jasper grabbed the kitty for comfort. He protested with a loud yowl, then relaxed onto her lap. "I like that about you, Proxy," Jasper said. "You're adaptable. I should learn to be so versatile."

"Good idea. Animals are such good teachers," Cookie said. "Great coffee. Too bad we don't have time for seconds."

"You mean we're gonna do this ghost business now?"

"Now is right. But about the 'ghost business' part -"

Jasper didn't pay attention to whatever else Cookie had to say about the proper language. She handed her the cat and bustled around getting ready to go. She put extra kitten food in Proxy's bowl and made sure his water fountain was full to overflowing so it wouldn't run dry and burn out the motor. One thing about working at an auction house, she could spot some pretty good finds nearly every week. She glanced in the bathroom mirror, tugged her uncombed hair back into a ponytail, and sprinkled some baby powder onto the palms of her hands. She patted her forehead, nose and chin with the powder. Then she pinched her cheeks and bit her lips for a little color.

Jasper wished she could instantly change her clothes from the khakis and red Biggs Auction shirt that were pretty much her daily uniform. She settled for a dab of rose-scented deodorant under each arm so that people would know she was a girl. When it came to looking good on a moment's notice, her sister seemed to have it all down pat. Of course, Cookie had sprung this house clearing on her at the very last minute. Cookie was wearing another casually elegant outfit with a high-necked silk blouse of faded violet and a rhinestone and onyx necklace that might have come from a Victorian era estate. That is, as Jasper thought, if one didn't know of the psychic's ability to find vintage-looking clothing online and at every resale shop in the vicinity. Cookie had teamed the blouse with a pair of powdered gray slacks and matching flats. Her large hoop earrings shimmered with each movement of her head.

Jasper grabbed the green canvas purse she had saved from its scheduled demise in the dumpster. "I'm ready," she told Cookie. "Ready as I'll ever be."

"That's the spirit," Cookie said.

"Is that a pun?" Jasper asked.

"You're the one who's good with words. I'm just the humble psychic."

"Uh-huh." Jasper picked up the kitten and kissed the top of his head. "Don't let in any mice," she said. Proxy meowed like he meant business.

Soon she and Cookie pulled up in front of the Clippert bungalow. Mary Clippert was already waiting for them.

Cookie took her hand. "Now this time it's important that you let me do all the talking," she said with gentle firmness.

Mary, dressed in another of her red and black outfits, harrumphed. She said, "This is my house now. And it's my father we're trying to reach. I don't see why you have to be in charge. And I don't see why she always has to tag along."

Jasper studied the overcast sky. If Mary had been a friendlier soul, she might've said aloud, *Don't make the psychic sister mad.* Instead, she let her lips settle into a neutral smile.

"It's like this," Cookie said with great timbre to her voice. "This is what I do. We're not playing around here. Either you agree with my terms, or we don't get this house cleared for you and you'll probably lose the deal with the Austrings. Jasper is here to assure that the deal goes through. You may not realize it but you need us both."

Mary dug the heel of one black boot into the vulnerable spring lawn. "I bet I could do this on my own. After all, he's my father. And if I tell him to leave, he'll leave," she added stubbornly.

"Did he listen to you when he was on this side?" Cookie asked.

"We were getting to that point." Mary's voice had lost its edge. She sounded more like a little girl.

"Uh-huh."

Go, Cookie, go. Jasper cheered her sister on silently.

Cookie continued. "Getting there and being there are two different things. Your dad's death hasn't changed him into a different person. He's the same as he was when he was in the body. He didn't do what you said when he was alive. He's not going to do what you say now." Cookie paused to let her words sink in.

Mary glared at her. She stamped down a patch of tender moss. "Okay, okay. You win."

"It's not about winning." Cookie was about to launch into one of her metaphysical lectures.

Jasper interrupted. "So, all right then, ladies. Let's get started!" she sing-songed.

Cookie led the way up the walk and then the front steps. She and Mary do-si-doed in a minor power struggle before Mary plunged her key into the lock. Mary hesitated, then uncharacteristically moved over to let Cookie go first, following her in. Jasper brought up the rear.

Whew! More fetid air. It smelled as if the house had been shut up for years.

"Sis, secure the door," Cookie ordered her. "We don't want any interruptions. And both of you turn off your cell phones."

Jasper closed the front door almost completely, but left it cracked open to let in a tiny bit of fresh air. Anything helps, she said to herself. She joined Cookie and Mary in the empty living room.

At Cookie's direction, the three women joined hands. Jasper wished for a fourth person so she wouldn't have to hold hands with the mean-spirited Mary whose fingers were just as icy and rough as Jasper would have expected. OK, so her own hands could use a good long soak in warm soapy water and a slathering of moisturizer. At least her personality wasn't cold and callous.

"Everyone, concentrate now," Cookie said, squeezing Jasper's hand. Sometimes it just wasn't fair having a psychic sister.

Suddenly the front door blew open.

Mary gripped her hand so hard that Jasper thought for a second she might break it.

"Ouch?" Jasper whispered.

"What the hell are you witches up to?" Ted Phillips strode into the room, waving his phone. "Jasper, I've called your cell five times. Oh, g'afternoon, Miz Clippert. Cookie."

"Join the circle," Cookie said. "Turn your phone off."

"We've got business to attend to," Ted protested.

"This *is* business," Jasper and Cookie said at the same time.

"All right, already," Ted said. He switched off his phone and jammed it back into his jeans pocket.

Mary mumbled under her breath. Jasper thought she heard her say, "You big dumb oaf. I'll give you 20 bucks to fuck off." In a louder voice, Mary said, "Come here, sweetie. You can hold my hand."

"Kind of you, ma'am," Ted said in that obnoxious imitation of gallantry that drove Jasper nuts. He inserted himself between Mary and Jasper. His hand at least felt warm to the touch.

Cookie led them through a chakra clearing, starting with the base chakra, and climbing steadily upward. Jasper could swear that her sister took on an extra shimmer of light when she was in the middle of her mediumistic work. Soft swirls of silver and lavender floated around Cookie's head. Jasper tried to focus and the colors disappeared.

"Let's go from room to room now. We'll clear each one of any spirits who have lingered behind. Then we'll bless the room and close any open portals," Cookie said.

Jasper shivered. She had heard words very much like this last time she and Cookie had started to clear the Clippert house. That was the day they discovered the body of Ray Clippert lying at the foot of the basement stairs. Would his ghost show up today? Would he reveal how exactly he had fallen? What or possibly who had tripped him and sent him careening to his death? Was that the secret he wanted to impart?

Cookie squeezed her hand, and Jasper returned her attention to the words her sister was reciting. "Now focus on the heart chakra where a beautiful blue light resides…"

Or would it be Jimmy Biggs who stepped forward from the ethereal realm to make some kind of pronouncement? Or dispense some sort of wisdom. *Don't take less than fifty for that pile of crap scrap iron on the back table.* Jasper giggled.

Cookie cleared her throat. "Even as we release our hands, we are connected in a blessed circle that will not allow any negative energy to enter its midst. You can let go now, everybody."

They all dropped their hands. Cookie continued, "We are here to help. Is there anyone here who wishes to communicate with us?

"Ah. A father figure has joined us. He wants us to step into the kitchen."

They regrouped in the kitchen which was now devoid of furniture. Cookie quieted everyone down and closed her eyes. "He says that he met his end after a fall down some stairs."

"That doesn't narrow it down much," Ted said.

Jasper shushed him.

"I'm just saying that two men have died here in the last short while. Who knows how many more fell down those old steep steps to the cellar? This is a house where every ghost must have taken a tumble," he said.

"What a fascinating perspective," Mary said. Her voice was super sweet.

"Yeah, really fascinating, Ted," Jasper said.

"I've got my own falling down the steps story," Ted said with some pride. "One time my dog Bear tripped me up – or down I guess you could say – when I was carrying a pile of dirty jeans to the washing machine. Damn dog. I thought he loved me like I loved him."

Jasper and Cookie exchanged a look.

Mary Clippert wiped away a fresh wash of tears. "I know exactly what you're talking about." Her eyes took on the look of dried mud balls, inhuman and unseeing. "He did not love me the way I loved him."

"Jimmy?" Jasper asked.

"Your dad?" Cookie asked.

"My mad dad." Mary began to laugh in a way that would've been part of the background sounds in Wisconsin's Northwoods. A loon, a frightened cub, a child tossed into a newly unfrozen lake. She tore the heavy beaded bracelet off her left wrist and threw it into the kitchen sink. "Women never did understand me," she said between bursts of laughter. She switched on the garbage disposal and it sounded like a wood chipper.

"Wait now," Jasper said. She took a step toward Mary.

Cookie grabbed her arm and pulled her back. "Let her be," she said in an even voice.

"That's what my mother said. 'Let things be. You can't do anything to change them, so why even try?'

"Men need action," Mary yelled over the noise of the disposal which had lowered to a continual growl. "Oh, hell." She flipped the wall switch down. She turned to Ted, "You get me, don't you?"

"Well, little lady."

"I'm nobody's little lady!' Mary shouted. She moved fast. Without warning, she slammed her hip against Jasper. Jasper sprawled sideways.

Cookie stooped down to help her sister. "Let's everybody take a break here."

"I don't want a break! I want to get this over with once and for all," Mary said. She clumped toward Ted and grabbed him in a chokehold.

"What the hell?" he sputtered.

Mary roared like a field coyote caught in a trap or a lonely cat screaming for attention. Her eyes were wild. She released Ted's neck and her nails raked down his arm. She jumped up on his back, surprisingly deft for such a large woman. Ted staggered toward the stairs.

"Get away from me, woman!" he yelled. But Mary, clinging now to the back of his belt, kept him off balance. The rotten old basement door stood open. Ted stumbled closer to the stairs.

With Cookie's help, Jasper regained her footing. She rushed after Mary and Ted.

"Sis! What're you doing?" Cookie shouted.

"I don't know," Jasper said. She crouched and dove for whatever leg she could grasp. She ducked closer to the floor to avoid a kick in the head. She clenched her eyes shut. She grabbed for fabric. She didn't know whose pant leg she clutched. Without pausing to think, Jasper jerked the fabric as hard as she could. A boot stomped her direction. Jasper rolled clear. She forced herself to open her eyes. She focused on Mary's dark slacks. Jasper reached again, higher this time. She jammed the heel of her hand against the back of Mary's knee.

"Dammit, that hurt!" Mary said, releasing Ted. He stumbled backwards and fell through the open basement door.

Some sickening clunks sounded. His moans carried upward. "Call 911!" he yelled. "I think I broke my arm."

"You meddling better-than-thou bitch," Mary said. "You think you're something special because you got to work alongside your father." This time she landed a kick to Jasper's side.

Cookie started toward them. "Stay back!" Jasper yelled. She struggled to her feet and wrestled Mary back from the door. The larger woman tumbled over her. Jasper made herself as long as possible so she could wedge herself against the doorway. She didn't know where her power was coming from, but she had it. Mary backed across the room, then reversed direction and charged toward Jasper.

Cookie screamed. With a mighty effort, Jasper jackknifed herself and flew clear. Mary Clippert kept going straight through the doorway. Her head struck against the wooden overhang with a loud clunk. Then she went rolling down the steps. Ted yelled, "Get me an ambulance. I think she just broke my other arm!"

Cookie hurried over to Jasper who was huddled on the floor, one hand on her injured side, the other holding out her cell phone. Jasper spoke calmly, "We need an ambulance. We need the police. Will you please tell Detective Relerford that it's me, Jasper Biggs calling?" She gave the address.

Cookie knelt beside her. "Are you okay, Sis? Are you okay?"

Jasper gasped for air. "I'm fine," she said just before she passed out.

♦

She came awake in an emergency room bed, with Cookie sitting alongside her.

"You have some bruised ribs, Sis. But nothing's broken," Cookie told Jasper.

"How's Ted?"

"He'll be all right. He broke his left arm in the fall. Then when Mary landed on him, he broke the other one. He's not going to be doing much auctioneering for a while."

"What about Mary?"

"She's all bruised up. But she didn't break anything. Ted cushioned her fall."

Jasper started to laugh but it hurt too much.

The curtains at the foot of her ER bed parted, and Glenn Relerford entered. "You're lucky," he said. "You met up with one crazy lady. Have you told her?" he asked Cookie.

She shook her head.

"What's going on?" Jasper asked. She struggled to sit up higher.

"It's Mary Clippert," Cookie said. "She said that she pushed her father down the basement steps." Cookie placed a protective hand atop Jasper's. "She said she tried to push you into the river."

Jasper shivered. "And Jimmy?"

Glenn Relerford stepped closer. "It may be hard to hear but we think she did him the same way. Right now she's denying it."

"She did it all right," Cookie said. "Jimmy told me."

"He won't make much of a witness, but we're looking into it," Glenn said.

"I feel kind of sorry for her," Jasper said. "She doesn't really like people."

"Especially men," Cookie said.

"And some women," Jasper added. She took a shallow breath. It hurt to inhale.

"She's started to tell us about all that," Glenn said. "She had a pretty rough childhood with that father of hers. From what she's said so far, her mother knew all about how he was abusing her and never stepped in to help." Glenn stayed just long enough to take statements from Jasper and Cookie and make sure that Jasper was feeling well enough to go home. He said he would talk to her soon. If that was okay. Jasper said it was. "Oh, I almost forgot," Glenn said. He set down an envelope on the hospital bed.

Later, in Jimmy's old apartment at the back of the auction house, Jasper and Cookie talked quietly over cups of tea that Cookie had brewed. Proxy curled up in Jasper's lap and would not leave her. Jasper ran her hand gently over the little cat's fur. Without saying a word, each of the twins handed the other a check.

"$201?" Jasper asked.

"$201?" Cookie echoed.

They shared a laugh, a hug and a long, deep sigh. "At this rate we'll never get that $401 Jimmy left behind divided up," Jasper said. "What are we gonna do about that extra dollar anyway?"

"Don't think we can ever really split it up."

"Nope." She tore up the check from Cookie. Her sister did the same with Jasper's.

"Guess we'll just have to keep up this twin sisterly togetherness thing. Maybe we could take a little trip together. Maybe to Galena," Cookie said.

"Or just stay home and use it up on lattes and exotic tea at the Forester," Jasper said. "We can tip wildly."

"The world is ours."

"Or, give it to the animal shelter." Jasper stroked Proxy's head. "Poor Mary Clippert. When you get mad at one man, you can end up mad at all men," she said. "Sometimes it lasts a lifetime."

"We're lucky, Sis." Cookie took Jasper's hand.

"You said it." The sisters sat side by side holding hands for a good long while without needing any more words. Proxy purred away louder than ever.

Epilogue

"So who'll give me fifty-dollah bid and start it right off?" Jasper called from up on the back table where she stood among the well sorted displays of iron doorstops, old postcards, and power tools. "I'll take 25 right there!" she pointed. The auction was off and running.

The auction bidders crowded around the table. Noisy bunch. Esteban and Tony handed up the next item for Jasper to sell. The bids came fast and furiously with Kelly wielding cards for absentee bidders. Jasper sold a flat of doorknobs for $35, then a stack of old Look magazines for $20. Not bad for a run-of-the-mill auction. And it was a full house. In addition to the 50 or so people crowded around the back table, jostling in closer when items they were interested in came up for bid, the folding chairs on her left between the back table and the auction block where the action would be focused after this first table full was sold, held an additional bunch of auction-goers. She knew from looking around before things got underway that most of the empty chairs had bidder numbers taped to their backs to reserve them for people who would take their seats later.

"What do you have, Estie?" Jasper asked her helper.

"It's a clock," he said, stating the obvious.

"Mantel clock!" Jasper refined the description of the small brass and cherry wood clock that the ringman held above his head. "It's a winner, folks! What-am-I-bid?" It was a back table item, so the seasoned bidders knew that it probably didn't work, and the metal might have a ding or two. But sometimes people didn't care and auction fever swept them up no matter what.

"I got 10!" Kelly yelled with enthusiasm, waving one of her absentee bidder cards.

"And I'll take 10!" Jasper said, honoring the other woman's hard work by accepting the low starting bid. She and Kelly had made peace with one another and had become the next best thing to friends. "Now 15, 15, who'll go 15, now 20! 25, 25, now 30 and 35!" The bids came in enthusiastic rhythm and Jasper kept pace with her chanting. She tried to jump the increments from 5 to 10 dollars. "We're at $50, now $60. Who'll go $60? You know it's gonna get there!" But the crowd fought back with fingers drawn straight across throats to signal they wanted to cut the bid. Jasper said good-naturedly, "You wanna do it the hard way? I can keep going all night! I have $55, now $60 and $65…" At last the bidding slowed down just shy of $100. Jasper pushed hard to see if she could break that marker. "We're at 90 dollars now, folks. S'great ol' clock." Half words dropped away in the slur of the auctioneer's rush. "Who'll give me a hunnert dollars? One-one-one hundred dollar bid now, hundred dollar bid?" She kept chanting. She glanced skyward. "This is for you, Jimmy!" she said to the ceiling.

Cookie, out in the audience, clapped her hands with excitement. She pumped the air with her fist. Tony pointed over to her, but Jasper didn't take Cookie's enthusiasm as a bid.

"Man, she's got her daddy up there helping her along!" said one gruff but good-natured man in the crowd. "I'll give you $100, girly," he said.

Jasper grinned.

A bright light flashed in her face. Sean Solberg was there, snapping away with one of his old 35 mm cameras. "You're beautiful, babe!" he yelled

Jasper kept her chant going steadily. Soon she reached $200, then $250. The bidding finally topped out at 300 even. "Sold! To the lady in the green hat!" she called. "Number 133."

"Atta girl," Ted said from where he stood back in the office area. Weeks after his fall down the stairs at the Clippert house, his arms were still healing. Molly cuddled their baby, bringing her up to kiss her Daddy Ted's cheek now and then, for indeed, the baby had been born vanilla and after a paternity test confirmed Ted's fatherhood, he had, surprisingly, become a real Dad to the little girl. He and Molly continued to call her Baby even six weeks after her birth. "All we know is her name ain't Mary," Ted would say.

Mary Clippert was in jail awaiting trial for the manslaughter death of her father. She recanted her original confession of outright killing him, now claiming that he had stumbled during an argument they had.

Jasper and Cookie held a little ceremony in which they officially forgave Mary for whatever part she had played in Jimmy's fall down the bungalow steps. Jimmy made no more appearances so as far as the twins knew, his spirit was at rest.

Jasper continued to visit Sean Solberg whom she still found attractive albeit somewhat cheap. Glenn Relerford and she took in an occasional movie together. Both men seemed to like her new style: Cookie had given her a makeover head to toe, adding highlights to her dark hair, helping her find the right rosy-toned makeup and learning how to use it, and choosing inexpensive but fashionable skirts, jeans and tops along with shoes that fit. Jasper's marriage to Tim Rowe still haunted her dreams. She hadn't yet filed for divorce. Mostly she didn't think about him. But she was in no hurry to commit to a new relationship.

She stayed on with Proxy in the apartment at the back of the auction house. Her nice neighbor from Hickory Lane, Ginny Gardner, had invited her and Proxy to move in with her and Alice but Jasper was busy looking around for a new more private home for herself and the cat who had become the love of her life. Her "like new" life. It wasn't perfect but it was all hers, and Jasper was looking forward to whatever it would bring.

The End

Acknowledgements

I owe a lot to a lot of people – everyone from my partner Davey and my twin sis the psychic medium Karen Richards to all the other friends, mentors, heroes and helpers along the way. These include writers Nancy Christiansen, Erle Stanley Gardner, Joanne Lenz-Mandt, Carolyn Lieberg, and Gertrude Stein; retired detective Steve Zandler; the Beloit and Milton, Wisconsin police departments; and the Rock County Sheriff's Department.

Any mistakes are my own. Except for those made by some very determined characters. Okay, alright, Jasper, we will drop the matter. Time to get ready for your next adventure in The Case of the Belligerent Bidder, the second book in the Auction House Mystery Series.

About the Author

Like her fictional pal, Jasper Biggs, **Sherry Blakeley** knows auctions. She has worked as a professional auctioneer, and published many articles on auctions and antiques. Sherry grew up in Illinois and Colorado and returned to the Midwest where she earned her degree from Beloit College in English Literature and composition. She lives in the Midwest in close proximity to her husband, the artist David Lundahl.